YOU MADE A
WITH Y

Shortlisted for Foyles Fiction Book of the Year

Nominated for the Goodreads Choice Awards for Best Romance

Shortlisted for the Indie Book Awards 2023

One of the *Evening Standard*'s Blockbuster Book Trends of the Year

'Rousing, celebratory . . . it could appeal especially to people who, living through an isolating pandemic that has accelerated loss, hunger for more joie de vivre.' **New York Times**

'The perfect novel for the summer. With sections of searing prose and serious moments exploring the grief of loss, this story about relationships ticks all the right boxes for me. I absolutely loved it!' **Karen Angelico**

'Full of sensory detail . . . Emezi disrupts and refreshes a genre that is typically the preserve of straight, white protagonists. Here, wealth and unabashed sexuality are reserved for a black woman, who is allowed to make messy and questionable decisions and to prioritise her own happiness despite her trauma.' **Financial Times**

'A sharply original novel about love, friendship and the journey grief takes.' **Good Housekeeping**

'I wish I hadn't already read this so I could take it on holiday. Refreshing and magnificent, poolside or not.' **Jo Browning Wroe**

'A once-in-a-generation voice.' **Vulture**

'Emezi once again absolutely slays a new-for-them genre, with tender-hearted characters and an immaculate balance of realistic dialogue and lyrical prose.' **Buzzfeed**

'One of the most anticipated books of the year . . . a seductive summer read about the pursuit of identity and happiness.' **Tatler**

'Messy, moving, heart in-your-mouth stuff, told in dazzling prose.'
LoveReading

'Exuberantly queer, smart and sexy, this sizzling romance manages to be simultaneously about grief and joy. So perfect for posing by the pool.' **Nikki May,** *iNews*

'A riveting and emotional exploration of grief and taking a second chance on love.' *PopSugar*

'One incredible romance you won't want to miss!' ***BookRiot***

'This contemporary romance [is] filled with Akwaeke Emezi's powerful and beautiful writing.' ***Business Insider***

'A scorching tale of love after loss.' ***Kirkus Reviews***

'*You Made a Fool of Death With Your Beauty* is fun, sexy, sensual, and everything in between. A vibrant celebration of love, loss, art, food, nature, and learning to live again in grief. Highly recommended.' **Fíona Scarlett**

'One of our greatest living writers.' ***Shondaland***

'Emezi has created a dazzling celebration of the messiness of living and feeling with their signature gift for articulating characters' inner voices in raw and expressive detail. Couple that with a thrilling story of forbidden love, and Emezi has created a seductive and powerful novel that will make readers feel renewed.' ***Booklist***

ALSO BY AKWAEKE EMEZI

Dear Senthuran
The Death of Vivek Oji
Freshwater

Young Adult

Bitter
Pet

Akwaeke Emezi

You made a Fool of Death with your Beauty

faber

First published in the UK in 2022
by Faber & Faber Ltd
The Bindery, 51 Hatton Garden
London ECIN 8HN

First published in the USA in 2022
by Atria Books, an imprint of Simon & Schuster, Inc.

Typeset by Faber & Faber Ltd
Printed and bound by CPI Group (UK) Ltd, Croydon, CRO 4YY

This paperback edition first published in 2023

A CIP record for this book
is available from the British Library

ISBN 978–0–571–37268–3

Printed and bound in the UK on FSC® certified paper in line with our continuing
commitment to ethical business practices, sustainability and the environment.
For further information see faber.co.uk/environmental-policy

1 3 5 7 9 10 8 6 4 2

For my darling Kathleen,
who is love itself in flesh.

**You made a Fool of Death
with your Beauty**

Chapter One

Milan was the first person Feyi had fucked since the accident.

They hooked up in a bathroom at a Memorial Day house party in Bushwick, with Feyi's glass of prosecco spilling into the sink and Milan's large hands sliding behind her thighs as he lifted her onto the bathroom counter. Speckled tiles stretched around them, washed bloody in the light of the red bulb someone had screwed into the ceiling, and a linen shower curtain hung around the bathtub, thick with monstera leaves. Feyi threw her head back, his mouth at her throat, and her long pink braids dripped over the faucet, the tips dragging against the draining bubbles of her drink.

"Tell me if you need to slow down," Milan said, his voice all tangled up, busy with want. "I know we just met or whatever."

He said it as if it could matter, or as if it was a reason to stop instead of a reason to go even faster. Feyi had first seen him back on the rooftop, when the party was in full force around them. She'd liked the way his eyes followed her as she walked, how tall he was, how broad. Her best friend, Joy, had leaned in, linking her arm with Feyi's.

"Whew, check out those thighs!" she'd whispered. "He thick as *fuck*. I'ma need him to turn around so I can see that ass."

Feyi had rolled her eyes. "So glad you don't have a dick," she said. "You'd be a fucking menace."

"I'd be *particularly* interested in his ass if I had a dick," Joy replied.

"I take that back. You're already a menace." Feyi snuck another look at the thighs in question. "Besides, you can just use a strap, you know."

"Nah, it's not the same. I wanna feel him *squeeze* around me." Joy had flexed her fingers into a fist to illustrate the grip, and Feyi stifled a laugh, her braids sweeping across her collarbone. Milan glanced in their direction, catching Feyi's eye and smiling at her from across the roof.

Feyi had already decided who she wanted to be that night, so she stared right back at him, unabashed, drinking in his terra-cotta skin and dark copper beard. When he nodded to his boys and started walking toward her, Joy squealed and vanished, leaving the two of them alone. Feyi wanted to cut through any potential small talk—just slice it away neatly— so she touched the buttons of Milan's shirt as soon as he was close enough.

"You're hot," she'd said, before he could even open his mouth. "Are you seeing anyone?"

A flicker of surprise had crossed his face, but Milan recovered quickly. "Nah," he replied, tipping his head to one side as he held her eyes. "You?"

For a moment, there was the scream of tires and the mad chime of broken glass, the soft petals of white lilies, and a clod of dirt breaking apart in Feyi's hand, but she brushed it all aside like smoke.

"Single," she'd said in return, stepping right into his personal space. He smelled of rain and bergamot. "And—how do they say it?—ready to mingle."

It would have been a corny line if she wasn't so beautiful, and Feyi knew it—knew how to part her lips in their full wine red, how to look up at him from under thick black lashes, how to inject a lifetime of suggestion into her voice. It was all a game, a simple formula, and there was nothing wrong with using these cards she'd been dealt. Besides, if she looked closely enough at the whole thing, none of it really mattered. He was a different kind of beautiful, and that was enough.

Although she and Joy had been drinking since brunch, Feyi wasn't drunk yet, just tipsy enough to choose him, to dive back into the deep end with his body. From the way this terra-cotta stranger had placed his hand on her lower back, welcoming her against him, he seemed to be on board with her plan. Joy was somewhere by the bar, surely restraining her glee at seeing Feyi make such a blatant move.

"I'm Milan," the stranger had said, his wide and delicious mouth curving into an amused smile.

Do we really need names? Feyi had thought, but she smiled back anyway, her hand splayed against his chest, his heart galloping steadily beneath her palm. "I'm Feyi."

Milan had glanced around the roof. "Wanna get out of here?"

Nice. He was playing along perfectly, no hesitation, no coyness.

"Not too far. I came with my girl."

He'd nodded and looked back at her. They were close enough for his breath to brush against her skin, for her to see the dark flecks in his brown eyes as he took in her face, his gaze lingering on her mouth. When he spoke again, his voice had dropped, low and rough. "Downstairs?"

3

Feyi had raised an eyebrow, hiding how his lust was like a match igniting hers. He *wanted* her, badly enough to ask only the important questions. "You're solution-oriented. I like that."

Milan took her hand, and they left the rooftop, squeezing past people on the stairs, then ducking around a corner as he led her into the bathroom. Feyi watched the muscles in his back move under his shirt as he closed and locked the door, then tracked the caution in his eyes as he turned back to her.

"So . . . ," he said, giving her space, not assuming.

It was sweet. It was so unnecessary. Feyi did not need to think about this. She put her drink down on the counter and pulled her blouse off over her head, her pink braids getting briefly caught in the black cotton, leaving her breasts covered in nothing but a thin bralette, small gold rings pressing through the sheer mesh.

The stranger—*Milan*—inhaled sharply, the want in his eyes going aflame. "You're fucking beautiful," he growled, still holding himself back. "Your skin, it just . . . drinks up the light."

Feyi smiled and said nothing. Instead, she stepped up to him, pulling his face down to hers, his mouth down to hers, his willing and ready tongue down to hers. He seized her greedily, his hands digging into her flesh, his hips pressing an iron length against her stomach. Feyi felt like a monster and a traitor, but it was fine, it had to happen.

It was precisely what she had come here for.

. . .

The accident had been five years ago, which felt like both forever and yesterday to Feyi. She'd been living up in Cambridge, near her parents' house, but she couldn't handle the roads afterward, couldn't handle driving or the way her mother's eyes were weighted with pain and pity every time they saw each other. So Feyi had moved down to New York, because if she was a monster, then so was the city, glorious and bright and everlasting, eating up time and hearts and lives as if they were nothing. She wanted to be consumed by the relentless volume of a place so much louder than she was, a place where her past and her pain could drown in the noise. Here, Feyi could keep her name and her unruined face, yet become someone else, someone starting over, someone who wasn't haunted. No one in New York cared about the vintage of the sadness tucked behind her eyes and in the small corners of her smiles. She didn't have to drive, and she could cry on the train and no one would look, no one would care, because she didn't matter, and it was, honestly, such a relief to stop mattering.

Feyi moved into a brownstone apartment with Joy, her best friend from college, and paid for it with the life insurance money, trying to ignore how ghoulish that felt. Everyone said it's what he would've wanted, but she was fairly sure he would have wanted to live. Most people didn't get what they wanted. Feyi didn't want the money, but she needed it, that obscene check, and maybe she even needed the accompanying guilt. It was a punishment that felt necessary, like balance. He was dead, and what was she doing? Being alive, making art. How frivolous.

She and Joy lived on a green and sunny block, around the corner from Baba Yusuf's botanica and the Trini shop that sold doubles at inconsistent hours. They smoked joints on their fire escape, and Joy convinced Feyi to dye her hair pink. "You're in Brooklyn now," she'd said. "Try a different look. It's not a big deal."

There was something in the air that first summer that made Feyi play along. She rented out a studio on the next block and made her work there. Grotesque as it was, nothing she painted or stitched together could bruise her the way her own life had. Feyi began to hope that her past could fade, thinning out like an old song, turning her sadness into just a vague layer under her skin. All that would be left was its residue, giving her a certain spicy and inexplicable melancholy that some men could smell. It made them want to save her. Feyi knew it was already too late for all that, so she dipped and ducked away from their hands, their hungry mouths. She liked the city as an entity better; it didn't care who you were or what your damage was, it ate everyone up indiscriminately.

Once the full summer heat hit in a wave of wet air, Feyi felt like she was being seduced into being a stranger, and she found that she wanted nothing more. She and Joy rented a car and drove down to Riis Beach, lying out topless in the sun under layers of coffee and coconut oil until their skin darkened into deep brown and gold. Joy shaved her head on a whim and tattooed a black dot on each lower eyelid. Feyi pierced her nipples and braided her bubblegum hair down to the small of her back. They turned off the news and ordered edibles instead, redecorated their apartment with plants instead, started making pizzas on Saturdays instead. There was nothing to stop them from being whatever they wanted.

"Do you think we're having a quarter-life crisis?" Joy had asked once, while rolling up a joint in their living room.

"First of all, we're a few years too old for that," Feyi had replied. "Second, I think we're just figuring out how to survive a world on fire . . . that it's okay to be alive."

Joy had looked over with a soft smile. "I'm proud of you," she said. "I know it isn't easy for you to say that."

She wasn't wrong. It wasn't easy for Feyi to do a lot of things, but now, with Milan kissing her against a bathroom mirror, Feyi found that it didn't quite catch in her chest the way she thought it would. She was a monster and a traitor, but only if someone else was alive, and he wasn't. She had to remind herself that he wasn't. Feyi still felt wrong, yes, but in an unfamiliar way, which made sense because she had become a stranger and it takes time to turn into someone new. If she let go and existed only here and now, without a past, it was actually easy. It was fun, in fact.

"I'm serious," Milan gasped, seizing air in between their desperate kisses, his palms hot against her thighs. "We can stop at any point. Tell me."

Bass thumped through the walls, and Feyi unbuttoned his jeans, sliding her hand inside. Milan had small diamonds in his ears, and his breath was ragged as he looked down at her.

"Don't stop," she murmured into his mouth, and Milan hissed in a sharp breath as her fingers wrapped around him and pulled him out.

"Are you sure?" he asked, and Feyi tried not to roll her eyes.

"Such a gentleman," she mocked, keeping her tone soft, then she kissed him again, slipping her tongue between his teeth as she tightened her grip. God, he had *girth*.

7

Milan made a torn and rough sound, then shoved her skirt up to her waist, his hands eating her skin. Feyi heard a rip, and she laughed in delight as he tore off her lace thong. Her laugh melted into a soft gasp as he tossed the delicate scraps aside, sliding his fingers inside her.

"Let me make that up to you," Milan growled.

He curled his fingers forward and Feyi cried out, her back arching. Milan laughed into her mouth, still hard and pulsing in her hand. She had forgotten what this felt like—the frenzy, the way lust could almost hold a shape within her, something big and loud and so very demanding. It felt rushed, dangerous, exactly how she wanted it, too quick to think, too fast, too hard, too wet to remember anything or anyone. She pushed away his hand and pulled the tip of him closer. Reckless.

"Hold up," he said. "I have a—"

Feyi wrapped her legs around his hips. "It's fine."

Reckless.

"But—"

"Shh. Here." She brushed him against her slick self and Milan swore in the back of his throat as his common sense slid away.

"Oh, you're *bad*," he whispered, pushing into her slowly, committed to their mistake. It was something she was beginning to like about him, the way he made decisions, abandoning uncertainty once the choice was done.

Her mind spun off as he stretched his way in, floating away on sharp pleasure. Feyi bit down on his shoulder as he sank into her and whimpered as he started to pull back out, tortuously slow. Fuck, it had been so long, how had she even made it this far? No wonder Joy kept telling her to get laid.

"Faster," she gasped, and Milan chuckled.

"Ask nicely."

"Oh, you fucking bastard."

He pulled all the way out and Feyi's breath hitched, the ache suddenly roaring and furious. "Ask nicely," he said, his smile wicked. "And I'll give you everything you want."

She needed him not to stop. He didn't understand. There were so many things she was keeping at bay. "Please," she said, giving in. "Please fuck me."

Milan's smile left immediately, and something shadowed took its place, but he gave Feyi what she wanted, slipping back in and burying himself deep with one hard stroke. He slid his arms under her knees, lifting her legs and splaying her open, then pushed even deeper. Sound blossomed from Feyi's throat as he reached up to twist one of her nipple rings.

"Like this?" he asked, watching her cry out, not breaking his gaze.

Feyi put a hand to his neck, circling it lightly, barely touching his skin. It was almost perfect.

"*Harder*," she ordered, her voice fracturing, and Milan obliged, his hands bruising her, her skirt bunched up with her waistbeads, his jeans caught around his ankles. They both still had their shoes on. Feyi's heels were trembling in the air over his shoulders, and she didn't care how loud she was being, if anyone could hear them above the bass and through the door—because there it was, that blessed blinding white space, that searing nothingness even as she was alive, so clearly alive and in his arms, strangers coming undone, and she was coming around him, begging him not to stop, and Milan kept going, his own voice twisting into low and uncontrolled sounds. When he gasped a warning and made to pull away, Feyi grabbed his hips, keeping him deep inside her and putting her lips by his ear. Men were easy; there were some keys you could use that unlocked them like a quick password.

"Come inside me," she whispered, her voice a silken filthy plea, making it sound like she was begging, desperate for him, and in some ways, she was. Since they were already mad and reckless and human, Milan cursed, his face contorting, his sense lost, and obliged her once more, pushing as deep as he could, growling against the glass and tile and her, their skin slippery with sweat and half of each other. Feyi felt another orgasm wash over her, and she welcomed it in all its illicit carelessness. She didn't call out his name—in that moment she didn't quite remember what it was anyway—but when he kissed her again, she kissed him back, and then they stayed still for a minute, their foreheads pressed against each other's, trying to catch their breath as the air settled around them.

"Sorry," Milan managed to say. "I usually don't . . . do that." He straightened up and pulled out of her, turning to grab some tissues and zip himself up as Feyi wriggled off the counter and tugged her skirt down.

"It's fine," she said, picking up her blouse.

"I got carried away. I shouldn't have." Milan handed her a wad of tissues and didn't smile. "I always use a condom, usually."

Sure. Feyi didn't believe him for a second; it had been way too easy to convince him not to bother. "I'm on birth control," she said, since they were playing this game. "I wouldn't have . . . you know. If I wasn't."

Relief flashed across his face. "Oh, okay. Cool."

They stood for a moment staring at each other, then Feyi pushed her braids back. "I should probably take a piss," she said, enjoying how blunt the words were.

"Oh! Of course." Milan turned toward the door, then paused and turned back. "Actually . . . can I get your number?"

Feyi raised an eyebrow. "It was that good, huh?"

Milan laughed. "I'm just saying. I wanted to take you out, soon as I saw you up on the roof."

"And you still want to?"

He frowned. "Why wouldn't I?"

Feyi shrugged. "No reason." She held out her hand for his phone and typed in her number. "Shoot me a text, I guess."

Milan leaned in to kiss her cheek, his lips soft as a wing. "I'll call you," he said before closing the bathroom door behind him as he left. The music from the party leaked through in a quick slice of sound, then quietened out again.

Feyi pulled her skirt back up and sat down on the toilet, listening as her pee hit the water, a smile half playing across her face. What the fuck had just happened? She wiped away his come and groaned. Joy was going to kill her for fucking him raw, but Feyi didn't know if she could explain it. There was just no way she could've watched him come in his hand or on her skirt or against her thigh, that arcing white. She couldn't bear to see it, not yet, not like this. It would have tipped the stranger thing too far to the other side, something sordid and used, something ugly and frantic. It felt better to be close, pressed against each other, intimate. As if they meant something. As if this was beautiful. She had just needed it not

11

to stop, because if she was lost in Milan and his skin, if there was nothing except his momentum in and against her, hard and fast, driving out everything else, then there would be no ghosts.

There would be no memory of a fine-boned man with almond eyes and braided locs, no memory of how slow and gentle he liked to move inside her, how his voice sounded when he whispered how much he loved her. Feyi shook her head and flushed the toilet, picking up her ruined thong from the floor and tossing it in the trash. She stepped into the hallway and bumped straight into Joy, all purple sequins and long legs.

"There you are! Where did you run off to? You ready to head out? They started doing lines on the roof and you know I don't fuck around with that shit."

Feyi grimaced. "Yeah, let's go home. Call an Uber?"

"Already did, it's like seven minutes out." Joy looked over Feyi's shoulder at the reddened bathroom. "Wait, were you in there the whole time? With *him*?"

Feyi smiled. "I mean. You *did* want me to get laid."

"*My* bitch!" Joy threw her arms around Feyi and squeezed her tightly. "Oh, you smell of sex; I'm so proud of you!"

"Yeah, yeah. Let's get out of here." They wound through the rest of the party and out of the house, pushing through the front doors and spilling out onto the stoop.

Joy stopped and pulled out a pack of cigarettes, passing one over. "Did you tell him . . . you know . . ."

Feyi flipped open a lighter and leaned over, the flame flowering in her hands. "Did I tell him what?"

"That he's the first since the accident?"

Feyi had decided to stop smoking, but this occasion rather called for it. She made a mental note to get Joy to quit too, even as she cut her a look. "Did I tell him that he's the first guy I've fucked in the last five years?" She took a drag, then tipped her head back and blew a plume of smoke out into the air. "Of course not. Fuck I look like?"

Joy raised her hands. "I was just wondering."

"Mm-hmm." Feyi looked out at the dark street and sighed. Time to come clean. "You're gonna be mad, though."

Joy stabbed a finger in her direction. "See, I *knew* this was too good to be true. What the fuck did you do? And if it's nasty, say it quick, before the car gets here."

Feyi groaned. This was going to suck. "Okay, so what had happened was . . ."

"Uh-huh."

"We kinda sorta . . . didn't use a condom."

Joy choked on her cigarette smoke. "You *what*?"

Feyi gave a weak smile. "Heat of the moment?"

Her best friend clenched her jaw. "Tell me he pulled out. Please, Feyi, tell me he pulled out, at *least*."

Well, fuck. "I have an IUD in, remember? It's not that big of a deal."

"Not that big of a— Bitch, have you lost your mind? You let him hit it raw *and* you let him nut in you?"

Feyi looked down and scuffed at the concrete with her toe. "I know, I know."

"*Clearly* you don't."

"Hey, it was my first time since, you know. Cut me some fucking slack."

She recognized the look on Joy's face—her best friend was

fighting between being sympathetic and cursing her all the way out.

"You know what?" Joy took a deep breath and closed her eyes. "I am going to pop by the bodega because you are killing me with this shit. Stay right here, and if you see a white Hyundai, make him wait."

"Aw, it's like that? You're just gonna dead it?"

"Oh, I'm not deading a goddamn thing. You and I are going to have a long conversation after we get home, once I stop feeling the urge to push you down some stairs, bitch." Joy reached in her purse, hunting for some cash as she grumbled under her breath. "How you gon' fuck up a perfectly good night by letting a nigga you just fucking met hit it raw?"

Feyi shrugged. "I take it you're not buying my 'heat of the moment' defense?"

Joy cut her a look, and Feyi hid a smile. It was hard to play contrite when she really felt magnificent, when just thinking back to the bathroom was sending little aftershocks through her. Feyi sat on the stoop as Joy started walking away, then called out after her. "Hey, babe, can you get me some gum while you're in there?"

Joy held up a middle finger without looking back. "Nope!"

The streetlights reflected violet off the sequins of her dress until Joy ducked into the store, and suddenly, Feyi was alone, except for the faint music from the house and the soreness of her inner thighs.

It didn't feel that bad, to be on the other side of it. She took a deep breath and stared up at the sky, leaning back to rest her elbows on the steps. There were no stars, just a blurred moon hanging over the brownstones. Feyi could feel her pulse between her legs, a rhythmic reminder of the stranger with diamonds in his ears and bergamot on his neck. For a treacherous second, she wanted to tell Jonah about it, to hear his smooth laugh again. He'd ask her if she'd had fun. Feyi pressed her elbows against the brownstone steps to drive the thought away, hard enough to hurt. It was the start of summer, she was alive, and she was so fucking close to becoming what she wanted—someone who had moved on, someone who had a life that wasn't dressed in black, someone who Milan had held like he was dissolving into her, like she was real flesh under his hungry hands, under a raging red light bulb. Someone who trapped pleasure in a small bathroom and pulled it out of herself, a roiling sweaty mess of alive on a bathroom counter. If she could do tonight, she could do anything—the rest of a life, for example.

"You got this," Feyi whispered to herself, her voice catching, her cigarette dying and gray between her fingers. "You can do this."

The music filtered down from the party, and there was no one to say anything back to her. Feyi stubbed the cigarette out and waited for their car to get there.

Chapter Two

The accident was an easy secret for Feyi to keep. What had happened on that cold night outside Cambridge was far enough in the past that the few scars she'd walked away with were unremarkable on her body—intermittent islands of hypertrophied tissue falling like stars down her left leg, a raised and jagged line across her palm, an everlasting bruise on her forearm from when they dragged her out of the car, scraping her across the road. When Milan called, like he said he would, and invited her over to his place in Bushwick, Feyi thought about telling him, but by the time he was opening his front door with a spilling smile, she decided not to. He would've thought it meant something, that it came with some responsibility. Feyi didn't want him to touch her like she was fault-lined glass, or watch him fumble through the awkwardness of a forced intimacy when, let's be honest, he'd only signed up for a fuck.

She felt okay with him, and that felt like enough—his body felt like enough, over and under and inside hers. They kept seeing each other for a few weeks, nothing serious. Milan was sweet but reserved, a city boy with manners his Southern grandmother would have been proud of. He didn't want to crawl inside Feyi's feelings and take a look around, which Feyi was grateful for. Letting someone touch her was already a big deal—it made her flesh real, just having it exist in his hands and eyes.

"I feel like I'm using him," she told Joy one night, after they'd gone out for dinner, walking down Second Avenue as the city spilled people around them.

Joy laughed. "Babe, I don't think he minds. He gets to fuck *you*, hello?"

"A valid point." Feyi hopped over a puddle. "He's good at it, too." She had steady orgasms with him, they cuddled and all, but Feyi always left in the morning. No breakfasts, no dates. It was clean and simple that way.

Joy looked over at her. "I'm glad it's still going well, babe. You deserve some fun."

Feyi's throat caught with feeling. There had been so much darkness after the accident, years and years of thick numbness, when she couldn't bear for anyone to touch her, yet she was here, now, on her way to meet her fuck buddy and his friends at a bar. Feyi linked her arm in Joy's and pulled her close.

"How's it going with that bartender girl you were seeing?" she asked.

Joy lit a cigarette and allowed the tangent. "Found out she's married; can you believe it?"

Feyi laughed. "You still fucking with her, though, aren't you?"

"Absolutely." Joy exhaled a feather of smoke. "Fuck I care about a husband."

One of these days, Feyi knew she was going to have to talk to Joy about how she kept going after straight girls, but then again, they had been friends for a long time and it wasn't like Joy didn't know her own patterns or the gnarled roots they came from. Everyone had a right to keep some hurts buried and private. Like Milan, for example, who kept lightness and fun wrapped around him like armor. Some nights, Feyi would see him staring up at the ceiling when he thought she was asleep, heaviness sedimenting in his eyes. She always pretended not to notice; she had a whole country of open wound inside her and no desire to brush up against his own rawness. It was nothing to feel guilty about. Feyi had spent a very long time building salves for herself, and they were finally working—Joy's face laughing through a mist, the arms of a casual lover waiting at the end of a night, an insomniac city with enough lives in it to forget the ones she had before.

So she said nothing, crossing the street with her best friend as the moon shone down on them. It was almost enough, or it would have to be, because they didn't have anything else.

. . .

At the bar, Joy twirled her straw in her drink, and her eyes glittered as bright as the gold mesh of her dress. "Fuck him, and then fuck his friends," she suggested, with a wicked grin. "I think that's the only sensible option here."

Feyi laughed and handed her card to the bartender to start a tab. "Nah, I can't be out here moving *that* mad."

Joy tilted her shaved head, her honeyed skin reflecting a thousand small lights. "I know we just got here, but I feel like I need to remind you. Have you *seen* his friends?"

Feyi flipped her turquoise braids over her shoulder and glanced to where Milan was drinking with his boys. Joy had a point—Milan's friends were gorgeous, ridiculously so, and the cumulative effect of them rolling in a pack was utterly unfair.

"Shit, you right." Feyi giggled. "I almost wish I'd gotten to choose from the menu back at that rooftop party. How the fuck are they *all* this fine?"

"Why you asking questions when you could be catching trains? Choo-choo, motherfucker."

Feyi choked on her drink, and Joy laughed, throwing a shot back.

"I'm just saying!" She slammed her shot glass on the bar. "Y'all aren't really together; it's not like his friends are off-limits."

Feyi rolled her eyes. "Girl, you know they be sensitive. Bro codes and shit."

Joy scoffed and gestured to the bartender for another shot. "One more time, have you *seen* these niggas? Man, *fuck* a bro code."

Feyi snuck another look just as one of the guys lifted his head from his phone. Their eyes met, and she found herself staring again, just like when she'd first seen Milan. This one was lean, his skin a smooth deep brown, and he was wearing a casual suit, his shirt unbuttoned at his throat. At first, the air between them was neutral, just two people caught in a glance, registering each other's features. Feyi wondered what she looked like within an evaluation like that, from inside his eyes. He was relaxed, slouched against the wall and sitting on a barstool, his jacket open. A few seconds passed, and he didn't look away. Neither did she.

The air between them tensed like a dare, like a challenge. When he put his phone aside and straightened up, interest now prowling through his narrow face, Feyi suddenly felt like she was in the path of something, but she wasn't sure

19

what. She watched as he leaned over to Milan, speaking softly while still looking at her, blatant with those interested eyes.

Joy caught on and squealed under her breath. "Oh, bitch, that man is *gunning* for you."

"Shut the hell up," Feyi hissed, keeping her mouth still and her lips curved as Milan turned and smiled warmly at her and Joy, gesturing for them to come over. The man next to him hadn't taken his eyes away, not bothering to cloak the curiosity that sharpened with every step Feyi took closer to him.

"You're fucked," Joy whispered back, keeping her smile equally fixed as they walked over.

"Hey, babe," Milan said, sliding an easy arm around Feyi and kissing her cheek. "This is my homeboy Nasir. Nasir, this is Feyi."

A corner of Nasir's mouth turned up, a glimpse of white teeth underneath, and she held out her hand.

"Hi," she said. "Nice to meet you."

He took her hand, and his skin was dry and warm against hers. "Pleasure," he replied, holding her gaze and her hand a moment too long. Milan didn't notice.

"You must be Joy," Milan was saying, letting go of Feyi to extend his arms in welcome.

"Yes, hi— Oh, we're hugging!" Joy said, widening her eyes over his shoulder at Feyi.

"Hell yeah. Heard only good shit about you."

"Ah, then she didn't talk me up enough," Joy replied, and everyone laughed. They did a quick round of introductions for the rest of the group—Grant the doctor, Tolu the finance guy, Clint the architect. Nasir was a consultant in some field or the other; he didn't seem as keen on talking about his work as the others. Tolu kept dropping clumsy hints about how hard he was balling, where he was vacationing, all while casting sidelong glances at Joy, clearly trying to impress her. Feyi fought back a yawn—she hated pretending like she gave a fuck about some random man's small talk.

Nasir slid next to her. "Milan says you're an artist?" His cologne was a faint musk, slithering notes of spice.

"Yeah," she replied. It still felt weird to call that her job, even though it had been years now. "I make things."

"That's a great way to put it." Nasir angled his head toward her and smiled. "I'm a bit of a collector myself. Just starting out, but I'd love to see your work if you're open. You got any shows coming up?"

His hair shone in tight black curls, and Feyi tried not to notice how his shirt stretched over his chest.

"Not at the moment. I've done a few group shows, and I had my first solo show up in Boston last year."

"Oh, you from there?"

Feyi made a face. "Not really. My parents teach in Cambridge."

"Well." Nasir reached into his pocket and pulled out his wallet. "Maybe we could set up a studio visit sometime?" He handed her a business card, and Feyi took it gingerly, surprised at the weight of the embossed black paper. It had only his name and a phone number on it.

"Oh, you're serious, huh?" she said.

He laughed. "I'm always serious."

Damn, she thought, even his laugh was sexy. His eyes crinkled up at the corners, and as he stared at her, Feyi reminded herself that she was there with Milan, not to check out his homeboys. She slid his card into her purse. Nasir's eyes flickered past her, and his face lit up with a joy that surprised her with how much it transformed his face. "Lorraine!" he called out, then directed the brilliance of his delighted smile at Feyi.

"My sister," he explained, "she just flew in this evening."

A short girl with flawless skin and long blond sisterlocks threw herself into his arms, her duffel bag smacking against Feyi's arm. She and Nasir laughed with the same full, wide mouths, spinning around, and Feyi took that moment to slip away and find Joy, who had escaped to the bar and was checking out the new arrival with shameless interest.

Feyi nudged her with an elbow in the ribs. "You're drooling," she said.

"Can you blame me?" Joy replied. "Look at her! You think she's into girls?"

"Like that matters when it comes to you."

Joy winked. "Good point. I'm gonna see if she'll let me buy her a drink."

Feyi shook her head and laughed. "Go on with your bad self." She knew better than to try and stop Joy from shooting her shot. "Good luck."

"Ha. Don't need it."

Joy left with a prowl in her shoulders, and Feyi headed to the roof, tapping people on their arms or the smalls of their backs as she pushed through the crowd, murmuring apologies and thank-yous until she made it through the doors. There were a few clusters of people outside, some smoking in a corner, most just standing and talking. The city was a spread of buildings and lights below them. Feyi braced her hands against the cool iron of the railing and closed her eyes, feeling the air against her skin, listening to the layers of sound, the DJ inside, the chatter and music around her, the faint cars all those stories down. She wanted another drink. She wanted to get in a car with Milan and go back to his place, come against his mouth, leave while he was still asleep so she could spend the night in her own bed without his flesh breathing beside her. She wanted to forget she was real.

"Mind if I join you?"

The voice came in low and unexpected, close to her ear. Feyi stumbled in her heels as she whipped around, startled. Milan's homeboy was right there, sliding a hand across her back and pulling her away from the railing, his palm against her bare skin. Feyi had a moment of regretting her outfit, how little her dress covered, how much of her skin was exposed and rippling with goose bumps at his touch. His name was still fresh in the front of her mind, his scent, and he was close, too close, throwing her even more off-balance. Feyi planted a hand on his chest to stop herself from falling entirely against him.

"You're touching me," she complained.

It felt electric, small shocks shooting through her. Heat radiated off his body, and Feyi's traitorous flesh responded, her pulse quickening.

Nasir smiled. "First of all, I'm helping you not fall off a building," he answered. "Second of all"—and here he made a point of looking at her hand on his chest and dropping his voice a little—"*you're* touching *me*."

Feyi recovered her balance and took her hand off his chest. "There," she said. "You can take your hand away now." She

23

wondered if he could tell that her breathing was a little too fast, her pupils stretching.

Nasir lifted his palm off her back, but only a little, leaving his fingertips grazing the skin over her spine. "Are you sure?" he asked, his words soft and playful.

Feyi's breath tangled in her lungs. The words were too close to Milan's in that bathroom the first time, too intimate. They had too much weight, and Nasir was looking at her with greedy eyes. Suddenly, whatever was happening between them felt too fast and too dangerous, like she was right at the edge of a cliff with dark but hungry unknowns waiting for her to tip over. His mouth looked soft; his teeth sharp behind those full lips. Feyi felt it at the back of her neck—he was *hunting* her. That unwavering look by the bar, now finding her up here, tracking her under the city's sky.

"Don't do that," she said, throwing up reflexive walls. "I don't know you like that."

Nasir stepped away immediately, slipping his hands into his pockets. "You're right. I'm being . . . inappropriate." He ducked his head and his mouth twisted. "I thought we were both feeling something, but—never mind. I sound like a dick. My bad."

She hadn't been expecting such quick contrition. He looked almost awkward, like his charm had been a front, and Feyi wasn't sure what to say. "You're very . . . obvious," she managed.

Nasir smiled a little and shrugged. "Yeah, so I've been told."

"But also, what's the point?"

He looked up, surprised. "Excuse me?"

The words had slipped out unexpected, but Feyi kept

24

going, wrapping the mild aggression around her like a shield. It felt better than all the uncertainty.

"Nah, for real. You're here flirting with me, touching me like you want something, but what's the point? You wanna hook up?"

Nasir looked aghast at how blunt she was being. It amused Feyi to see it. Men were never used to being called out on their bullshit.

"What's the point, my nigga?" she pressed. "What's your end goal?"

He laughed, bringing a hand up to cover his mouth, suddenly awkward. "Aw fuck, you're going in."

Feyi shrugged. "You didn't think first? You just went for it, thought, *Hey, let me hit on the girl Milan's here with*? Don't you niggas have a code or some shit? Or you thought Milan wouldn't mind sharing?"

As soon as she said that, whatever little ease that was left in the air between them drained away completely.

"I didn't mean it like that," Nasir said, his face sobering up.

Feyi wrapped her arms around herself, a heaviness crawling in, touched with real anger. "How else do you mean it when you try to fuck the girl your boy is fucking?" She shook her head and started walking past him. "I need to go find my friend."

"Feyi."

She ignored him as she pushed past, shoulder-checking him. Nasir grabbed her arm.

"Feyi!" He dropped his hand when she gave him a look that dragged white-hot from his grip on her to his face. "Just listen, please. It's not like that."

25

She did not care. She couldn't even articulate how much she did not care. Maybe this was a thing with Milan and his boys, passing a girl around. Maybe they did threesomes, or trains. She just wanted to find Joy.

"It's getting cold out here."

"I *felt* something." Nasir was standing close to her again, his eyes searing above his cheekbones. "I'm not trying to fuck you. From the second I saw you, I *felt* something. I don't know what it was, what it is, but it's not how you're making it sound. Like, I love Milan, that's my boy! Swear to God, I'm not trying to play him."

Feyi frowned. He was babbling, his eyebrows pulled together, his voice urgent, and it was making her curious. He seemed to care so much about how she saw him, so she let him continue, her arms still crossed over her body.

"All I know is I saw you and— Look, just now, I only asked that because I didn't want to stop touching you. I didn't want you to stop touching me. I just—" Nasir dragged a hand over his face and exhaled. "Fuck, I sound unhinged. I don't know. I'm sorry."

Feyi stared up at him. God, he was fine, even if a little unhinged. She wanted him closer. She wanted him far, *far* away. For a moment, she considered taking his hand and leading him into the bathroom, finding out if he fucked as desperately as he talked. Maybe that could become her signature—an apparition who flitted about the city, pulled men into small rooms, and had her way with them. Small fractions of time, not enough for her to become real in. It could become addictive; it felt so good to be on the receiving end of these men's hungers. It felt like power. Feyi wanted Nasir to put his long hands to her face and kiss her like their friends weren't there, kiss her precisely *because* she was with his homeboy, burn up their friendship because he wanted her that much. After years of numbness, that was something that could turn her on. Feyi liked the proofs of want, like Milan making reckless choices in that bathroom, like this man making a fool of himself right now.

Except, he just said he wasn't trying to fuck her, even if that was a virtuous lie. All this was just desire, blind and stupid, and it had nothing to do with who she was, so it wasn't even personal, no matter how deep he was trying to make it sound. They'd just met. He didn't know her; he'd just seen someone pretty with turquoise cornrows and a plum mouth, a body leashed in black sequins, so of course he wanted to touch her and be touched. Of course he wanted to fuck her, no matter what he said. If anything, Feyi was irritated that he was acting so heartfelt. What she had with Milan was sure and simple, honest from the start, not with all these masks Nasir was placing on top of his lust.

"You're just describing attraction," she told him, her voice cutting. "It's not that deep, plus there are a thousand ways to handle it better than how you did." She looked around and spotted Joy holding two drinks and trying to wriggle through the dance floor. "I gotta go." If she didn't know better, she'd say he looked distraught—his brow still furrowed, his eyes worried. She relented slightly, enough to give him a small smile, a throwaway parting gift. "It was nice to meet you, Nasir."

He hesitated before leaning in and kissed her cheek, quick and light, a daring butterfly of a goodbye. "Pleasure," he murmured, his eyes dragging over her one last time before he turned away.

Feyi watched him leave, the touch of his lips fading on her skin as the bass thumped around her.

Chapter Three

Feyi broke up with Milan two weeks later. It wasn't because of Nasir, not exactly, and it wasn't quite a breakup, because they technically weren't even dating. It was just that somewhere along the way, Feyi had started to feel like it wasn't enough.

"But he's so pretty!" Joy whined over brunch. "He can't be that bad in bed."

"He's not bad at all! It's just . . . it's good. It's nice."

Joy winced. "*Nice* is not how you want your stroke game described."

"It's . . . pleasant?"

"Oh God." Joy laughed. "Just stop. You're killing both me and that poor guy's reputation." She signaled to a waiter for their mimosas to be refilled and looked at Feyi, tapping her acrylics against her empty glass. "What more did you want from him? A relationship?"

"Nah, fuck that." Feyi dabbed at the corner of her mouth with her napkin, then dropped it into her lap, sighing. "I don't know, really. More . . . oomph? More sparks? That first night in the bathroom was amazing, but the more we did it, the more . . . settled he became?"

"Same shit every time, huh?"

"Yo, like a restaurant where the menu never changes." Feyi shook her head. "I tried asking if he wanted to switch it up, but it just . . . never happened."

"So you want, like, more passion."

"Maybe? Doesn't that just fade eventually?"

"Oh, please." Joy leaned back to let the waiter refill her glass. "Y'all weren't some married couple going on their eleventh year of monotonous fucking or some shit. Doesn't apply."

Feyi smiled a thank-you at the waiter, then ran a finger along the cool edge of her glass. "He felt comfortable. Like a friend."

Milan hadn't seemed bothered when she told him she wanted to stop the sex. He'd asked if they could still hang out once in a while, and to her surprise, Feyi had been open to the idea, curious to see what it could look like without the fucking.

"Yikes." Joy grimaced. "So what you're saying is, Milan's a goddamn teddy bear."

"Shit. I guess I didn't wanna fuck a teddy bear."

Joy put down her mimosa. "Bye. You're done."

"I'm sorry!" Feyi laughed. "But it's true."

"Well, he had a good run." Joy raised her glass. "To Milan, the teddy bear who'll always be there if you do need your guts rearranged."

Feyi mock gasped, her lips curving in amusement. "That's cold. He's a *person*."

"Like you give a fuck. Toast, bitch."

They tapped their glasses together, a clear bell over the table.

"To Milan," Feyi said.

Joy put down her glass and narrowed her eyes, already done with him and plotting ahead. "Okay, now, think about what you want next. Like what you *really* want."

"I might take a break from this," Feyi replied. "I don't know if I want to get all intimate with someone else, you know?"

Joy ignored her completely. "Ooh, you need someone real nasty. Suck your toes and shit. Let you put a thumb in they ass. Keep it spicy."

Feyi gave up. "I worry about you sometimes."

"Worry about yourself. You're the one who just cut off your dick supply."

"Whatever. Tell me what's going on with you."

Feyi ate her poached eggs, listening as Joy told her about the married woman she was seeing, her therapist's strong disapproval, the thrill she got from sneaking around with her. She made the appropriate sounds, but Joy's question about what she really wanted still simmered at the back of Feyi's mind, like an irritating splinter. She knew what she wanted, and if she was being honest, she'd known it since that night at the bar, but Feyi didn't *want* to want like that. She didn't want to think about Nasir's fumbling declarations or the way he looked at her, like he wanted more than her body. Feyi preferred to believe that he didn't know what he wanted, and she most certainly preferred to ignore how good it had felt to be seduced by that kind of attention.

Milan would have never done what Nasir did if their places were switched, moving to her like that, because it was just a fuck. He could find it anywhere else; of course he hadn't cared when she broke it off. He was probably fucking someone else already. Feyi wasn't special, even if she'd felt that way at first, when he'd been so close to her in the bathroom, losing control like he was starving for her. She couldn't tell Joy this, because Joy would immediately point out how there was absolutely nothing to romanticize about what they'd done. In the light of day, it was just reckless and foolish. In the bloody glow of that bathroom, it had felt different, but Feyi knew Joy was right. Milan had done what felt good for his dick, and then there was Nasir, insisting he didn't want to fuck her, as if he wanted her more than her body.

That was what Feyi wasn't sure she was ready for. Maybe she didn't have anything to give other than her body, not right now. Not when she kept dreaming of glass and tarmac and white lilies. She was glad Milan hadn't gone looking for more. She was a little hurt he hadn't gone looking for more. Could he sense the wounded expanse she held inside, was that what had kept him guarded? Was that what Nasir was hunting?

Feyi forced herself to stop wandering off, dragging her attention back to the table as Joy told her a story that seemed to be mostly about marital indiscretions and increasingly complicated sex toys. It was only later, after they'd parted ways and Feyi was back home on her couch, ignoring an incomplete grant application, that the thought popped up again—what if she was only interesting as an unknown, before you actually spent time around her? Had Milan been . . . underwhelmed? Would Nasir lose interest the minute she became real, not a mirage against a city skyline? *Why did any of it matter?*

Feyi put a cushion over her face and groaned into it. This was a spiral she didn't need to fall into. It would probably be a good idea to see if she could move up her appointment with her therapist to earlier in the week. She lay there for a moment, just the soft darkness of the cushion against her eyes and the bubbling whir of her aquarium in the background, until her phone began to ring. Reaching out blindly with one hand, Feyi swiped at the screen and brought it to her ear.

"Hello?" she said, her voice muffled.

"Feyi? It's Nasir." His voice sounded just like it did on that roof, sleek and much too close for her comfort. Feyi sat up, throwing the cushion aside, her pulse racing.

"Um, who?" She was a whole-ass liar, she'd totally heard his name, but it didn't make sense that he'd be calling her. Who had given him her number?

"Nasir. Milan's friend? Joy gave me your number."

When did *that* happen? Never mind.

"Oh, hey, Nasir! This is . . . a surprise."

He laughed softly. "I know. I'm sorry I didn't text first, I figured I'd just try my luck with a call. Surprised you picked up a number you didn't know."

"Shit, so am I."

There was an awkward pause before he cleared his throat and kept talking. "So, um, I was wondering if you'd like to have dinner with me."

"Ah, so you heard about me and Milan." The words slipped out, and Feyi winced at how blunt they sounded. She might as well have called him an opportunistic vulture.

Nasir made a small amused sound. "There's that directness again," he said. "And yes, I heard about you and Milan. I also heard you when you said there were other ways to deal with attraction; I figured asking you out to dinner was a better way than how I handled things."

"I mean, you're not wrong," she replied, even as her mind

33

sped through what he was saying. A date. He was asking her on a date. "Did you tell Milan you were doing this?"

"No, I didn't." Nasir's voice was firm. "I don't think you're Milan's property or that I need his permission to ask you out. And besides, it's just dinner."

"So . . . it's not a date?"

"Oh, it very much *is* a date, Feyi, trust. I would just like to see how it goes first. If there needs to be a conversation between me and Milan, no offense, but that's between me and Milan. You can tell him whatever, whenever you want."

He sounded so clear, like he'd carved out a road to her, like he wouldn't even entertain the possibility of drama. Feyi smiled, glad that he couldn't see her face.

"So," Nasir continued, "will you go to dinner with me?"

Ah, fuck it. "When?"

"You free tonight?"

Feyi laughed. "You don't waste time, huh?"

Nasir's voice stayed even. "I want to see you," he said, and it was that, that simple sentence threaded with the hunger she now thought of when she thought of him, it hooked itself into Feyi.

"Okay," she said. "I can do tonight. Around seven thirty."

"Can I pick you up?"

"Sure," she said, letting her smile seep into her voice. "I'll text you the address."

"Perfect," Nasir replied, then, "I can't wait."

Feyi hung up, texted Nasir her address, then immediately called Joy on video.

"Hey, girl, how's it going?" Joy answered, her face filling the screen.

"Bitch, did you give my number to Milan's friend?"

"Ooh!" Joy rolled over on her stomach and propped the phone up, white pillows clouding around her. "Did he call?"

Feyi raised an eyebrow at her best friend. "First of all, whose fucking bed are you in? I thought you were going shopping."

"I'm in a hotel, bitch, mind your business. Tell me if he called!"

"Yeah, he did, but it's whatever. He wants to take me out to dinner tonight."

Joy shrieked in delight, kicking up her legs. "Yes, bitch! Get in there!"

Feyi shook her head. "I fucking can't with you. When did you even give him my number?"

"Shit, I texted him right after brunch. He gave me his card that night at the club, told me he was into you but he'd blown it, and if it ever looked like he could have a shot, I should give him a chance."

It was the last thing Feyi had expected to hear, Nasir charming Joy over to his side. "What the fuck? Why didn't you tell me any of this?"

Joy shrugged. "Girl, you were kinda shook that night. I was going to trash his number but honestly, I kinda appreciated his strategy. He a sneaky motherfucker. Plus, I saw the sparks between y'all, so it hit me after brunch—maybe that's what you were missing with Milan, you know?"

Feyi sighed and pressed her fingers against the bridge of her nose. "I can't do it, Joy. I don't know why I said yes. This is some ho-ass shit, working my way around the friend group."

Joy rolled her eyes. "Well, excuse me, I had no idea you had plans to fuck him in the middle of the restaurant tonight."

Feyi glared at her, but Joy was unrepentant.

"Nobody's calling you a ho except you," she continued. "Milan wouldn't say that shit and *clearly* Nasir doesn't give a fuck. Just go have fun."

"Maybe it's time to hit pause on this dating shit." It would've been easier to fuck Nasir than to go on a date with him. Feyi considered inviting him up to her apartment instead, getting it over with. It couldn't be that hard now that she'd gotten back in the swing of things with Milan; it was just a different bicycle.

"Why? Because this one feels like he could be serious?" Joy's face softened on the screen. "I know it was easy to get rid of Milan, and I know it's scary, love, but one day you're gonna have to give something serious a chance again. Maybe Nasir is it—not the serious thing itself, but just the chance. Don't run away from it."

Feyi groaned, her stomach dropping. "I hate growth."

"I know, hun. It's a bitch. What are you gonna wear tonight?"

"I'm gonna go take a nap."

"Boring. But sure, get your rest in case y'all get it in tonight."

"You're disgusting. Don't you have a married woman to be turning out?"

Joy winked. "She's in the bathroom."

"Oh my God. Goodbye."

"Call me after the date!"

Feyi hung up and flopped on her bed, her concerns about the date paling a little next to a blossom of worry for Joy. She'd seen her best friend actually fall in love with women like this before, and it always ended in a messy breakup once Joy realized they wouldn't leave their boyfriends or husbands to go play happy lesbians with her. Those women never wanted to live that openly, but Joy fell for them anyway, playing the same story out over and over again. She wasn't wrong about Feyi's forming patterns, either, the way she chose Milan because he didn't want anything deeper than what she was offering yet worried there was something wrong with her because he wanted only what he wanted and not more.

It was impossible to nap, so Feyi went through her favorite playlists and got ready instead. By the time it was seven thirty, she was a ball of jangling nerves and Joy's words about Nasir being a chance were sticking to her like a wet and heavy skin. What if Joy was right and this could be something different? Just thinking about it made Feyi nauseous.

She paced the apartment, her mules clicking against the hardwood, her dress swirling around her legs. She and Milan would never have gone on a date. Maybe she was too dressed up. Maybe she should've worn jeans and slides to show that this wasn't a big deal, that she didn't care.

"It's just a first date, calm down," Feyi told herself, turning her phone in her hands. She wished Joy was home. "You got this. Relax. It's not serious."

Her phone vibrated with a text from Nasir saying he was downstairs, and Feyi blew out a relieved breath and grabbed her keys. Getting the date over with was better than waiting.

Nasir flashed his headlights once she stepped out onto the sidewalk, and Feyi climbed into his sports car. It hugged low to the ground, and the seats inside were a buttery leather. Nasir was wearing a jewel blue shirt, his thighs encased in denim. When he leaned over to kiss her cheek hello, Feyi wondered if he'd ever feel a comfortable distance from her— he was always too close or too far away, or often, both at the same time.

"You look amazing," he said.

Feyi shrugged. "You look aight," she replied, and his laugh unfurled something warm in her chest.

"I'll take it," he said, pulling the car out into the street.

. . .

"So," Nasir said, after they'd put in their orders at the restaurant, some bougie farm-to-table place everyone kept talking about. "Joy told me you're not looking for a relationship, probably just something light and fun, and I've been wondering why ever since."

Feyi tore off a piece of bread from the basket and slathered a dab of herb butter on it. "What's there to wonder about?"

"Look, no judgment. We're all around the same age, right? I just turned twenty-seven."

"Twenty-nine," she said. So, he was younger. Interesting.

"Close enough. And I feel like either people spent their early twenties fucking around and are thinking about if they should settle down, or they were in a relationship that whole time and are catching up now."

"That's a whole lotta generalizations."

Nasir made a face. "Fair enough. I don't really care about other people. Just been wondering, why *you* against a relationship . . . like, some guy fuck you over, or what?"

Feyi narrowed her eyes, focusing on her bread. He was asking pointed questions, and it wasn't the question she minded as much as the assumptions he was wrapping around it. "So, some guy had to have fucked me over for me to not want a relationship now?" she asked, not bothering to keep the bite out of her voice.

"Ah, fuck. I didn't mean that—" Nasir took a deep breath. "Let me try again. I'm dating because I'm interested in being in a long-term committed relationship. I'm a little nervous because Joy seemed to make it clear that you're . . . not. And I'm being hella clumsy right now in trying to find out why, okay? I'm sorry."

Feyi looked at him for a few moments, partly just because it was nice to see him squirm. He was sounding surprisingly old-fashioned for someone who hadn't opened her car door for her.

"Look," she said finally. "I could tell you the real story, but I don't think you want that. Most people don't. Y'all want the simple explanation. I'm bitter and jaded and fucking around because of it, or I'm a party girl who just doesn't want to settle down, or I'm just a ho. Everyone prefers something that's easy to swallow."

"I'm not Milan."

Feyi raised her eyebrows. "Whoa there."

Nasir shrugged. "I know my friend. He's dealing with some heavy shit with those kids he works with, day in, day out, and he runs away from anything else that's got some weight to it. I'm not him. I want the real thing. I don't need it to be light and easy."

She wondered if he was telling the truth. She was almost sure he was just talking shit. *Take a chance*, Joy's voice said in her head. *Don't run.*

"All right, then. Since you asked for it." Feyi put her hands in her lap, resting them against the smooth white napkin. It had been so long since she'd talked about this to someone new. Milan had never asked enough questions to get here in the weeks they'd been involved, and she'd been grateful for it. Feyi wasn't even sure where to start at first, but she wanted to keep it short. So, the beginning and then the end, skip the in-between. Nasir's eyes were fixed on hers as he listened.

"His name was Jonah. We'd been together off and on since high school. Got married right out of college."

Nasir smiled. "That's sweet," he said. "You don't get to hear many stories like that anymore."

Feyi tried to smile, but her face couldn't quite get there. "Yeah, um . . ." She took a deep breath, hating the tears that were already trying to show up. "We were in a car accident five years ago. Nothing much happened to me, but Jonah . . . Jonah died." She shrugged and didn't look up at him. The table and her plate were already a blurry mess behind the tears. "That's the end of the story." Feyi pressed her napkin to her eyes. "Jesus. Sorry."

Nasir reached across the small table and touched her arm, his voice gentle. "No, don't be. And thank you for sharing that with me, and I'm sorry if I pushed too hard."

Feyi ignored his apology. She was the one pushing herself, trying new things, telling old stories. "Yeah, well. It's not the best first-date material. More like a third date, or really, a never-bring-it-up kinda thing." She laughed shakily and blinked the rest of the tears away.

"You okay?" Nasir's worry was almost palpable.

"I'm fine," she lied. "But yeah, I haven't wanted to date seriously since, and Joy took it upon herself to try and get me out on the scene again. Milan was the first person I dated since, and that was only a few months ago." She folded the napkin in her lap. "Light and simple is all I've been able to handle."

Nasir nodded. "I hear you. Let's just . . . take it slow, then? Like incredibly slow-motion slow. Like, friends first, maybe?"

Somehow, he sounded like he meant it.

Feyi smiled at him, feeling surprisingly raw and tender. "I'd like that."

He smiled back at her. "Now, let's talk about your work."

Feyi groaned. "Do we have to?"

Nasir's face had lit up as soon as he'd switched the topic to art. "I wanna know! My dad's a big collector; he's actually the one who got me into it. Said it was never too early to start."

"Oh, word? Who're you into?"

The waiter came by with their plates, duck breast with risotto for Feyi and a glazed pork chop on a bed of veggies for Nasir, who twirled his steak knife as he thought about her question.

"I mean, definitely Kehinde Wiley."

"Of course." Feyi laughed. "I bet you'd like a wall-size painting of yourself reclining in velvet and silk."

41

"Um, obviously. Hang that shit above my bed with a quickness."

"That's sexy right there."

Nasir grinned at her, his eyes crinkling. "I like you," he said. "But don't think I didn't notice you avoiding the question about your work."

"Technically, you didn't ask a question about my work."

He raised an eyebrow. "Touché. What do you make? Painting, sculpture, collage?"

"Eh." Feyi cut into her duck, and a caper rolled to the edge of her plate, small and dark and green. It felt odd to be talking about her work on a date. She was used to keeping it in a whole separate world. "Little bit of everything."

A stiff shirt splashed in dry brown, the jagged tears. A gold ring spinning. Another, then another, then another. It was better if it all stayed in that other world.

"You'll see it one day," she lied. "It's always better to see the work than to hear about it."

"Can't wait," he replied. "I'm still down to do that studio visit if you're up for it."

Feyi paused, startled. He wasn't supposed to do that, keep following up like he meant it.

"How about next week?" he continued. "Where's your studio?"

"Brooklyn," she replied automatically. "Not far from my place."

Nasir smiled. "It's a date."

Feyi's smile mirrored his, even as her mind raced, trying to find somewhere else to shift things to. "Is your sister still in town?"

42

"Nah, she flew back to the islands a coupla days ago."

"Oh, that's home for y'all?"

"Yeah, my dad lives there. Runs a restaurant."

"Nice. With your mom?"

Nasir paused and moved some veggies around on his plate. "Um, no. She died when I was a kid."

Feyi stopped eating. "Oh." So he knew death, too. "I'm so sorry, Nasir."

He looked up and smiled. "It's all good. It was a long time ago. What about your parents?"

"Oh, they're up in Cambridge. Professors. You know how Nigerians are."

Nasir laughed as their waiter started to clear their plates. "Y'all overachievers are everywhere."

"I mean, facts, though. We can't help being amazing."

"Yeah . . . I don't think you can." Nasir's eyes were reflecting the softened lights of the restaurant, and Feyi caught the weight in his voice. She looked down at her hands, the stacked rings she wore, and made small talk as they declined dessert and he picked up the check. When they stepped out of the restaurant, Feyi turned to him. She had to ask, because she was deciding whether she could believe him or not, and there was no point moving forward if she couldn't.

"Did you mean what you said?"

Nasir was shrugging his jacket back on. "About what?"

"Being friends first. Or was that just a line to get me comfortable?"

He touched her elbow to move her out of the doorway as another couple walked out, guiding her to the side, then looking down at her with a careful seriousness.

"Of course I meant it. Why wouldn't I?"

Feyi cut her eyes at him. "Come on. Y'all niggas will say anything."

"Feyi." Nasir took her hand in his. "I'm trying to get to know you. However you want, at whatever pace you like. If you want to go slow, that's fine with me."

"Even though I already hooked up with Milan?" The words felt like a weapon in her mouth, or a shield, or a spear pushing him away. If he was serious, then Nasir had to look at her, the real version, not whatever he was spinning in his head.

He didn't let go of her hand. "Woman, I told you already. I'm not Milan. I'm not looking for what he was looking for." Nasir shrugged. "This is different, and I don't take friendship lightly."

Feyi kept her voice casual. "Shit, I'm just making sure."

"Nah, that's fair. I'm sure niggas be talking a lot of game around you." He smiled at her. "You doing anything this weekend?"

"Maybe. Why, what's up?"

Nasir pulled her hand into the crook of his elbow as they started walking to his car. "There's a Moses Sumney concert Saturday night and Tolu has VIP tickets. Thought you might like to come."

Feyi laughed. "Yo, Joy would kill me if I went to see Moses without her."

"She can come, too. Shit, Tolu would probably wet himself if she did."

It would be fine if Joy was there. Feyi could handle anything if Joy was there. "Okay, cool. Let's do it."

Nasir opened her door for her, his face creased in a smile.

He looked delighted that she'd agreed. "Sounds like a plan."

Feyi watched as he walked around to his side of the car, his silhouette graceful and dark. She felt a little jumpy, like this was moving too fast, even though being friends was a *slow* step. It was supposed to be nonthreatening. It wasn't meant to feel like she had set off on a river marked with white water, an insistent current taking her around a bend she couldn't see.

Nasir played one of Moses's albums as they drove back to her place, and Feyi watched the city speed past her window. The music didn't need them to talk, so they didn't, and Feyi wrapped it all around her—the sounds, the feeling of Nasir sitting next to her, the heat off his body, the comfort of knowing he wouldn't try to press himself against her, not after watching her cry about Jonah. A wave of embarrassment warmed her face, and when Nasir pulled up in front of her building, Feyi unlocked her door quickly.

"Guess I'll see you on Saturday," she said.

Nasir grinned and reached over to hug her. "I had a great evening."

"Same," Feyi agreed, as his arms slipped around her. She felt his gaze searing at her back as she stepped out of the car. If Nasir was hunting her, then he was patient and he was very good at it. Feyi had stayed lost for a very long time, though. She had no intention of being found.

Chapter Four

Feyi leaned against Nasir's chest at the concert, his arm wrapped around her waist. They were standing close to the stage, next to Joy and Tolu, watching Moses Sumney sway under the lights with green netting draped around his shoulders. The singer's eyes were closed as he stretched out his carved arms, his voice piercing the air and glitter shining off his bare chest. Nasir pressed his cheek to Feyi's braids and sang the lyrics softly to her—" 'I'm not trying to / go to bed with you / I just wanna make out in my car.'" Feyi giggled, warmth rippling over her skin, Nasir's breath brushing against her ear. He was wearing a black T-shirt and jeans, so casually handsome that both men and women around them kept stealing glances.

"Everyone's checking you out," Feyi told him.

Nasir laughed. "Nah, that's all you." He dropped his voice as he whispered to her. "You look so fucking beautiful none of us know what to do with ourselves."

Feyi couldn't stop the smile that spread over her face in a spill of pleasure, so wide that Joy gave them both an appraising look as she passed Feyi a cocktail in a plastic cup.

"Y'all keep it PG, now," she warned.

"Mind your business, my friend." Feyi winked at Joy as she took the drink, and Joy laughed, her voice blackberry rich, then turned her attention back to the stage.

"That body!" Joy said, gazing up at Moses. "How do we get backstage? I would like to get . . . acquainted."

Nasir chuckled. "Ask Tolu, he's the one who got us the tickets. I think he went to school with Moses."

Joy rolled her eyes. "And break his heart?" Tolu was standing behind her, bright and hopeful in his crush, smoothing down his blazer. "He still thinks this night is gonna end well for him."

Nasir shook his head. "Whew, you're cold."

Feyi listened to their banter, noting how comfortable she felt in the circle of his arms. Her body fit against his as if they were something—a unit, lovers safe in a harbor. All four of them had gone to dinner before the concert, at a vegan spot on Fifth Avenue, and Nasir had passed Feyi plates of tofu kebabs and seaweed salad, his thigh and shoulder pressed against hers. It hadn't felt like she was being crowded, more like he was reassuring her with solid touches, saying he was there, he was real, he meant what he said about being friends, look at the easy comfort, how smooth things could be. It was a story Feyi could fall into, a thick blanket wrapped like an exhale around her. Moses finished a song, and the crowd exploded into applause. He sketched a bow on the stage, skin gleaming under the lights, and Feyi lifted her head to speak to Nasir over the noise, as she handed him her drink.

"Hey, I'm gonna go to the bathroom real quick."

"Ooh, same!" Joy threw back the rest of her drink, then gave her empty cup to Tolu, grabbing Feyi's hand. "Try not to make out, boys, we'll be right back."

They pushed through the crowd as Moses began his next song in Hebrew, the sound waxing ethereal through the air, turning the venue into a cathedral, staining the air with

47

something holy. The crowd settled into a transfixed stillness as Feyi and Joy joined the line for the bathroom.

Feyi took a deep breath, loosening her shoulders and rolling her neck around. "I love this song," she said. "It feels so peaceful, you know?"

"Mm-hmm." Joy leaned against the wall. "You and Nasir look cute together."

Feyi pushed her braids out of her face and smiled. "Yeah . . . he's nice."

"Girl, here you go with that nice shit again."

"You know what I mean. It just—it feels weird to be doing things like this."

"What, going on an actual date?"

"Yeah. I feel . . . I feel a little guilty, I guess?" Feyi looked down at her leather mules, but Joy reached out and tilted her head up.

"Hey, don't even go there. Jonah would want you to be happy, you know that. It's been five years, boo. You gotta move out of mourning at some point."

"Yeah, I know."

"Besides, you not even fucking this nigga."

Feyi threw her hands up. "I know, but that's what feels so fucked up! We out here going on dates and building a friendship—"

Joy snorted. "I see his mouth all up on your neck, that ain't no damn friendship."

"Right, whatever, my point is—it feels like it's leading up to a foundation for something . . . something real. And I'm not ready for that. I don't want that shit."

"Oh my God, Feyi, it's been one dinner and a concert."

Joy rolled her eyes. "No one's proposing to you. Chill."

"Ugh." Feyi pinched the bridge of her nose. "You're right. I'm jumping way ahead. I should be in the moment."

"Yes, bitch! And might I say, it is a sexy-ass moment—how much longer are y'all gonna play this cuddling abstinent game? Nasir looks like he loves to give head, I'm just saying."

Feyi snorted out a laugh. "I know, right? Like he'd just stay down there for hours."

"Pass that nigga a snorkel."

The girls laughed together as the line shrank and they stepped into the bathroom, waiting for the next stall door to open.

"Nah, it just feels weird, though," Feyi said. "Like, it was easy with Milan. I already cried in front of Nasir, shit feels too . . ." She waved her hands about vaguely.

"Too open," Joy filled in. "I feel you."

"Yeah, too open. I'm not ready to have sex with someone who's actually trying to *see* me. Can you imagine me freaking out in the middle, just fucking bawling for no reason?"

"Yikes. That's not cute."

"Thank you! So I'ma just keep it tucked in for now."

Two stalls opened next to each other, and they went in as Joy kept talking, her voice carrying over the divider. "Personally, I think that you should keep seeing Milan. Fuck him on the side while practicing the whole emotional shit with Nasir."

Feyi paused in the middle of folding up some tissue. "You know, if that wasn't such a terribly messy idea, it would be fucking brilliant. Goddammit. Why did they have to know each other?"

Joy flushed and went to wash her hands. "Cockblockers. Men ruin everything, I swear."

Feyi joined her, and they touched up their makeup in the mirror, passing each other a tube of lip gloss. They were heading back to the guys when Joy grabbed Feyi's arm and hissed in her ear. "Don't look, but I swear that's Milan over there."

Feyi turned her head, and Joy pinched her.

"I said don't look!"

"How the fuck am I supposed to know if it's him without looking?"

"Oh. Good point. Okay, look, but make it subtle. I know that's hard for you Nigerians but try."

Feyi shoved her gently and glanced over. She was right—it was Milan, standing there in a white tee, all tall and copper with his diamonds in his ears.

"I'm gonna go over and say hi," Feyi said, surprising even herself.

Joy gave her a look but didn't argue. "You want me to come with you?"

"Nah, I'm good. I'll come find y'all in a sec."

"Aight." Joy gave her a light smack on the ass. "Don't trip and fall on his dick now."

"Girl, we are in public!"

"Like that ever stopped either one of us." Joy laughed, and the sound disappeared into the crowd with her.

Feyi exhaled and cracked her knuckles, pulling the music of Moses's voice around her like armor as she walked over to Milan, hoping that he wouldn't flinch at the sight of her face. She hadn't done anything wrong; there was no reason why everything shouldn't be fine. Feyi pushed her way through people, and when she was a few feet away, Milan looked up and saw her. There was a short moment in which her heart sped up, but then his face broke out into a wide smile and he held out his arms for a hug. Feyi buried a sigh of relief as she stepped into him.

"Good to see you, girl," he said, squeezing her tight.

"You too," she said. Milan's body was familiar, his beard soft and brief against her cheek.

"Nasir told me y'all might be coming together."

Feyi felt blood rush to her face. She hadn't told Milan about her date with his friend yet. "Oh, he did?"

She tried to keep her voice casual and steady, but Milan saw through it anyway and put his hand on her shoulder. "Yeah, don't worry about it. I'm not tripping."

"I wasn't sure if you'd be cool with it," Feyi admitted.

They were leaning their heads together to be heard over the sound of the show. Milan's eyes flickered, and he threw back the rest of his drink, then shrugged.

"My ex and I are trying to work things out," he said.

Feyi couldn't hide her shock. He'd never even mentioned an ex before, let alone one recent enough to revisit. "Oh, word?"

Milan winced at the look on her face. "Yeah, I know. I should have told you about her earlier, but the breakup was ugly. Like, real ugly. I just didn't wanna get into all that."

Feyi held up her hands, pressing her feelings down. It didn't matter now. "Hey, it's cool. You didn't have to fill me in on your whole backstory." She let a memory call up a little smile on her face, the two of them that first time in the

51

bathroom, the red light. "It's not like we did much talking anyway."

Milan's face creased up in a smile. "Facts." He sounded a little relieved, and Feyi decided to let the moment stay as it was, pleasant and close to sweet.

She touched his arm and smiled back. "I hope things work out with your girl. I'm gonna go find Nasir and Joy."

"It's always good to see you, Feyi. Don't be a stranger."

It felt too much like a goodbye. "Hey, maybe we'll all go on a double date," she said, wondering if they ever would. Maybe it would be awkward as hell, or maybe it would be something else.

Milan laughed. "Wouldn't that be something. Stay sexy, mama."

They hugged once more, then Feyi left, slipping between the crowd as she made her way toward the stage. Moses was singing into three microphones, layering his voice over itself, eerie and beautiful. A bright halo of light shone behind his head. Feyi could see Nasir's face in the audience, the sharp line of his jaw, the black of his hair. When she came up to him, he pulled her back into the circle of his arm and dropped a kiss on her temple, like she'd barely left, like she was back where she should be. It felt too easy, and Feyi wondered if she should be more on guard, more careful. Just then, Nasir bent to speak into her ear.

"Isn't this amazing?" he said, and Feyi looked around. The air was threaded with music, with the ache of a violin and the warp of Moses's voice as strangers gazed up at him, entranced. Joy was laughing at something Tolu had said, her face split open with amusement, her eyes warm.

It was a fiercely alive moment, down to the flesh of Nasir's arm around her, and although Feyi didn't answer him, she reached for his other arm and pulled it around herself, and they stood there, caught up in each other.

. . .

Over the next few weeks, Feyi discovered that things with Nasir almost *were* that easy. He made no secret of his attraction and interest in her, but he kept it light at the same time, flirty and warm, never trying to push it further. He didn't even mind when she kept avoiding the studio visit by coming up with excuses or just sidestepping it altogether. Feyi couldn't stop being suspicious at first, waiting for when he'd cross the line, when his act would drop and his real face would twist out into the light, but then they went on more dates, spent more time together, and the moment never came.

One night, both of them fell asleep on the couch after binge-watching *Black Mirror*, Nasir's head weighted on Feyi's shoulder. Joy took a picture of them on her way out to meet her married lover and texted it to Feyi. *Y'all are too cute*, Joy had said, and Feyi had stared at the picture, at his lashes against his skin, the calm on her face. They looked good together; they looked like friends, like they were safe with each other.

If she wasn't seeing it for herself, she wouldn't have believed that someone like him—or any guy, really—would be okay with how close to platonic this was. Maybe he'd think she was leading him on, if this didn't end up where he wanted, or maybe this was just her using him for emotional intimacy, a convenient kind of comfort, someone who was easy to hold. Nasir had said that it was fine to go slow, sure, but this was *glacial*. The worry, once it crept in, kept growing, taking up more space, until Feyi had to do something about it. She and Nasir had just finished seeing a movie together and were stepping back out into the street when she pulled him aside, under an awning.

"Hey," she said. "Are you sleeping with anyone?"

Nasir took a half step back. "Damn, okay!"

"It's cool if you are." Feyi kept her voice steady, praying he wouldn't lie to her, praying he wasn't waiting for something she wasn't sure she could give him. "I just wanted to know."

Nasir rubbed the back of his neck but met her eyes. "Well, kinda. There's this girl I hook up with once in a while, but it's just a casual thing. No strings."

Somehow, it was the perfect answer. Feyi exhaled, relieved. "Okay, good."

Nasir raised an eyebrow. "Good?"

She reached out and adjusted the collar of his jacket. "I mean, I'd feel bad if you weren't getting laid because of me."

That light energy between them was always easy to find, like sunshine scattering clouds.

Nasir caught her hand and kissed the scar on her palm. "You are . . . so thoughtful," he teased. "Thinking about not just me but my dick."

"What can I say? I'm generous like that."

He laughed as they kept walking, and a passing streetlight caught on his smile, glinting off his teeth. Feyi loved seeing him laugh. He did it so freely, with his throat thrown back and his mouth wide. She slid her arm through his, and they walked a few more blocks in an easy silence before Nasir spoke again.

"I got a question for you, too."

Feyi squeezed his arm. "Shoot."

"You gonna let me see your studio or nah?" His face was half turned to her and serious. "It's cool if not—"

"No, no." Regret shot through Feyi. She'd been pushing him away, and he didn't deserve that. "I want you to see it."

Nasir stopped, and uncertainty flickered across his face, so swift and surprising that Feyi barely caught it. "You sure?" he asked, and his voice was steady. Light draped across his cheekbone, and Feyi felt a rush of affection tighten her chest. She let it carry her and stepped out into the road, flagging down a cab.

"Come on," she said, opening the door. "Let's go."

He laughed. "Right now?"

"Yes, nigga, right now. Get in." She climbed into the car after him and shut the door, giving the cross streets to the driver. Nasir watched her as the car pulled off and shook his head, taking her hand in his across the vinyl seat.

"You know, being kidnapped by a Nigerian is turning out to be way more lit than I expected," he said.

Feyi smacked his arm. "Shut up." She laughed and scooted closer to him, dropping her head on his shoulder. They sat together as the cab went over the Williamsburg Bridge, watching the streets turn until Feyi directed the driver to pull over. She took a deep breath as they climbed up to the third floor, and she unlocked the door to her studio, flipping on the lights. The electricity crackled as the space lit up, and Feyi exhaled. This felt more intimate than anything they'd done so far. Nasir took slow steps, tracing his fingers along the rough edge of a workbench, running his eyes along the walls. Large photographs were hanging pinned from a clear line, images of gallery walls.

"That was one of my first group shows," Feyi said, wrapping her arms around herself. Nasir stepped in for a closer look. The pictures showed stained clothes displayed behind clear glass. A pair of jeans, splashed dark on the thigh. A ripped T-shirt frozen in stiff folds.

"Is that blood?" Nasir asked, his voice soft.

Feyi pulled her artist persona over her face, polished control sliding smoothly over old scarred flesh. "I recovered the clothes from the accident," she explained.

He let out a low whistle. "That's heavy."

"Yeah. I lost a lot of lightness back then." She glanced at him. "It's been nice to find some of it again."

"You still have these pieces?"

Feyi nodded and gestured to the other end of the studio. "Stored out of the sunlight." Her movement encompassed a freezer against one of the walls, with a transparent door showing neatly labeled plastic buckets.

"What's that?" Nasir asked.

A small smile pulled at the corner of Feyi's mouth. "It's blood," she answered, and laughed at his raised eyebrow. "I work a lot in blood now. Since the accident. It's so . . . it's necessary to be alive. I think there's something in using it deliberately now, versus the accident pieces, you know? There wasn't much . . . choice there."

Nasir missed the way her voice shifted into the past, he was still staring at the freezer. "Human blood?" he asked.

"Nah, pig blood." Feyi reached up and pulled off a large covering, exposing a thickly painted canvas, taller than her and stretching across the wall. It was covered in rows of neat bloody handprints, each of them with a jagged line marring the middle. "Been using it to make things like this."

Nasir came up next to her and took her left hand in his, touching the scar on her palm. "It's you," he said. "Over and over and over."

"Yeah."

"It's beautiful, Feyi." He laced his fingers with hers. "I had no idea your work would look like this. Shit, I had no idea it would . . . feel like this."

She ducked her head. "Thanks, man."

"It's wild. For real." Nasir turned to her fully. "Okay, so I have a proposition for you."

Feyi raised an eyebrow. "Sounds promising already."

"Remember when I told you my dad's the one who got me into collecting?"

"Yeah, for sure."

"Okay, so he's on the board for the National Museum back home *and* he's best friends with Rebecca Owo—"

"Shut up! The curator?"

"Yup, and get this—she's curating this group show for the museum that's opening next month. Black Diaspora artists. Apparently, there was some drama and one of the participants pulled out or got kicked out? I'm still waiting to get all the tea on that, but here's the fun part. Rebecca was gonna just close up their slot, but I got my dad to put your name in the mix."

Feyi pulled her hand out of his. "Don't play with me, Nasir."

He grinned, his teeth white and broad. "You're welcome."

"You're fucking with me."

"Nope. If you want it, it's yours. I gotta give him an answer by tomorrow, though."

"You hadn't even seen my work! Did you look it up?"

"Nah. I figured I'd wait till you were ready to show me yourself. But they looked you up for sure. Guess they liked what they found."

Feyi's breath was seizing in her lungs as she tried to process what he was saying. "Wait, wait. So you're telling me Rebecca Owo is putting me in one of her shows, last minute? That's crazy, Nasir. That doesn't happen."

He smirked. "You don't know my dad. Mans is swimming in clout."

It wasn't any easier to understand. "Why would you do all that for me?"

Nasir shrugged. "Why not?"

She cut her eyes at him. "Come the fuck on."

"Okay, fine." He gave her a charming grin. "I was going home for a few weeks anyway, and I thought this would be a great reason to have you come take a vacation with me. As friends. My dad likes hosting artists; he'd love to have you."

Feyi stared at him incredulously. "You want me to meet your dad?"

Nasir rolled his eyes. "You real cute and all, but it's not even like that. I'm just asking if you wanna come show your work on a tropical island and sneak in a vacation while you're at it." He tugged on her arm gently, his way of reassuring her that it wasn't awkward, or that it didn't have to be. "Feyi, my dad's fucking loaded. He flies me and Lorraine's friends out there all the time. It's not a big deal, I promise, but I understand if you're not comfortable."

"Excuse me, but that show is *absolutely* a big deal."

Nasir laughed. "Okay, yes. But the rest of it isn't. And if it feels like too much, just let me know."

"And you're offering all this just as friends." She couldn't help the way her voice colored skeptic, but she also didn't take it back once it was in the air between them.

"Hey." Nasir stepped in front of her and held both her hands in his. The skin of his palms was cool and dry. "When I said we could take things slow, I meant it. When I said you're my friend, I meant that shit, too. There's no way I'd try to rush you into something you're not ready for, Feyi."

She winced. "I know, I'm sorry. You're being so generous, and I hate feeling like you have to reassure me over and over."

"That's what friends do." He shrugged. "Trust is built. I could say the same shit a thousand times, but it's what I do that matters."

Feyi swore internally. See, the problem with Nasir was that he was always like this, saying things that sent tendrils of warmth curling through her, being so unflinchingly gentle that he seemed too good to be true. She cupped his cheek in her hand, affection hot and sticky in her chest. There wasn't anything enough to say, so Feyi hugged him instead and let her breath unwind out when he hugged her back, his arms strong around her body.

"Thank you," she whispered.

Nasir dropped a kiss on her braids. "Anytime," he replied. "Is that a yes?"

"I need to sleep on it! I have to go through all my work and see what I can show, if I have time to make something new, figure out transport—"

"I'll handle the logistics," he interrupted. "You just focus on the art."

Feyi shook her head. "So, let me get this straight. Your dad flies you *and* your friends out? Y'all just out here giving island vacations like you Oprah?"

Nasir winked. "First-class flights, baby. And you get your own room at his ridiculous house in the mountains."

"Shit, forget the show, you making this sound like a whole-ass resort!"

"It low-key is. I don't offer to host just anyone, you know?"

"Ah, just the homies?" she teased.

"Just the beautiful homies." He grinned back at her. "Look, take tonight, think about it. You're welcome to stay for just the group show or for as long as you like. Either way is chill."

Feyi touched his arm. "Thank you, for real. Putting my name forward was amazing enough, but covering the whole trip is next level."

"It's not my money, so fuck it." Nasir laughed. "But nah, you deserve it. Especially now that I've seen your work? We gotta talk about me buying a piece off you. You know, before you blow up and some gallery snatches you."

Feyi covered the bloodprint up, cloth floating through the air. "You'd like something like this, for real?"

"I'd like anything by you, Feyi."

She blushed and glanced around the studio. "Okay, I'll see what I got. Wanna head back to mine?"

"Yeah, sure." Nasir took one last look around the studio as they left. "Thanks for showing me this. I can feel how important your work is to you."

Feyi hit the light switch, and the room fell into darkness. They walked a few blocks back to her building, and as they stepped through the first front door, Feyi felt her pulse quicken. There was something small but important happening in her chest, a tiny leaf of want that wasn't detached, that wasn't armored and dismissive. It felt terrifying, like it would bruise and break if she touched it the wrong way, but this was Nasir. He was slow and gentle, he was making her believe that everything would be okay. She paused in the foyer, her keys hanging from her hand. Nasir placed his palm on the small of her back, one of his thousand familiar touches.

"You okay?" he asked, concern lilting in his voice.

Stop thinking, Feyi told herself. *Stop thinking and just move.* Before the fear could stop her, she turned and slid a hand behind Nasir's head, pulling his face down to hers and kissing him with a mouth full of trust. It felt different from Milan—she had been sure and reckless then, certain that nothing there could hurt her, that she was absent enough to be invincible. With Nasir, it felt like a risk, like something sweet and dangerous, like flames licking around them. He kissed her back, but gently, carefully, and Feyi pulled away.

"Don't do that," she said. "Don't hold back." If he treated her like she was fragile, that was the one thing that would make her break. Feyi didn't think she could stand it, to be touched so tentatively. People had turned her into webbed glass after Jonah died; it made her feel like a relic, not a person.

Nasir held her face in his hands, his eyes searing into hers. "Are you sure?" he asked.

Feyi bit her lower lip and nodded.

Nasir raised an eyebrow. "It's not because I seduced you with a show and a fancy vacation now, is it?"

"Oh my God." Feyi started to laugh, then broke off because he was kissing her again, unrestrained this time, his tongue sliding into her mouth, his hands trapping her face, and Feyi found herself pressed against the mailboxes, old brass cutting into her back, soft sounds being pulled up from her throat. Nasir tasted like the peppermint gum he liked, sharp and clear, like the start of a second chance. Feyi's heart was thundering, blood roaring in her ears, Nasir's hands sinking into her braids, his lips moving to the side of her neck, her pulse jumping against his teeth. She clutched at the back of his neck and looked at the tin ceiling of the foyer, feeling the world around her melt into something unreal, blurred at the edges.

Nasir nipped at her earlobe. "I've been dying to kiss you since the first time I saw you at that bar," he whispered, his warm breath swirling on her skin.

Feyi hid a smile. "I hoped you would," she confessed. "Just for a moment, when we were fighting on the roof."

Nasir pulled back, his eyes surprised. "Really? I thought you were going to tear out my throat back then."

She lifted and dropped a shoulder. "I didn't know you back then."

Nasir's eyes softened, and he ran his thumb across her lower lip, gloss smearing off its fullness. "But you know me now," he said, and Feyi could feel the weight of the question behind it. *Do you trust me now? Do you know I don't intend to hurt you, that I mean everything I say? Do you know that I care?*

He was so sweet, so terrifying in what he could represent, the possibility of someone actually seeing her. A world after Jonah.

Feyi forced her fear back and smiled at him. "I do," she said, pulling him down so she could kiss him again, feel him press against her with all that want he'd been holding in his body. "I think I know you now."

"Good," he murmured, and the word trailed like smoke from his tongue, losing itself in her mouth.

Chapter Five

The next morning, Feyi and Joy went for a run, breaking open the weekend with sweat so they could feel like they'd done something useful before they partied it all away. The sun was coming in jagged through the trees, and someone was playing soca from an open window over a fire escape, the music wafting through the heat. Joy's skin shone a clear amber, gleaming with sunscreen, and her hair was growing back slowly in tiny dark curls on her scalp. Feyi had knotted her gray braids into a bun on top of her head and was trying out a new running set in bright red, shorts and a strappy sports bra. She looked like a gorgeous alarm, a warning splashed over the sidewalk.

The butch lesbian who lived on the corner of their block whistled from her stoop when she saw the girls. "All right, dark chocolate in red!" she called out. "I see you, sexy caramel!"

Joy laughed and yelled back. "Q, you better stop before I tell your wife!"

"Go 'head witcha bad self!"

Feyi blew her a kiss as she and Joy went past the storefront church and down to the bodega on the corner that was being renovated, jogging along a shaded block.

"Nasir asked me to come home with him," Feyi said, dropping the news casually as she waved to Baba Yusuf through the window of his botanica.

Joy whipped her head around. "I'm sorry, what? Like, to the islands?"

"Yeah. He goes every summer, for a couple of weeks."

"Isn't that kind of a big step? You meeting his family?"

"Technically I already met his sister."

"Mm, that's right, the little thick one."

Feyi shook her head. "Stop drooling. Besides, he invited me as a friend. And also, for work reasons. Apparently his dad can get me into a group show—"

"As a friend?" Joy let out a short barking laugh. "Yeah, right."

"What? I'm serious."

"You paying for the trip?"

"Nah, but—"

Joy tugged at the waistband of her running shorts, tucking her keys back into a pouch as they tried to slip out. "Then that's not some friend shit."

"Oh, come on." Feyi wiped a trickle of sweat out of her eye. "As if you and I wouldn't pay for each other."

"Yeah, but we're us. Nasir is a nigga who would fuck you in a heartbeat if you let him."

Feyi put a hand to her chest, pretending to gasp. "What, you mean you wouldn't fuck me in a heartbeat if I let you? I'm hurt, Joy."

Her best friend rolled her eyes. "Been there, done that, got the neck cramp to prove it."

"Oh, that's bullshit, I totally ate you out."

"Uh-huh. Pillow princess."

Feyi shoved her, knocking her out of her stride. "That's not what you were calling me by round three."

65

Joy laughed and fell back into pace. "Whatever, that shit was years ago. What I'm saying is, quit acting like what y'all have is a real friendship. It's different and you know it."

She was right, but that was no reason for Feyi to agree with her. "Look, I don't know what it is exactly," she said, "but the important part is that his dad is rich as shit and paying for first-class flights."

They jogged in place at a red light, and Joy let out a short whistle. "For real?"

"And I get my own room at their family house up in the mountains."

"Ooh, shit. That low-key sounds amazing. And the work hookup doesn't hurt."

"Right? It's like going to an all-inclusive resort and getting to move my career forward at the same time."

"I'm not mad at it."

The light changed and the girls picked up their pace as they crossed the street. "I'm just worried that he's going to think it's some big step if I say yes," Feyi continued.

Joy blew out an exasperated breath. "You are so fucking paranoid, always acting like this nigga's tryna marry you or some shit. Just take it as what it is."

"Yeah, you're right. He's hooking up with someone else anyway, but I did kiss him last night."

Joy stopped and caught her breath, her hands on her knees. "Wait, you did *what*? And he's seeing someone else? Since when?"

Feyi jogged a circle around her. "Dunno, he said it's an off-and-on thing."

"Don't act like you didn't just tell me about a kiss, bitch.

And besides, that boy can't take his eyes off you, so if he's fucking someone else, he's probably just imagining that she's you the whole time." Joy knelt down to retie her laces and looked up at her. "How was the kiss?"

Feyi stopped and started to stretch her quads, trying to sound casual. "It was nice."

"I swear to God, Feyi—"

"Nah, it was amazing." She tried not to blush and felt herself failing. "We were downstairs by the mailboxes, and he had me all up against them . . . it was super hot, actually."

"Okay, and then what? I swear I didn't hear any fucking in the apartment last night."

"That's because there wasn't any, you pervert. We just . . . made out." Feyi shrugged. "It was cute."

"Wow. You fully on a high school tip right now."

"Whatever, man. You done? Wanna walk back?"

Joy straightened up and pointed down the block. "Nah. The ice cream spot is officially open for the summer. Mama needs some matcha honey in her life."

"Bitch . . . did you seriously get us to run this way just so you could get some ice cream?"

"You fucking bet. I waited all winter for this shit."

Feyi threw up her hands as they got in line behind a mom and her three colorful and sticky kids. "Unbelievable."

"I think it's a big step," Joy said, "but not necessarily in a bad way. He's trying to be your friend while y'all take it slow. He's looking out for your work. It sounds lit as fuck, if you ask me, and besides, you don't have to stay there the whole time. Just go for like a week and check it out, do the show and come back."

"Maybe . . . I feel like I'm gonna miss him for the rest of the summer if I don't go anyway."

"Aw, look who's catching feelings!" Joy crowed.

"Man, fuck you," Feyi replied, and flinched as the mom whirled around to glare at her. "Sorry, ma'am."

Joy snickered. "You kiss Nasir with that mouth?"

"Shut up," Feyi hissed, but she was smiling. "I'm tired of talking about him. Tell me how things are going with you and what's her name?"

Joy blushed. "Justina."

"Whoa, whoa! A name *and* you turning red? When did this get serious?"

"I don't know." Joy was usually slick and light when she talked about her affairs, but this time, there was something real there, and it was uncomfortable in her mouth.

Feyi didn't even feel like making fun of it. She knew there was a part of Joy that believed she wasn't going to get a happy settled-down story, something Feyi suspected came from her Ghanaian parents, something about being deviant, maybe not even deserving what "normal" people got. Other people's stories could sink in like that and fuck you all the way up, especially when it was family.

"You really like her, huh?" Feyi asked gently. "Is it a culture thing? I don't think you've ever dated another Ghanaian before."

Joy nodded. "I didn't think it would matter, you know. But then Justina started telling me how she got married because her parents pressured her into it, and whew, I remember when mine tried to do that to me. It's like, I got out, but she didn't, you know?"

68

"You think she wants to?"

"Yeah, I know she wants to. And that's the scary part. It was different when what we were doing was just fun and games, but now it's, like, real. And if it's real, then so is her husband. Is she gonna blow up her whole marriage? For what, for me?" Joy shook her head. "Nah, that's too much pressure."

Feyi adjusted her bun and looked at her best friend. She could feel the sun against her shoulder blades, warm and steady as the ice cream line moved forward. Joy was biting her lip, clearly worried, and a creeping suspicion made its way into Feyi.

"Do you love her?" she asked Joy, and it was incredible, how quickly Joy's face shut down into a careful and managed blankness, walls spinning up out of nowhere.

"Bitch, please. It's not that serious." Her tone was dismissive, and Feyi knew the conversation about Justina was over. She could feel a cloud gathering around Joy, so she changed the subject quickly, before it grew too gray, too heavy.

"Wanna help me pick out my outfits for this trip?"

Joy spun around with a gleeful smirk. "Oh my God, you're going! Yes!" She did a fist pump and a little dance. "Your Instagram is going to be on *fire.*"

They came up to the ice cream window and put in their orders, Joy all but vibrating with glee. The kid behind the window scooped out their cones and handed them over while Feyi tapped her phone to pay.

"Thanks, sugar mama." Joy licked the cool green of her matcha honey scoop as they started heading back to their apartment. "When are y'all flying out?"

69

"I think he's flexible; it didn't sound like he had set dates."

"Okay, cool. We need to decide your look for the trip. Gotta get new braids; those ones are getting a little fluffy."

"Yeah, I was thinking maybe blond?" Feyi took a bite out of her ice cream and caught a rivulet of chocolate running down the side of the cone.

"Nah," Joy replied. "That's too basic. How about gold?"

"Ooh, that's hot." Feyi would look unreal, which was perfect. "Okay, so I want them to be curly, and dammit, I'm gonna have to dye my hair. I don't want dark roots, you know?"

"Ah, you don't like what you have now with the gray?"

"It's fine, but I just think the gold will look better if there's no black braided in with it."

Joy nodded. "Halimat can do it, no problem. When has she ever let you down?" Halimat was a Senegalese friend of theirs who ran a private hair salon out of her Flatbush apartment while going to school at NYU. She'd been braiding Feyi's hair since Feyi moved to Brooklyn, cycling through colors as they experimented with a new look every six weeks. Everyone had always told Feyi growing up that she should stay away from bright colors, that they would be too garish against her dark skin, so it was a delight to stop listening to all of them, to lean into pastels and neons and metallics, rainbows cascading down her back.

As they walked home, Feyi let herself imagine the trip with Nasir, a version of it that was easy and perfect. The two of them swimming in the ocean, salt in their hair, sand on their skin as they lay out in the sun. Mangoes falling apart in their hands, the wet color of a sunset, the road up the mountain blanketed in green. She took out her phone and texted Nasir. *Hey, I'm down for the trip. Thank you again.*

He replied within a minute. *Fuck yes! Call you later to talk flights?*

Sure, she typed. *I can't wait.* To her surprise, she meant it.

. . .

A week later, Feyi sat in the back of a cab as reggaeton played over the radio, a comforting beat that wrapped her rib cage with a steady thump. The cabdriver had a stuffed dog perched between the two front seats, light blue with large sparkly eyes, staring endlessly. Feyi smiled and shook her head, lifting her phone to take a video for her Instagram story, the eerie dog and Bad Bunny singing in the background. *Gotta love Brooklyn*, she captioned it. The car turned onto Nasir's block and pulled up to his building. Nasir was standing at the curb in jeans and a hoodie with a large duffel bag hooked over his shoulder. He threw it into the trunk of the car, then joined Feyi in the back seat, kissing her on the cheek.

"Good morning, gorgeous," he said.

She smiled at him as he touched one of the gold pigtails snaking out from under her headwrap. "Oh, you *ready* ready for the plane," he teased. "Got that hydration mask on?"

"You know it," she replied. "You can have your skin dry out if you want, that's your problem."

"I'll take the risk." He smiled. "I got them natural oils." Nasir's eyes were bright with excitement, and Feyi could feel it running through her as well, a quick river of possibility, rapids of anticipation. She'd spent four days packing, trying

71

on every single outfit under Joy's critical eye, picking out jewelry and sandals and sundresses, makeup and a bottled array of oils, from coconut to coffee to jojoba laced with tea tree for her scalp. They'd gone to get mani-pedis, and Feyi chose a metallic gold polish for both her fingers and toes, a different shade from her hair, but rich brass nonetheless.

"You look expensive," Joy had said, with a wicked grin, picking out delicate gold chains for her to layer over her collarbone. "Like a goddess dripping in offerings."

Feyi winked. "As it should be." She stacked gold circles on her fingers and tried to decide which nipple rings to pack. "Bars or hoops?" she asked Joy, who raised her eyebrows.

"Remind me why it matters? I thought y'all weren't fucking."

"We're not, but you know I don't like all that padding in my bikini tops, so . . ." Feyi smirked and held up the options. "Which ones look better through the fabric?"

"Oh, you a *tease*."

"Just because we're going as friends doesn't mean I can't stress him out." Feyi laughed.

Joy put her hands on her hips. "I'm actually impressed. Bars, then. No silver."

"Obviously. We're going with consistent opulence for this trip."

She'd promised Joy pictures every step of the way, so Feyi pulled Nasir in for a selfie in the back of the cab. He pressed his lips to her cheek, and she broke out into a wide smile as she took the picture.

"We look good together," he said, but there was no suggestion in his words, just a plain statement of fact.

"We look amazing together," Feyi agreed, turning her head to kiss him. There was always a microsecond of a pause before he kissed her back, as if he couldn't quite believe she wanted him, as if he needed a moment for it to register. Ever since that night in the foyer of her building, she and Nasir hadn't gone much further than making out. It was slower than Feyi could ever remember going with a guy since she was a teenager, but with him, it felt right. It felt like they had all the time in the world to discover each other, so they could afford to be languid. Feyi never felt like Nasir was trying to rush her, and quite honestly, that in itself felt like a small miracle. She couldn't remember the last time someone had been content to just kiss her desperately and then lie in bed breathing each other's air. No—that was a lie. Jonah was the last time. Sometimes, the terror and guilt leaped up in her and Feyi would pull away from Nasir, break off a kiss or break away from his eyes. He never said anything, thank goodness, because she didn't want to talk about how it felt to try to learn how to be safe with someone who wasn't the dead love of her life.

"I feel mad inconsistent," she'd told Joy. "Like, half the time everything is chill, and I feel fine, but then I remember who he is and that this is so new, and it totally freaks me out."

Joy had shrugged. "He knew what he was getting into with you, and besides, you're worth it, Feyi. You can be yourself, as messy and contradictory as you like. He's lucky to be even near you."

At the airport, Nasir lifted Feyi's suitcase from the trunk of the cab and wheeled it into the terminal for her, his duffel

73

bag slung over his shoulder. They went through security together, stashing their jackets in the same bin, and Nasir held her hand as they boarded the plane. Feyi settled into the window seat and watched as he cleaned off their screens and seat belts with a disinfecting wipe.

"Hey," she said, touching the sharp plane of his cheekbone. "Thank you for this. For real. It means a lot to me."

Nasir took her hand and kissed the scar on her palm. "You deserve more," he said, and this time his voice was loaded with the outline of promises. A sudden spike of warning shot through Feyi, but just as quickly, Nasir's face shifted, wiping away the weight with his usual teasing lightness, the incorrigible flirt. Feyi told herself that the glimpse of something else was a glitch, an error. They were just friends, with fairly innocent benefits, true, but just friends.

She couldn't afford for it to become anything else.

Chapter Six

When the pilot announced they were twenty minutes from landing, Feyi pulled up her window shade and stared out at the sea, a brilliant blue with beaches undulating along it.

"You grew up here and *left*?" she said to Nasir. He leaned over to look out, his hand warm against her thigh.

"To be fair, I didn't appreciate it as much as I should've when I was growing up," he said. "I'm just glad my dad stayed so I get to come back and still have a proper home base, you know?"

"Did you grow up in the house we're going to?"

"Nah, we had another house in town, but Lorraine lives in it now. Dad built this one a couple of years ago after his work really blew up. He went all out with it, too, got some fancy architect to draw it up and even put in an infinity pool outside. Shit is unreal."

"Oh, damn! That sounds amazing." Feyi watched Nasir smile faintly as he talked about his father.

"Yeah. Dad's restaurant is in town, but he wanted somewhere separate, private, you know?"

"For sure. Building a house up a mountain is a peak hermit move." She laughed. "Team Introvert unite."

Nasir cut his eyes at her. "Girl, you and Joy be out partying all week, don't give me that introvert bullshit."

"I can do both, thanks." Feyi flashed him a smile and stroked a thumb against his stubble. He was so beautiful.

Who would've thought that seeing him across the bar that night would lead to both of them on this plane together, that she could touch his skin so freely, have the memory of his mouth be so recent?

Nasir closed his eyes briefly at her touch, then opened them again to smile at her. "You excited to see my home?"

Feyi dropped her hand. "Absolutely! And to eat at your dad's restaurant. What's it called again?"

"Alusi. He has another one in London called Ori and one in Toronto, I think. Opened that one last year, I can't remember the name."

Feyi was frowning. "Alusi? That sounds mad familiar."

"What, you into fancy restaurants around the world like that?"

"Nah, Joy is. She's got a whole bucket list of them, and I swear I've heard her mention that one before." She tapped her brass nails against the seat arm, trying to remember. "What's your dad's name again?"

Nasir unplugged his headphones from the plane and started rolling them up to return to their case. "Alim," he said. "Alim Blake."

Everything slowed down for Feyi as her brain made the connections, clicking details into place, then it sped up again as she gasped and punched him lightly on his arm. "Hold the fuck up! Your dad is Alim Blake? Alim *fucking* Blake?!"

"Damn, girl!" Nasir rubbed his bicep. "What, you know him?"

Feyi glared at him and fought the urge to smack him upside the head. "Um, yeah, of course I know who he is. His restaurant has two Michelin stars, Nasir. Two!" She threw up her hands. "He's a goddamn celebrity chef."

Nasir laughed and zipped up his headphone case. "Oh, come on, 'celebrity' is pushing it a bit."

"Nasir, the man is *literally* on TV! He was a judge on that cooking show Joy got me sucked into; he did like two seasons!"

"Oh, damn, I forgot about that." Nasir shook his head at the memory. "Lorraine and I gave him so much shit for doing it. But that was a while back, he's just been chilling since then. Real talk, I didn't think you'd have any idea who he was."

The announcement system crackled with static as the pilot informed the passengers that they were beginning their descent. Feyi covered her mouth with her hand and stared at Nasir as even more realization dawned. "Wait, I'm about to meet Alim Blake. Oh my God! Joy is gonna lose her entire mind when I tell her!"

"Ma'am," said the flight attendant, leaning over their seats. "I need you to put up your tray table and fasten your seat belt, please."

"You're totally a fan," Nasir said, amused wonder tracking over his face. "This is hilarious—are you gonna be this hype when you see him? 'Cause you've got like maybe twenty minutes to pull yourself together, baby girl."

"Twenty minutes?" Feyi's eyes went wide with shock. "He's picking us up at the airport?"

Nasir winked and reached around to buckle her seat belt. "Welcome," he whispered, kissing the side of her neck. Distracted, Feyi felt her skin skitter with pleasure, and she put a hand to the back of his head, her fingers digging into his tight curls. Nasir nuzzled against her, flicking his tongue over her throat.

"Stop it," she giggled, "we're in public."

"I don't care," he said, kissing her mouth.

The plane jolted in its descent, and Feyi gasped, the sound losing itself as it wound around Nasir's tongue. He broke away from her reluctantly and caressed her gold braids.

"Thank you so much for coming with me," he said, his eyes earnest. "I know you've got work to do and all, but still. It's so dope to have you here."

Feyi blushed—she was never sure what to do when he was so affectionate, the words didn't spring into her mouth as easily as they did for him. Instead, she kissed him again and hoped he could feel it that way, as the plane dragged them down toward his home.

▪ ▪ ▪

After they got through immigration and were waiting for their bags, Nasir turned to Feyi. The air was hot and humid, you could almost smell the water in it. They were standing by a pillar, in the path of a loud air conditioner.

"There's something maybe you should know before you meet my dad," he said.

Feyi leaned her backpack against her calf and waited, listening. Nasir ran a hand through his hair and scuffed his foot. "It's just—he's a little different from how he appears on TV."

"Aren't most people?" she replied. She'd never seen him look this awkward, not since the first night they'd met at the bar. It was endearing but unexpected.

"Not like that," he said. "He's just more . . . effeminate in person." Nasir said this in a rush, like it had to be thrown out of his mouth, and then he kept going, the words tumbling over each other. "Sometimes it throws people off, but it doesn't mean anything, it's just how he is—so I wanted to give you a heads-up."

Feyi frowned. She wasn't sure where he was going with this, or why he was telling her. Maybe because things down here could be a little . . . somehow?

"Is your dad gay?" she asked, and Nasir flushed all the way through the deep brown of his skin.

"No!" he said, a little too loudly, enough that some people turned and looked. Feyi had never heard him raise his voice before, and she fought the urge to take a step away from him. Nasir dropped his head, shame cloaking his body, and lowered his voice. "No. It doesn't mean anything. He's just different, but he's not gay, okay?"

Feyi put a hand on his arm. He looked more scared than angry, and she didn't quite understand why. "It's okay," she said. "I'm sorry, I was just asking."

Nasir was knotting his fingers together, trying to compose himself. "It's fine," he replied. He slid his hands into his pockets and gave Feyi a small smile, meeting her eyes reluctantly. "We had some problems with the tabloids down here a year or two ago and things got ugly, that's all. I didn't mean to pop off like that."

"It's okay. That sounds like it must've been really stressful."

"Yeah."

The luggage carousel clicked into motion, motors grinding. Feyi and Nasir fell into silence as they waited for the bags to come out, watching for his duffel and her suitcase. It took several minutes before they spotted them, the red tinsel Feyi had tied to the handles curled into spirals. Nasir pulled the bags off the belt, then dropped a kiss on Feyi's cheek to show he was back, that he was okay now.

"Let's go meet my family," he said, his voice warm and light again, his mouth pulling into a broad smile. Feyi smiled back, relieved to see him clear, and followed him out through the doors and into the waiting heat.

. . .

It was easy to recognize Alim Blake in the crowd of people gathered outside the arrival hall—bodies and voices flowed around him in streams, a map of movement while he stood in the sun, a fixed point. The man had *presence*, gallons of it radiating out into the air like a force field. His skin was the color of wet coal, mineral rich against the white linen he was wearing—a shirt with rolled-up sleeves, buttons open to his chest, loose trousers. It was chaos out there, but no one bumped into Alim, no one so much as touched him, except those who stopped to shake his hand and greet him. He was charming with them, touching arms and shoulders, crouching to smile at a little girl in a pinafore who was babbling excitedly, her mother watching fondly. The child held out her arms, and as Alim was hugging her, Nasir walked through the doors of the arrival hall, wheeling Feyi's suitcase with his duffel over his shoulder.

Feyi was walking behind him, and she caught the exact moment Alim saw his son, when his eyes widened and filled with a love so radient it hurt to behold, transforming his face from something calm into something fierce and burning. Alim unfolded and said goodbye to the child, brushing a kiss against the mother's cheek, but he didn't move toward her and Nasir. Instead, he stood right where he was and held out his arms for his son to step into them. Nasir dropped his duffel on top of the suitcase and entered his father's embrace without a word. Feyi stood by the bags, noticing small details about Alim, Nasir's raised voice echoing in her head.

Alim's nails were manicured and shiny, there was a touch of a deliberate bronze on his cheekbones, maybe even some pigment on his lower lip, like a faint rouged memory. His body hung in the air, redolent with grace. When he kissed Nasir's temples, the corners of his eyes wrinkled with pleasure. His face was dotted with small sunspots, clustered on his sharp cheekbones, and his hair was shot through with silver, textured sections with tight coils. Nasir came up to his father's shoulders, and while Nasir was built from hitting the gym with Milan, Alim was lean and corded. With fresh alarm, Feyi noticed a twinge of attraction unfurling in her stomach.

It was the last thing she'd expected. When she'd met both Milan and Nasir, she'd been drawn to them because the want had started in *their* eyes. It had beckoned her over like bait, calling her until she built a mirror, reflecting it back to them. This was foreign, the want bursting small but insistent in her belly, a warm pool. Alim wasn't just a handsome face on a television screen; he was real, he was looking at Nasir, and now Feyi could see what love looked like on his face. It illuminated him from inside, much like how Nasir had lit up when Lorraine came into the bar the night Feyi had met him.

81

She held on to her suitcase handle, desperately wishing Joy was there with her.

Nasir turned back and reached out a hand to her. "Dad, this is Feyi," he was saying.

Feyi pushed a smile forward as she took Nasir's hand and came up to both of them. Alim put a hand on her shoulder.

"Feyi," he said, her name rolling off his tongue like coconut sugar melting. "I'm so glad to meet you. Welcome home." His voice was slightly accented, smooth and crisp, and her shoulder was aflame under his palm, like his skin was burning through the cotton of her T-shirt.

"It's a pleasure, Mr. Blake." Feyi braced herself, but she couldn't stop the want from boiling over inside her when she looked up at him. Alim's irises were gray, encircled by a corona of swirling brown that spilled into the oat-milk whites of his eyes. His eyelashes were long and black.

"Please," he said. "Call me Alim."

Feyi felt her knees buckle slightly and she could hear Joy's voice in her head, clear as day.

Oh, bitch. You're fucked.

Chapter Seven

The drive up the mountain to Alim's house was ridiculously gorgeous, as if it had been copied and pasted from a postcard. Feyi couldn't stop staring out the window. She'd made the mistake of glancing at the rearview mirror, but then she'd accidentally made eye contact with Alim, which left her flustered beyond measure. Nasir was telling his father about his latest client, a kid from San Francisco boasting of some new app that he was convinced was going to change everything. Feyi had heard the story about five separate times before, so she tuned out and watched the trees instead, the slope of the hills falling, the people they were passing. She could still see the ocean from the road, a blue rippling sheet of water lapping at the land. Often, Alim would honk his horn and wave an arm at someone who'd wave back at him, shouting greetings over the sound of the yellow Jeep's tires rumbling against the road. Feyi was holding her phone tightly in one hand, not sure if it would be too tacky or touristy if she just started taking pictures. She had tried shooting Joy a text before they loaded up the car, but the airport Wi-Fi was spotty and it didn't go through. She checked her phone to see if she was getting any service, but it stared emptily back at her.

"Feyi?" she heard Nasir say, and snapped her head up.

Alim was watching her in the mirror with those murky eyes of his. Feyi looked away from him and at Nasir instead.

"Sorry, what?" she asked.

"I was asking if you good?"

"Oh! Yeah, I'm great." She gestured out of the window. "This is amazing. I've never seen anything like it."

Alim made a sharp corner, throwing a question over his shoulder. "This is your first visit?"

"Yeah, I've never been to any of the islands before. I didn't know you could even get mountains like this so close to the sea."

Nasir noticed the phone in her hand and grinned. "You can take pictures if you want to. I know Joy's waiting for all the updates on the 'gram."

Feyi stuck her tongue out at him. "I don't have any service."

"There'll be Wi-Fi at the house. You can upload them soon as we get in." Nasir twisted in his seat to point out a massive tree to her, its trunk whorled and wider than any arms could reach. "No one's allowed to cut that down. They say it holds the spirits of ancestors."

Alim glanced at his son, curious. "You used to make fun of all that, calling it obeah business."

Nasir shrugged. "I was a kid. I thought it was cool to be skeptical."

"And now?" Feyi asked.

"I think it's nice to believe in something," he answered, watching as the tree receded into the distance. He continued pointing out landmarks and details to Feyi as they drove up the mountain. The road became more and more narrow, snaking precariously, and then they turned down a side road, the Jeep's wheels bumping over the dirt. Trees formed a thick canopy above them, sunlight glimmering through in fragments. Feyi held her breath as she looked around—it felt like a fairy tale, like they were passing through a gate between worlds. After a while, the road evened out, ending in a pair of black wrought-iron gates that towered above the car. Feyi gazed up at them as Nasir popped open the glove compartment and pulled out a remote that swung the gates open with a quiet hiss. Alim drove the car through, and Feyi's jaw dropped. It looked like a dream. She couldn't even see the house from the gate, just a long driveway lined with trees filled with pink and white flowers, hummingbirds darting through the air, monkeys peering between the leaves, and the sun washing gold over everything.

"I know, right?" Nasir was watching her, pleased with her reaction. "It's really something."

Feyi reached her hand out from the window and watched as petals fell over her skin. "This is surreal," she said, her eyes wide. "There's so much land!" It stretched out farther than she could see, lush and green, a kingdom unto itself.

"Family land," Alim said. "Our blood is in it." He drove up a bend in the driveway as a kaleidoscope of butterflies wheeled past the car, and the house pulled into view, a breathtaking tropical modern structure that was all cascading expanses of uninterrupted glass and dark timber, three stories high.

"Whoa," Feyi gasped. "That is gorgeous."

Alim glanced at her through the rearview mirror. "Thank you," he said. "I wanted to live in something open, as close to the air as I could get. The architect did well."

"Wait till you see inside," Nasir added. They parked under a steel-beamed trellis dripping with bougainvillea, and Feyi stepped out of the car. There was entirely too much to look at—her eyes could only snag on the details a few at a time: the soaring birds of paradise along the pathway, the albino peacock watching them from the grass, the side door inlaid with mother-of-pearl. Alim and Nasir took off their shoes as they entered the house, and Feyi quickly followed suit, dropping her sneakers on the teak rack next to the door. The ground floor was a stretch of black polished concrete, spilling into an open living area littered with sculptures, couches, and art. She spun around, taking it all in.

"You look like a kid," Nasir said with a laugh.

Feyi made a face at him, then stopped in her tracks, staring at a drawing that took up most of one wall. "No way."

Alim watched as she walked up and lifted her hand, her fingers a breath away from the glass protecting the art.

"You have a ruby onyinyechi amanze original?" she asked, glancing over at him.

When Alim smiled at her, her chest fluttered in response. "I thought you might like that," he said. "You Nigerians always know each other's work."

Nasir came up and stood beside her. "I don't get it," he said. "There's too much empty space, shouldn't it be filled up?"

Feyi immediately smacked his arm. "Never repeat that blasphemy!" she scolded, and Alim laughed, a deep low wave rumbling through the room. Feyi didn't dare to look at him. It was safer to keep her eyes on the drawings, the leopards and ghosts, the crashing aliens. "This is incredible," she said. "I've never seen one of her originals so close, especially one this size. I didn't even know she let individual collectors

86

have them these days. Unless you got it way back when, at the beginning?"

Alim came up next to her and looked at the drawing fondly. "No, you're right. Only museums and permanent collections now, but she and I made an agreement."

Feyi raised an eyebrow. "What kind of deal did you cut?"

"Only that I'd never sell it," he answered, and Feyi glanced at him.

"That's real," she said. "I've been so worried about who's going to end up with my work, it feels too close to just let it be in anyone's house, let alone some old white collector type, you know?"

He nodded. "You want it to be with its people. Whoever those turn out to be."

Feyi didn't dare look at him again. His body was too close to hers. "Exactly," she said, keeping her eyes on the drawing.

Nasir came and joined them. "Dad, don't start the whole art tour. We can do that another time, it's not going any-where."

Alim smiled at his son. "You heathen," he teased.

Nasir rolled his eyes and turned to Feyi. "Come on, lemme show you to your room." He grabbed her bags, then turned to his father. "Lunch soon?"

Alim sat down on one of the couches and flipped open a book, reaching for a pair of gold spectacles. "Three o'clock, but you're never on time," he said, then looked up at Feyi. "Make yourself at home, yes?"

She nodded. "Thank you, Mr. Blake."

He had returned to his book, but as Feyi followed Nasir

out of the room, she thought she heard him say, "Call me Alim."

When she looked back, he was reading as if he were already alone.

. . .

Nasir led her up a polished staircase and into a hallway lined with a stretch of floor-to-ceiling glass. Everything was jungle outside the window, cawing sounds and the rustle of branches and leaves.

"This is almost like being outside," Feyi said. "Low-key makes me a little nervous."

"Oh, there's a glass walkway on the third floor that connects to a guest tree house," Nasir told her. "I used to hate walking on it, I felt like it was going to break at any second, and you know I don't fuck with heights like that." He slid open a sleek wooden door and stepped to the side. "This is you."

Feyi laughed out loud as soon as she saw the room. "You've got to be fucking kidding me," she said. "This is like a whole-ass apartment!" The space was sprawling, marked by a platform king bed in the center, canopied with gossamer curtains. The entire outside wall was glass, looking out into a landscaped garden exploding with flowers, birds, and butterflies. A small stream sang through the garden, rippling over stones. Feyi walked over to the bed and ran her hands over the flax linen sheets, her fingernails golden against the olive green. "Nah, man. You did not adequately prepare me for how off the charts this place is."

Nasir grinned as he set her suitcase on a luggage rack. "I

wanted to surprise you," he said. "Besides, if I had even tried to describe it, you would've thought that I was bragging or some shit."

"Facts," she answered, staring at a line of sculptures installed on one of the walls. There were about five fencing masks in various states—pierced through with long feathers, smudged with black, covered in gold, dripping with tendrils. "I would not have believed a single word out of your mouth. That, for example"—she pointed at the masks—"is an entire Allison Janae Hamilton set. Do you know how wild it is to have them all together?"

Nasir laughed. "I see having you visit is going to be an entire art education." He came up to her and wrapped his arms around her waist, nuzzling his face into her neck. "How come you never took me to an exhibit when we were in New York? You don't want me to be cultured?"

Feyi giggled and placed a hand on his cheek. "Maybe I was shy about that part of my life. Like I know you said you were collecting, but . . . I don't know."

"Well, we can fix it when we get back. You know I'm down to do anything if I get to do it with you." He raised his head. "Except running. You cute, but you not *that* cute."

"Fuck off." She laughed. "I gotta shower and get changed."

"Aight, aight." Nasir let go of her and headed for the door. "I'll be back in a few. Wi-Fi password is on the desk."

As soon as he left, Feyi pulled off her headwrap and grabbed her phone. Joy had told her to text first instead of just calling.

"I might be with Justina," she'd said, "and she getting kinda possessive."

"Why is it always the married ones who be wilding?" Feyi had asked. "Doesn't she have a whole husband?"

Joy had just shrugged. "Lesbians," she said, as if it explained everything.

Feyi sat on the bed and typed out a quick message, hoping that Joy was alone. *BITCH. CALL ME NOW.*

It took only a few minutes before her phone was ringing, and Feyi quickly answered the video call. Joy's face popped up, grinning and full of mischief. She was wearing a new blond wig with bangs that fell almost into her eyes.

"What's the tea, my good sis?" she said immediately. "Spill all of it."

"Oh my God," Feyi whispered into the phone, looking around to make sure she wasn't close enough to the door for anyone to overhear her. "Joy, you'll never guess who his fucking dad is."

"Oh, shit. Who is it? We know him?"

"Girl. It's motherfucking Alim Blake."

Joy did a double take and flipped her hair out of her face. "Let me move my goddamn bang," she said. "Bitch, did you just say Alim Blake? Like from the cooking show?"

"Yes, bitch, he picked us up at the damn airport!"

Joy clapped her hands over her mouth. "I'm sorry," she said, her voice muffled. "But you're telling me that you met Alim Blake. That you're low-key dating Alim Blake's son?" Joy dropped her hands. "Oh my God, bitch, you're in Alim Blake's *house* right now?"

Feyi plopped down on the bed. "Yup, and it gets worse."

"The fuck you mean it gets worse?"

Feyi grimaced. "He's hot, Joy."

"Uh-uh." Joy held the phone away from her face so Feyi could see her full incredulous expression. "We all know Alim Blake is fine as hell, but I don't like how you're saying that, Feyi. I'ma need you to expand on that statement."

"Like, he's *hot*." Feyi groaned and fell sideways on the bed. "Like, *hot* hot."

"I know—" Joy paused and let out a deep breath. "Whew, chile, I *know* you're not in your boyfriend's daddy's house right now talking about how hot the man is."

"First of all, not my boyfriend."

Joy gasped. "Oh my God, that is *not* a loophole, Feyi!"

"Second of all, I'm not going to *do* anything!"

Her best friend leaned in toward the camera and shook her head. "You know, I really thought the day it became time for this lecture, you'd be the one giving it to me and not vice versa, but Feyikemi Ayomide Adekola, do *not* fuck your boyfriend's father in his own house, for God's sake."

Feyi spun around, bringing the phone close to her face. "You're on speakerphone, Joy! And he's *not* my boyfriend!"

"Well, now you're just being messy, Feyi, put your god-damn earbuds in."

"They're somewhere in my bag." Feyi paced the room, then stepped into the walk-in closet and closed the door, her screen lighting up her face. "I haven't unpacked because I've been freaking the fuck out," she continued. "Like, you think I *want* to be crushing on Nasir's father? That shit with Milan was already too close to home."

Joy snorted out a laugh. "I'm sorry, but you literally can't get closer to home than where you are right now."

"Oh my God, that's not *helping*."

"Okay, okay." Joy arranged her face. "Look, it makes sense."

Feyi cut her eyes at her best friend.

"No, it really does! He's rich and famous, I mean, he's basically an older, more successful version of Nasir, right? Makes sense that you'd find him attractive." Joy tapped a bedazzled nail against her lower lip. "Was he vibing toward you?"

Feyi groaned again. "No. He was perfectly polite and nice. This is just me being a completely inappropriate ho, that's all."

"Honestly, babe? I think you're also kinda scared about where you and Nasir might be heading. He's been low-key perfect, and maybe it's easier to think about blowing it all up than to keep going. There are lots of ways to run away, you know?"

Feyi rubbed the back of her neck. "Yeah, you probably right," she said. "I gotta get my shit together."

"Maybe if you'd just fuck Nasir already, you'd stop being a little horny bunny toward his dad," Joy suggested.

"Oh shit." Feyi laughed. "Where is the love, sis?"

Joy shrugged. "I'm just saying. That nigga is crazy about you, sexy as fuck, hooked you up with a dream gig, literally flew you over to paradise, and is two steps away from swinging you in a hammock and dripping coconut water into your mouth from an actual fucking coconut. Frankly, I don't know what else you're waiting for."

Feyi grimaced. "I don't know if I'm waiting for anything. It just hasn't felt right."

"Girl, you be sticking your tongue down his throat every other night. Do you wanna fuck him or nah?"

"I don't know." Feyi ran a hand over her face. "I legit do not know. Maybe I'm just not ready."

"You're never ready for shit, Feyi. Just jump in the deep end already and figure out if you remember how to swim."

There was a knock at the door, and Feyi stuck her head out of the closet to hear Nasir calling her name. "Fuck, I gotta go," she whispered to Joy. "I think it's time for lunch, and I haven't even showered yet."

"Yeah, please don't show up at a whole Alim Blake's table looking like *that*."

"Wow, rude. Is it that bad?"

"You look like you just woke up from a nap. The man has two Michelin stars, for fuck's sake. Put some makeup on and text me later."

Joy hung up, and Feyi scrambled out, tossing her phone on the bed and opening her door.

"There you are," Nasir said, smiling. "You do not look ready at all." He was leaning against the doorframe and had changed out of his airplane sweats into a white tee and some wax-print shorts. His hair was damp, and he smelled like mint and cinnamon.

Feyi gave him a puppy-dog look. "Okay, see, what had happened was . . ."

Nasir laughed and tugged on one of her pigtails. "Uh-huh?"

"I had to call Joy! And then we started talking and—"

He held up a hand, still laughing. "Say less."

Feyi batted her lashes at him. "I knew you'd understand. Gimme ten minutes?"

Nasir leaned over and kissed her cheek. "Take as long as you need. You want some company?"

She stepped aside so he could enter her room. "I'd love that."

Nasir plopped down on the bed as Feyi started rummaging through her suitcase for her toilet bag. "It's so weird seeing you here," he said. "Like two of my worlds are colliding."

"Are you kidding me?" she shot back. "It's extra weird knowing your dad's balling like this! How old is he, even?"

It was a decent pretense at an innocent question, but Joy would have seen through it in a heartbeat. Nasir suspected nothing, but then again, he had no reason to.

"Mm, I think he turns forty-eight this October."

Feyi looked up in surprise, her brain calculating. "Oh, he had you young!"

Nineteen years. Alim was only nineteen years older than her. It was much less of a gap than she'd thought, but Feyi could already hear Joy's voice in her head—*Bitch, that's still old enough to be your daddy! He was changing diapers while you were* in *diapers!*

"Yeah, he and my mom were high school sweethearts. Got married not long after they graduated."

The ghosts were always sudden. "Wow," Feyi managed to say, going back into her suitcase so he wouldn't see the shadow that had crossed her face. Jonah proposing a month before they finished grad school. The quick ceremony at City Hall, the proper wedding they were planning. The automated emails from the venues that kept coming long after he was a broken thing on a dark road. She cleared her throat. "So how come you're not living in some fancy loft in the city?"

Nasir shrugged. "I like to think of my dad's money as *his* money. We didn't grow up like this, you know? Like, he started making it big my freshman year in college, so this is new. Plus"—he gestured around—"this isn't quite my style."

"Oh, you're more simple, huh?"

Nasir laughed. "I really am, though! Like I don't wanna be stuck up in the middle of nowhere, no matter how pretty it is. I'm not into this hermit life."

Feyi grabbed a dress and draped it over her arm, turning to him. "Okay, so what would your ideal setup be? If you had this kind of money?"

"Real talk? I want a brownstone in Brooklyn. Somewhere near the park, where I can, like, ride bikes with my kids on the weekends."

"Oh, you wanna stay in New York?"

"Absolutely. Don't you?"

Feyi raised and dropped a shoulder. "Haven't really thought about it," she lied. "Taking it one day at a time, you know?"

"Ah, word, word."

"Be right back." She stepped into the bathroom, shutting the door softly behind her. It was all marble, from floor to ceiling, with gold fixtures and a banana tree leafing green in the corner. Feyi turned on the shower and tied up her braids in the mirror, placing her toilet bag on the limestone counter. She'd had no idea Nasir wanted kids, but it made sense. He was in his twenties, of course he was planning a home and a family who biked down to the park. Jonah had wanted to adopt, bleeding heart that he was. Feyi didn't want kids, she never had, but she would've tried with Jonah, for Jonah. Everything had seemed possible with him; she hadn't known how to be scared when she was around him. She'd felt invincible. It had never occurred to her that maybe he wasn't.

Stop thinking about Jonah.

Feyi pulled off her T-shirt and wriggled out of her jeans, tossing her dirty clothes into a rattan laundry basket and stepping into the shower. The hot water drove thought out of her mind, steaming off her skin as she stood in the spray. She let out a breath she didn't even know she'd been holding and listened to the water hit her shoulders. If she had more time, she could've stayed in there for hours, but Nasir's presence was loud on the other side of the door. Feyi grabbed her washcloth and scrubbed down with some of the shower gel that was on a limestone shelf next to the faucet. It smelled like grapefruit with something floral in it, tangy and sweet. She wondered if it had been picked out for her; this wasn't the kind of soap she'd expect Alim to keep in his house. Nah, his style would be something cleaner and sharper. The smell of cold air at the top of an avalanche. A salt breeze from an ocean leagues deep, the water too dark to see into. Feyi laughed to herself as she got out of the shower, drying off with a towel as white and thick as a cloud.

She had no business speculating on what Alim smelled like, not when his son was out there sitting on her bed. Was this deeply unwelcome want just misplaced desire, like Joy had said? Because, what, Alim was an older Nasir? Feyi grimaced as she pulled on a yellow slip dress with thin straps and a cowl neck, smoothing the silk down around her hips. She loved Joy, but that theory sounded like a reach. Feyi could tell the difference between the two men, it was blatant and obvious, and right now, it was distinctly not in her favor.

"It's just a crush," she whispered to herself. "He's hot and famous, and it's just a crush. Get the fuck over it."

"What d'you say?" Nasir called from the other side of the door.

"Nothing! Be out in a second!" She untied her braids and shook them out, the gold curls dripping down her back, then opened the door and smiled at him. "You wanna watch me do my face routine?"

Nasir got up from the bed to lounge at the bathroom door. "I wanna watch your face," he said, then noticed her dress. "Whew! You look like butter!"

Feyi laughed as she swiped toner over her skin and patted in a serum. "I look like *butter*? That's the line you're going with?"

"Mm-hmm. All that gold and yellow." He leaned toward her, his voice drawling into a singsong. "You look like ghee and honey, baby, you look like money."

Nasir kissed her cheek, and Feyi swatted him away.

"You better let me finish putting on my makeup."

"I'm so happy you're here," he said, his eyes going serious.

She paused with a mascara brush in her hand. "So am I." It wasn't a lie, it was so far from a lie, but Feyi could feel all the things she wasn't telling him curdling under her tongue, sour and forming a skin. She didn't know what to do with them, so she swallowed them back and took Nasir's hand as he led her down to lunch.

Chapter Eight

"Is this entire house made of glass?" Feyi whispered to Nasir as they walked through the dining room, which seemed to be built out of windows and skylights, braced by steel frames, opening up into a shockingly blue sky above and walls of greenery around.

"Real talk, it's a little creepy," Nasir whispered back. "I always wonder if someone's hiding out there, watching us."

"Wow, thanks, that's terrifying."

The dining table was massive, an organic single slab of wood with swirling dark grain, balanced on black steel legs. Delicate glass globes hung staggered from the ceiling, and several chairs in rust leather surrounded the curves of the table. Feyi ran her hand along the back of one, marveling at how supple the leather was, then she noticed that the table was empty.

"We're not eating in here?"

"Nah, Dad likes the breakfast nook better." Nasir slid a door open and waved her through into a large kitchen with accordion glass doors next to a casual seating area that was set for three. The air was thick with warm spices. Alim was bringing ceramic bowls to the table, steam wafting up from them. He was still in his white linen, and Feyi noticed a silver ring hanging from a chain around his neck, falling out as he bent to put the bowls on the table. It caused a twinge in her chest—she'd worn her wedding ring like that for years after

Jonah died, stopping only when she started thinking about dating again. What did it mean that Alim still wore his? Was it a mark of dedication to his dead wife? Why wouldn't he wear it on his hand, then; why put it around his neck?

More importantly, why was she even wondering about this? Feyi warned herself to be careful. These were dangerous paths to be thinking along; this curiosity was a risk. It had been safer with Milan, where she felt neither the urge to ask nor to answer questions, and even with Nasir, who held no caverns inside him. She sat down in the chair he pulled out for her, avoiding Alim's eyes, afraid that he'd see the accumulating interest in hers.

"It's all your favorites," Alim was saying to his son. "Curried goat, culantro rice and peas with a touch of saffron, spicy garlic grilled breadfruit."

Nasir whooped in excitement as he sat next to Feyi. "I've been dreaming about this all year," he said. "What's this, Dad?"

Alim sat across from them and spread a linen napkin over his thighs, his voice amused as he glanced at his son. "Just a homemade sauce, Scotch bonnet and passion fruit."

"See, that's a bomb-ass welcome-home meal." Nasir leaned forward and dapped his father. "You a real one."

Feyi wondered what would happen if she shared on Instagram that she was in Alim Blake's mountain house, eating a dinner he'd made himself. It was fucking surreal—she could still remember the first time she'd seen him on TV, sitting on a judging panel in an ash-gray suit, his hair cropped low. It was difficult for her to connect that man on the screen to the one sitting before her now. The real-life Alim had more texture. Feyi could see old acne scars on his cheeks, she could reach out and touch his long fingers if she wanted to, his nails cut short and oval, the rugged terrain of his palms. Nasir made a plate of food for her, heaping bright green rice next to a red spill of the curried goat, layering slices of breadfruit by the edge of her plate. Feyi thanked them both awkwardly, then ate in blissful silence as flavors unfurled in her mouth. Joy would kill to be here. Feyi tried to remember everything so she could describe it to her best friend later, the way the breadfruit melted in her mouth, how easily the curried goat dripped off its bone, how fragrant the rice was. She was barely listening to Alim and Nasir's conversation, noticing only when it dropped into silence and she looked up to find both of them watching her eat as they held back smiles.

"Don't mind us," Nasir said, with a grin. "You having a whole moment over there."

Feyi blushed furiously. "Oh my God, I'm so sorry." She dabbed at her mouth with the napkin. "I got so distracted. This is, like, the best thing I've ever tasted in my life."

"Never apologize," Alim said. "This is what food should be—more than a meal, a sensory experience." He put his hand to his heart, and his eyes crinkled. "It's a pleasure to share it with you."

Feyi felt her face get even warmer. "I have to confess, Mr. Blake," she blurted out. "I've seen you on TV, and I never ever thought I'd get to eat your food in person. I had no idea until our plane was landing, and it's just—it's an honor to be your guest. My best friend is, like, one of your biggest fans. She's been telling me about Alusi for years."

"Ah, we must have her visit one of these days, then," he

replied, giving her a kind smile, and Feyi could tell that he actually meant it. She couldn't wait to tell Joy.

Nasir patted her on the shoulder. "You did good, holding all that in up till now. I really didn't think you'd last this long."

"Look, I *tried* to play it cool," she said. "The food just broke me."

Alim laughed. "I am very much looking forward to seeing your work at the show. Rebecca wouldn't give me details; she's being quite secretive."

"Same here," Nasir added. "Feyi won't tell me a thing about what she's going to be showing."

"You'll see it when you're meant to see it," Feyi retorted. "Be patient."

"I'm sure it will be spectacular," Alim said. "Rebecca wouldn't have included you if it wasn't, not even as a favor to me."

Nasir smirked. "And that's saying a lot, because she's had a crush on Dad for ages."

Alim cut his eyes at his son, and Feyi paused with a forkful of rice in her hand.

"Oh, it's like that?" she said, trying to mask the way something in her chest had clenched at the thought. Rebecca Owo would be perfect for Alim, now that she considered.

"Ignore my son," Alim said. "We'll schedule lunch with Rebecca soon. I believe she's already been in touch with you about install and the like?"

Feyi nodded, her mouth full of rice and peas.

"Perfect." Alim stood up from the table. "You must excuse me; I have a quick call with São Paulo, but Nasir, you'll show her around, yes?"

"Of course."

"Thank you for the meal," Feyi said, smiling up at Alim. "It really was spectacular." *He* really was spectacular. How on earth was she going to make it through this trip sane?

Alim smiled back. "We'll have a simple dinner later, but if you're feeling peckish, help yourself to anything in the kitchen." He left the room, and Feyi turned to Nasir, squeaking with excitement.

"I cannot believe that just happened! I have permission to snack in Chef Blake's kitchen?"

Nasir laughed. "Bet. And this is just one of the kitchens in the house; he has a full professional kitchen on the next floor, where he tests out his recipes and shit."

"Oh, so this is like his play kitchen?"

"Basically." Nasir stood up and held out a hand to her. "Ready to see the rest of the house?"

"Will I ever be ready?" Feyi let him pull her out of her chair, and she stared wide-eyed for the next half hour as they walked arm in arm through the rooms and hallways, the soaring library, the gym and saunas. Nasir avoided some parts of the house, and Feyi didn't ask why. She could feel Alim's silence there, behind the doors, and she had no desire to poke into his spaces, the places where he was just himself, not the chef, not the father, just whoever was left behind when he took those faces off. There was so much of the house that she got completely disoriented halfway, unable to keep track of the staircases and bends.

"See, I can't even show you the grounds," Nasir said. "We'd both get lost if we went exploring."

"Are there other houses nearby?" Feyi asked.

"Yeah, Dad has some staff who maintain the property, and they have their own homes not too far from here."

"Ah, I was wondering who keeps the house up."

"There's a whole farm out there, and an orchard, even." They turned a corner, and Nasir made a sweeping gesture with his arm. "And here's the swimming pool," he announced. "Check out the view."

Feyi gasped. The pool was on the third floor of the house, an infinity edge with a stunning spread of mountainside beyond it. "Oh, this is going to look so lit on Instagram," she said. "Joy's gonna eat her fucking heart out." She walked to the edge of the pool and dipped her toe in the water. It was, of course, perfect.

"Should we take a swim?" Nasir asked.

Feyi was about to respond when Alim emerged from the other end of the pool, water sluicing off his back, his hair soaked. He turned and lifted a hand to them, then stepped out of the water and walked over to a lounge chair, throwing a towel over his shoulder and checking his phone. Feyi tried not to stare at his slick body, the dark length of it, the way water ran down his cheek, his neck, his chest. Desire hit her with an oppressive weight, punching the air out of her and weakening her joints.

"Um, I think I need to go take a nap after all that food," she said to Nasir, backing away from the pool. There was no way in hell she was going to strip down in front of his father. Nipple rings and skimpy bikinis aside, she just didn't trust herself to be around him. It was too unstable, these feelings he brought up in her, the way they made her feel out of control, like she was someone else—someone different from the woman who'd fucked Milan in a bathroom and kicked him out, who'd tentatively begun to open up to Nasir—a woman who made all these deliberate choices. This mountain, this man she'd literally just met, they were turning her into a woman who *wanted* so loudly that it was drowning out the logic of a choice, and that terrified Feyi. That felt dangerous, fast and menacing. She had to get away from it.

Nasir showed her back to her room and, thankfully, left her alone. Feyi didn't hit up Joy. She was too shaken by how insistent the want had become, how suddenly it had returned. Even when she tried to nap, all she saw behind her eyes was Alim's torso, the ease of his hips as he walked, the trail of curls descending from his navel into the waistband of his swim trunks, the muscles of his thighs and calves, and the hunger inside her grew even more. Feyi tried to ignore it. It was just a crush. He was rich and famous and a culinary genius, but she didn't know him. This wasn't real. So what if she got wet as fuck each time she thought about his hands or his eyes or his mouth? This was Nasir's *father*, for fuck's sake. What did it say about her that her feelings for Nasir could be washed away so quickly? She was just trying to sabotage something good because she was scared, because this was easier than doing the real work with Nasir. Feyi picked up her phone and scrolled through it, forcing her mind to be somewhere else.

At dinnertime, she texted Nasir that she was feeling tired, and he brought her up a bowl of cucumber gazpacho.

"Get some rest," he said. "I'll see you in the morning."

The soup was smooth and cool, and knowing that Alim's hands had made it only turned Feyi on more. She took another shower and changed out of the slip dress into an oversize T-shirt that she'd stolen from Milan, but even then she couldn't sleep, and she couldn't stop thinking about Alim. Finally, she flipped onto her back and started to rationalize it.

"Okay, bitch," she said out loud. "Why is this freaking you out? Because you feel like fucking this dude? It's not a real thing, y'all don't know each other, it's just attraction. So, what's the big deal?"

The ceiling stared back at her.

"You want him," Feyi said. "That's fine. That's normal. You want him." As she said the words, a sobering thought occurred to her. "You want him . . . and he doesn't want you."

It was like being dunked in cold water. That's what it was, this was coming from only her. He wasn't looking at her like Milan or Nasir or most other men did. He was unavailable, down to the wedding ring at his throat. It was safe to want someone she couldn't have; she didn't have to follow up on it, she didn't have to do anything except be drunk on her own desire. Feyi pushed away the irrational feelings of rejection (*He doesn't* have *to want you*, she scolded herself) and focused on what did belong to her—this desire. This desire that pooled like traitorous flame, that wasn't in response to someone else, that was coming from her and just her. She belonged to it, and it belonged to her, and that's as far as it needed to go. How long had it been since she'd felt this on her own, with and by herself? All her timelines stretched back to a dark road covered in glass. It didn't matter. She was alive, like her therapist had taught her, and it was okay to live.

Feyi reached under her pillow and pulled out the vibrator she'd stashed there while unpacking. She closed her eyes and reached between her legs. This was just hers, everything else was unreal, down to the picture that her mind pulled up, spinning it from memory and make-believe. Alim hovering over her in the bed, his palms leaving wet prints in her olive sheets, his eyes reflecting hers, full of hunger, inevitable, reckless.

When she came, her cry echoed through the room, against the glass of her window, and the night outside observed in silence. Feyi didn't care if either or both of them heard her; she was herself again, and it was none of their business. They were just men; they could dream about her if they liked. She rolled over to her stomach and fell asleep.

. . .

The next morning, Feyi woke up to the wind gently rustling through the trees outside her window. The morning light was clear and clean, leaking in through the glass and falling against the white walls of her room. There was layered birdsong in the air, high-pitched cheeps over longer warbling calls. Feyi yawned and curled up some more inside the soft olive linen. It felt too early in the morning, like it was just her and the birds and the trees and the eager sun splashing against the textured walls. She wanted to take a picture of it, but she already knew half the beauty would die inside a camera lens and she'd never quite catch the edges of how it felt.

For a moment, she wondered what it would be like to wake up with Nasir's head on the other pillow. The thought was surprisingly unwelcome—he'd want to share this morning quiet with her, he'd break it with his voice, with his hands. She felt possessive of herself, echoes of last night's reclaiming, perhaps. Feyi rolled over to look at the little clock on her bedside table: 6:35 a.m. It wasn't worth trying to go back to sleep. She threw off the covers and climbed out of bed, smoothing out the wrinkles in her T-shirt and stretching as she walked to the bathroom.

There was a cheep at the bathroom window, and Feyi looked over to see a small bird perched outside on the sill, with a black back, a yellow belly, and a white streak of feathers on its head. It hopped up and down for a bit, letting out short bursts of sound, then flew away. Feyi smiled—she couldn't remember the last time she'd seen a bird that wasn't a New York pigeon. It made her want to hurry down to see what the gardens looked like in the morning, to walk through the soft grass with bare feet and watch dew roll off leaves before anyone else woke up. She splashed water on her face and brushed her teeth before patting in a face cream and spritzing an oil sunscreen over it. Shaking out her braids, she tied them back into a bun and pulled on a pair of sweatpants and a light kimono, not bothering with a bra, then unlocked her bedroom door and padded out into the hallway, making a quick left to the top of the staircase that led down to the ground floor.

The house was resplendent in the morning. Feyi stood at the top of the staircase and looked out at the soaring windows, the riot of green and sunlight and flower bursts of color, the gorgeous wood in the floors and frames, the sheer abundance of light that poured in everywhere. She let her fingers skim the banister softly as she came down the stairs, feeling a little dramatic, a little regal, like there was someone at the bottom gazing up at her adoringly, like the light was a carpet unrolling before her feet. Feyi held the edge of her robe so it could billow out behind her, then spun in a circle at the bottom of the stairs, giggling to herself. She already felt lighter just being there, being back to herself, being alone in this paradise of a morning.

It was clear that the house was too big to go wandering in alone, so Feyi made her way to the breakfast nook where they'd eaten lunch the day before, knowing she could enter a courtyard from there. To her surprise, the table was already laid out with breakfast, the smell of oven-fresh sweet bread in the air, bowls weighed down with fruit—papaya, guava, and mango. Nasir's father was sitting at the head of the table, reading a newspaper with his glasses on, legs crossed at the knee, his feet bare. His toes were silver. He glanced up when Feyi came into the room, and she found herself stumbling over her own tongue, tugging her robe to hide the imprint of her nipples as they tightened under her shirt.

"Oh! Good morning, I—I'm sorry to interrupt? I didn't think anyone else would be awake."

"Good morning, Feyi. Help yourself." He drifted a hand through the air in a vague gesture and returned to his reading. Feyi hesitated, then came up to the table, taking a small plate and filling it with a croissant, a blob of roselle jam, and some fruit. She snuck glances at him, but Alim seemed to be comfortable with the early-morning quiet, the pages of his paper rustling as he turned them, a cup of espresso at his elbow. Feyi stepped into the soft quiet and sat down, pouring herself a glass of pineapple-mint juice. The room felt companionable, relaxed. She looked out at the impossibly blue sky as she ate, at the banana tree leafing loudly above its deep red fruit, the jeweled pink of the bougainvillea flowers, and occasionally, the white porcelain of the espresso cup as Alim lifted it to his mouth. He took up so much more space in person than she expected from seeing him on TV. Even silent and sitting, he was loud. The room felt crammed with his energy, pressed into every corner, but Feyi didn't feel out of place in it. Somehow, there was room for her, too.

She wondered if this aura of his was because he was famous, if there was just a level of assurance and presence that you couldn't help once you got to where he was in his career. A brief pang of envy shot through her—so much of her time was spent in uncertainty, wondering if she could be doing more with her work, if she was just coasting while funded with blood money. It was hard to imagine Alim ever doubting if he fit into wherever he was. Maybe that's where Nasir got his confidence, his ease in moving through the tech world despite all the spikes it threw at him, all the ways it told him that someone like him didn't belong. Feyi's parents were different—sweet people, but they hadn't understood why she chose the work she had, so when she talked about her impostor syndrome, they'd been loving but a little confused. Belonging was a thing they did, not a thing they thought about, especially not when it came to jobs. Her father had quoted Toni Morrison at her while explaining that a job was a job, you went to it and then you came home, and home was where you belonged.

"You're awake already?"

Feyi looked up to see Nasir in the doorway, wearing only a pair of pajama pants. She pulled her eyes away from his bare chest and composed her voice. "Trust me, I'm just as shocked as you," she replied. "How did you sleep?"

"Woke up because there was too much sunlight," he complained. "Dad, would it kill you to invest in some blackout blinds?"

Alim chuckled but didn't look up from his paper.

Nasir grumbled and went to pour a cup of coffee. "Whatchu wanna do today, Feyi?"

She looked out into the courtyard and thought of the land, of the river he'd pointed out on their drive up, the waterfall it ended in. Her body felt not just alive but strong and awake. It wanted sky and water, soil and air. Maybe she'd kiss Nasir with nothing around them but rain forest. Maybe she wouldn't even let him touch her. She was hers; she was alive; there was so much to do.

Nasir thought she was undecided. "We can do anything you want," he said.

Feyi looked at him and smiled. "I want to do everything."

Chapter Nine

Jonah.

Jonah at prom, kissing her in front of her horrified parents. Jonah on their college road trips, singing along to Beyoncé, his eyes sparkling. Jonah at City Hall, trying not to cry through his vows. Jonah making corn bread like his grandma taught them, breaking off a piece and slipping it into her mouth. Jonah's fingers. Jonah's hands. Jonah's bleeding hands, limp against the broken glass.

Her voice, screaming his name, over and over and over.

Feyi woke up with a start, sweat sticking her T-shirt to her body and tears sticking to her face, Jonah's name still tangled in her mouth. Her heart was pounding as she dashed her hands against her eyes and swung her legs off the bed, the soles of her feet smacking against the wood floors.

"Fuck," she said out loud. It had been months since the last nightmare. She checked the time on her phone and cursed again when she saw she'd been asleep for only a few hours. It was still the thick dead of night. Feyi blew out a breath and stood up, pulling on pajama pants. There was no point in trying to go back to bed; she would either lie awake for another few hours or fall right back into the nightmare if she did sleep, straight to the part where they were zipping his body into the black bag and she was raking her nails against the arms of the first responders holding her back.

She put her phone in her pocket and wandered out into the

sleeping house. It was her third night there, and through the glass walls she could see the night sky outside, rippling with stars between the trees. It had been ages since Feyi had seen full constellations. She walked along the wall, looking for a garden Nasir had shown her earlier, where the wall curved and the glass just dissolved into air and suddenly you were outside, no roof above you, large white stones under your feet. She ran her fingers against the glass as she walked, wondering if she was smudging it, wondering if she cared. Jonah would have loved this place.

The garden came upon her the same way it had before, like a gasp of surprise. It was flooded with moonlight, clear of tree canopy, just ink-blue sky crowded with those stars. Feyi stayed on the white stone path that wound through the garden, walking with her head thrown back, looking at the sky. There was gold bougainvillea crawling up trellises along the side, and a scattering of small fountains almost buried by greenery. Half the garden was a patio with rugs and poufs and curved daybeds arranged on it. Feyi glanced over and stopped walking when she saw Alim sitting on one of the daybeds, cross-legged and gazing up at the sky.

"Mr. Blake!" she blurted out, blushing when he turned to look at her. She hadn't seen much of him in the last day or two. Nasir had been showing her around town, they'd eaten jerk chicken and green juice down the mountain, cooked a few meals of their own in the play kitchen, driven to the beach. "I'm sorry, I didn't mean to interrupt."

"Come sit," he said, gesturing to the cushion beside him and ignoring her apology. "It's beautiful out here at night, isn't it?"

Feyi hesitated, then walked over and gingerly sat next to him. Alim was wearing a white shirt and a white sarong that draped to his ankles. He looked like a holy man, or a ghost.

"It's gorgeous," she agreed, looking up at the moon. A wisp of a cloud passed over it.

"And call me Alim," he added, still with his eyes to the sky. "Please."

Feyi was grateful that he couldn't see her face, the mild fluster that came with the intimacy of his first name in her mouth. "Sure," she said. "Alim."

He glanced at her then. "I like how you say it. It's a little different."

Feyi made sure she was looking at the rug under her feet because there was no way she was going to look him directly in the eyes while sitting in a garden full of moonlight at such close proximity. She didn't need that kind of trouble—she'd probably already found more trouble than she'd bargained for.

"You couldn't sleep?" he asked.

She nodded, still looking down, her gold braids a curtain against the side of her face, relieved when he looked back out into the garden.

"Neither could I. It's a terrible thing, insomnia. I'm never more grateful for this garden than on nights like this."

"What kept you up?" she asked, risking a glance at Alim's profile. His curls were so like Nasir's, thick and full, except for the moonlight glinting off his silver. His nose was steep, a sharp angle jutting from the bridge. Nasir must've gotten his from his mother.

Alim made a clicking sound in the back of his throat. "I wish I knew," he said. "You?"

"Bad dreams."

"Ah." He gave her a commiserating look. "Those are hard."

Feyi shrugged. Bad dreams had always sounded better than the terrors they actually were.

"What are they about?" Alim asked.

Jonah. Jonah. Jonah. Feyi almost laughed. The water in a nearby fountain sounded like it was singing. She was too tired to lie. "Oh, the usual. A car on fire. My dead husband."

She felt Alim's gaze on her again, but she didn't want to look and see the pity on his face. At least now it was almost impossible to crush awkwardly on him—bringing up Jonah usually stripped the fantasy away from any situation she was in, even if it did leave it bleak. And it felt true to call him her husband still. They'd never broken up, he wasn't an ex, he was just . . . dead. An image from the dream flickered back, Jonah's hand moving, even as mangled as it was. Feyi had forgotten about that.

"He was alive," she said out loud. "Sometimes my brain blurs out that he was alive when I came to." Then the black bag. "He died by the time the paramedics got there." It was amazing, she thought, how she wasn't crying already, saying all this.

Alim steepled his fingers under his chin. "Did Nasir ever tell you how his mother died?" he asked.

Feyi glanced at him, surprised. She was used to people bubbling over with discomfort whenever she shared details of the crash—either that, or they tried to touch her in ways they thought might be comforting but rarely were.

Alim looked back at her, his face still and open, and Feyi shook her head. "No," she said, "he never did."

114

He nodded, his eyes sliding back out into the garden. "She drowned," he said. "In a bay we'd gone swimming in a thousand times before. It was the most"—he shook his head—"it was the most unreal thing, the way the current took her. Nasir and Lorraine were so little. They were on the beach, I was trying to keep Lorraine out of the water. I didn't notice. I didn't notice it took her until it was too late." He paused and took a deep breath. "They found her body by the rocks."

Feyi put her hand on his arm, and he turned his head to her, surprised by her touch. "What was her name?" she asked.

"Hmm." He smiled at nothing. "Marisol. She was . . . everything." Alim shook his head and caught himself, placing a hand on top of hers. "But! I did not mean to trade war stories. Only to say, I know the particular pain of losing the one you love before your very eyes. I am sorry," he said, "for the hurt that lives in your heart."

Feyi opened her mouth and found that her throat was dry and empty. She was touching too much of him, his arm under her hand, his palm on top of it. She drew back her hand and swallowed nothing. "Thank you," she managed to croak out.

"What was his name? And how long has it been?" he asked.

Jonah. Five years, seven months, nineteen days. "Jonah," she said. "About five and a half years."

"I wish I could tell you it gets easier—"

"It doesn't," she interrupted.

Alim put his chin in his hand and propped his elbow on his knee. "No, no. But it gets . . . older. It grows with you."

Feyi looked over at him. "How long has it been for you?"

Alim chuckled. "Ah. Twenty years, four months." He

115

tilted his head to smile at her, boyish in the moonlight. "Eight days."

"Did you love again?"

Alim studied her, his head sideways, his eyes searching her face. "I see why Nasir calls you direct," he said.

Feyi blushed. "I'm sorry. It's an inappropriate question."

Alim waved his hand. "There's no such thing. I like your bluntness, and the answer is, I don't know. Maybe." He made an expressive twist with his mouth. "Not like that, though, no. Not in the same way. But I've loved other things."

"Like what?"

"My children. My work. My memories."

"Did you stay here because of her?" Feyi wondered if she was pushing too much, why she was even asking.

"Out of nostalgia, you mean? No, no. I stayed because of the restaurant, because of what I've been making here that I couldn't make anywhere else. It had to be on this mountain."

Feyi looked around. "I can't wait to see more of it."

"There is time," Alim replied, unbothered. "But I have a question for you."

Feyi laughed. "At this point, it's only fair."

"Do you love Nasir?"

She'd been opening her mouth, ready to quip a response to anything he'd asked—anything but that. Every word fled from her head, and Feyi stared at Alim in slack-jawed silence.

He blinked slowly, like a cat. "Hmm," he said. "You don't have to answer that."

Feyi scrambled for her words. "No, it's just that—we've only been . . . um . . . I mean—"

"Feyi." Alim was smiling at her. "It's fine. I was just

curious, not because he's my son. Only if you've loved since you lost Jonah."

It was then that the tears showed up, but Feyi tried to force them back. It would be mortifying if she started crying in front of this relative stranger simply because he'd asked her the same damn question she just asked him.

"I'm sorry," she said, hoping her voice didn't sound too thick. Alim looked closer and reached out, brushing his thumb against her cheekbone where a traitorous tear had already leaked out. His face softened.

"I didn't mean to make you cry," he said, and Feyi nearly unspooled at the tenderness radiating from him. She stood up, hurriedly, before she could make an even bigger fool of herself.

"I think I'll go back to bed now," she said, starting down the path toward the house. It didn't matter if she seemed rude, she just had to get out of that garden before she started bawling.

After a few steps, she paused and turned around. Alim had stood up as well, a specter holding her secrets.

"Don't tell Nasir," she said, a plea threaded through her voice.

"I won't," he answered, not even asking which parts she meant. "I promise."

Feyi hesitated, wanting to say something more, maybe a thank-you, but instead she spun on her heel and rushed back to her room.

The next morning, when Joy asked her how her night had been, she lied.

Slept like a baby, she texted. *It was amazing.*

Chapter Ten

"Dad, yuh real obsessed, you know?" Lorraine poured honey into her oatmeal as she spoke, her braids in a low bun and her lined eyes sparkling at Alim.

It was Feyi's second week at the house, and Nasir's sister had come up from their house in town to spend some time on the mountain. She'd been a little cool toward Feyi, but Feyi didn't take it personally. She was the guest in their home, after all, a stranger who wasn't even Nasir's girlfriend. The lines were indistinct, and Feyi couldn't blame Lorraine for keeping her at arm's length.

"Is he going on about the orchard again?" Nasir asked, passing a pitcher of cucumber water to his sister. "Don't get him started, I heard enough about erosion and irrigation the last time I was here to educate me for a lifetime."

"No, he just talking about walking up the damn peak again," Lorraine replied.

"My God, how did you two end up as such city children?" Alim replied, cradling his cup of espresso. He'd made them a spread—a soft scramble with grilled spring onions, black pepper French toast, cinnamon date sticky buns, collard greens with fennel, fried plantains and sumac. Now he was watching them eat, his smile indulgent as he sat at the head of the table in an indigo jalabiya, the silk caressing his shoulders.

"Like a mountain peak?" Feyi asked. "That sounds dope."

118

Nasir laughed. "See, it *sounds* dope, until what you realize is that Dad is talking about waking up at the ass-crack of dawn so you can hike for hours up the mountain just to watch a sunrise through the trees."

"When was the last time you went up there?" Alim countered. "You don't even remember how it looks."

"Dad, no one waking up that early to watch a damn sunrise," Lorraine said. "It's not *that* dope."

"Let Feyi decide for herself," Alim said. "Perhaps she's not like you two heathens."

"I mean, I'd like to see it," Feyi said, looking around the table. "At least once."

"Fine," Lorraine said, giving her a saccharine smile. "Leh the *tourist* go see it."

Feyi wondered if she was the only one catching the barb in her words. Nasir didn't seem to notice.

"I'm not coming with y'all," he said, "that's too goddamn early in the morning." He poured out some fresh orange juice. "But you should go see it, Feyi, like you said, even just once."

"That's the kind of support I'm talking about," Alim said. "Grudging but present."

"She's going to regret it when she has to wake up at four thirty just to start heading out," Lorraine said. "Have fun!"

Nasir grimaced. "Yeah, that's going to suck." He stood up and took his plates over to the sink. "I'm off to take a call. You good, Feyi? Is your meeting with Rebecca today?"

"Nah, day after tomorrow. She said I could come start install on the weekend."

"Sweet. Catch you later?"

"Yeah, come find me."

As Nasir left, Lorraine got up and followed him out, leaving Feyi and Alim alone together. Feyi glanced over as Alim sipped on his espresso and watched a hummingbird dive through the honeysuckle vines out in the courtyard. She wondered if she should say something, strike up a conversation, fight off the vague but annoying guilt she felt whenever Nasir left them alone together. Her initial attraction to Alim at the airport had been bad enough, but it had deepened into new shapes since their conversation in the midnight garden. Nasir had noticed when she began to withdraw, no longer kissing him the way she used to, but they'd talked about it during one of their trips into town.

"It's just a little confusing being around your family," Feyi had explained. "Like, if I'm here as your friend, then let's let it be that for real. At least for now. I don't feel comfortable sneaking around and making out in your dad's house, you know?"

Nasir had squeezed her hand and grinned. "Do we get to make out when we're back in Brooklyn?"

It was a good question. Feyi ran a thumb over his lower lip and let herself imagine for a moment that things could return to the way they were, like she'd never been on this island or felt anything for his father, like they could just pick up where they'd left off.

"We'll totally get to make out," she'd said, forcing herself to believe it was true.

Now she was sitting alone with Alim, watching the porcelain of his cup press against his lips, denting the soft dark flesh. It was too easy to get caught up in the details of his face, to wonder how his skin would feel under her fingertips, imagine his tongue—

"How's your work going?" she blurted out, wincing as she heard herself. "I mean, I know the restaurant is on hiatus and all, but I was just wondering."

Alim put down his cup, and Feyi watched his throat swallow, distracted.

"It's going well," he replied. "It's one of my favorite times of the year. My staff and I get to reflect, experiment, discover new ideas. Taking time and space to do that is important."

"Could I sit in on some of that? It sounds amazing." Feyi heard her voice ask the question and cringed at how forward it was. Why on earth would she think someone like Alim Blake would want her getting in his way while he worked? It was ridiculous, but she'd already suggested it like an idiot, so there it was, floating in the air between them.

Alim tilted his head. "You would like to?"

Feyi blushed, looking for a safe way to backtrack out of this. "Don't mind me, I'd probably just be in your way," she started, but Alim interrupted her.

"I'd love to have you," he said, and a small heat twisted in Feyi's stomach as a quick fantasy flashed through her head— Alim in her bed, looking down at her with those swirling eyes of his. *I'd love to have you*, and she'd reach up to him because, yes, of course, a thousand times—

"Do you like to cook?" he was asking.

Feyi pulled herself together and forced out a laugh. "No, I love to eat. And watch other people cook."

Alim chuckled, the sound warm and low through the kitchen. "Then we're a perfect match," he said.

121

Oh, the worlds of possible innuendo. Feyi kept a straight face. "You don't mind being watched?" she asked, feeling a little mad and reckless, but Alim just looked thoughtful.

"Sometimes," he said. "It's not always serious in my kitchen; I find a certain level of playful alchemy useful. Another presence can help create that."

"Yeah, but I know, like, *nothing* about cooking on the level that you do, come on."

Alim's eyes were steady and kind. "I like teaching," he replied. "And if you love food, I'm sure you're not as averse to cooking as you claim."

"You and your Michelin stars are offering me a lesson?"

This time, Alim laughed out loud, and it rolled through Feyi's bones like a tide. "Yes, Feyi. As much as you'd like to learn."

Her name in his mouth sounded obscenely delightful. It was time for her to go. Feyi pushed her chair back from the table. "Can't wait," she said, and Alim's eyes followed her as she stood up.

"Sunrise tomorrow?" he asked. "For the peak. I'll knock on your door?"

Reckless. She could feel it in her thighs, a simmering warning. Alim was just being polite, hospitable. There was no invitation in his eyes, and Feyi knew she was the only one in danger. There was a reason she'd fled from the garden that night, and a certainty that going on an early-morning hike alone with this man was a terrible idea. And, because Feyi was Feyi and she was alive, there was no way she could say no.

"Four thirty," she replied, with a damned smile and a traitorous chill burning through her veins.

. . .

By the time the sun rose the next morning, Feyi was standing at the mountain's peak, her dark skin glowing and damp with sweat. The sky was bursting apart with tender light and pale color, the air was full of dew and birds, and it felt like she and Alim were the only two people in the world. He was standing just behind her shoulder, watching the sunrise with her, and she could smell him—the salt from their walk, a touch of orange she'd caught when he knocked on her door earlier. Waking up that early had been more brutal than she expected, like fighting through a blanket of air, and it had taken all her willpower to drag herself out of the house, grab a beef patty, and hit the hiking trail with Alim. Thankfully, he hadn't talked much, just led the way as she followed. It had taken maybe half an hour before she felt awake, and she'd been too tired to even think about her crush on him. None of it had felt reckless then, just exhausting.

But now, with the cool air folding around her arms and Alim's body so loud and close, Feyi needed him to take a step back, just far enough so she wouldn't be tempted to turn and pull his head down and kiss him. No one but the mountain would see. Secretly, she cursed Joy's optimism that the crush would go away, or even that this had anything to do with Nasir, who clearly trusted her so much that he thought nothing of sending her to watch a gorgeous romantic-ass sunrise with his obnoxiously handsome father. And why would he? Most people would be maintaining some boundaries in their heads, not letting fantasies erode all the lines that marked common sense.

"This is one of my favorite moments," Alim said softly, gazing out. "Thank you for sharing it with me."

"Thank you for inviting me," Feyi replied, plopping down on the grass and wiping her forehead. "It's worth the hike."

It really was, too. The view was spectacular, delicate pink and gold sunlight pulling across the hills like a veil, as billowing blue clouds hung in the sky and a layer of fog rolled over the deep green rain forest. "I've never seen colors like these."

Alim sat down next to her and passed over a bottle of water. His fingernails were painted an iridescent pearl. "I used to try to capture it in a camera when I was younger. It was . . . so futile." He laughed. "Some things are only meant to exist in our eyes, I think."

She glanced over at him. "I know what you mean."

They sat there for a long time as the sun climbed and climbed. Feyi took slow deep breaths, feeling warmth crawl over her skin as the light hit her. Her mind felt blessedly blank, catching up to her sore muscles. Alim pulled out a thermos of hibiscus tea and slices of upside-down pineapple cake wrapped in thin cloth. They ate together in silence, passing the thermos cup between them. Feyi's attraction to him was still there, at a low and consistent hum but under control. When Alim finally spoke, it took her utterly by surprise.

"I wasn't honest with you the other night," he said. "In the garden."

Feyi turned her head just enough to see the slope of his nose, the curve of his mouth, the damp dark of his skin, and waited for him to continue.

"You asked me if I'd loved since Marisol, and I told you I didn't know."

She watched his mouth twist again, just as it had in the garden. "You did love someone," she said, shifting so she could see all of his face.

An old melancholy drifted through Alim's eyes and his jaw tightened. "I did," he said, the words sounding creaky and rusted. He cleared his throat and ran a hand over his hair. "A long time ago."

Feyi wasn't sure why he was telling her, but it felt like something he needed to say, and it was something she wanted to hear—what it was like to fall in love again after your heart had been shattered. She could feel Jonah's presence on the mountain peak, gentle and curious.

"What happened?" she asked.

Alim pulled a hand across his mouth. "I had to choose," he said, and Feyi could hear a faint fracture in his voice. He cleared his throat again and stitched the break together. "I chose my children."

Feyi couldn't stop herself from reaching out and touching his arm. He always felt so alone, and sometimes she wanted to change that, even just for a moment. His skin was warm, dusted with hair.

"Why did you have to choose at all?" It sounded wrong, to have to sacrifice that, to lose it again but this time by choice. "Why couldn't you have both?"

Alim looked at her, and she could see storms and calculations running through his gray eyes. He took her hand in his, and her heart staggered at his touch, but she kept her face still. Alim wasn't looking at her like he felt how she did; he was looking at her like he couldn't decide if he could trust her, if he could tell her the truth. Feyi squeezed his hand tightly. There was a hurt in him, and she could feel the edges of it, how sharply they cut.

"I told you about Jonah," she reminded him softly. "You can tell me anything." The air around them was filled with leaves rustling and birdsong.

Alim sighed and gave her a sad smile. "Devon," he said. "He was a painter. Loved coming up here." He shook his head, catching himself. "He's still a painter, somewhere out there."

Several things clicked together in Feyi's head at once — Nasir's raised voice at the airport, his insistence that Alim wasn't gay, his mention of the tabloids, even Alim's reluctance to tell her about this lost love of his. She kept hold of his hand and met his eyes, showing him that she wasn't pulling away in the slightest, that she was listening.

"Nasir was in college," Alim continued. "He came home for the summer, and I introduced Devon to him and Lorraine. It . . . didn't go well." A muscle in his jaw spasmed, and Feyi tightened her fingers around his.

"I'm so sorry," she whispered.

"I thought they knew," he said, a shadow of confusion resurrecting within the memory. "I thought they already knew about me. I'd never hidden who I was from them or Marisol. And maybe they did, but . . ." Alim shrugged. "They were so young. It was difficult."

"And you had to choose."

Pain spread like the tendrils of pigment through the whites of his eyes. "And I had to choose." Alim smiled at her, and it was sad, yet so terribly genuine. "I chose well. They are the lights of my life."

Before she could think about it, Feyi leaned over and hugged him, throwing her arms around his neck. "You shouldn't have had to choose," she said, her voice thick with feeling.

How brutal, to be torn between such points, how painful the ripping away must have been. Feyi barely registered what she had done until Alim let out a breath and returned the hug, wrapping his arms around her, pressing her body to his. That was when the alarm bells finally went off, a deafening clanging, a siren screaming inside her head. The skin of his neck was millimeters from her mouth, an insignificant breath of distance, her breasts were pressed against his chest, the gold nipple bars sending insistent nerve impulses back to her brain. Her joints were turning into water.

"Feyi . . ."

When he said her name, she stopped breathing. She couldn't tell what was in his voice, other than it was heavy, surprised, and clean with the shock of some revelation. He drew a ragged breath, and the moment seemed outrageously long, like someone had paused the whole mountain and Feyi could smell the sweat from his neck, feel his hair rough against her wrist, the muscle of his shoulder under her palm, his hands burning on her spine, his exhale brushing her ear.

"Alim," she whispered, and it sounded like a sin, like she was admitting to blasphemy. She let too many secrets fall into the syllables, a foolish accident that threaded a vein of hunger into her voice, and so Feyi was not that surprised when he hissed out a breath and pulled away from her, standing up. She scrambled to her feet as well, and adjusted her waist beads, shame and desire tangling thickly inside her.

"I'm sorry," she started. "I—"

"No." Alim didn't meet her eyes, looking down at the ground as he clenched and unclenched his hands. When he lifted his head to look at her, he relaxed his hands and his eyes were controlled murky ponds once again, a surface that might as well have never rippled. "I am sorry. This . . . this was inappropriate of me. I've disregarded boundaries that should have been common sense; I—I've been shockingly careless and a poor host. Please"—he waved one hand in an apologetic gesture and smiled at Feyi—"forgive me. I grow sentimental at my age."

She wanted to tell him he was wrong, but the way Alim was holding himself apart reminded her that he wasn't. This was Nasir's *father*. Why were they talking about dead and lost loves in gardens and on mountain peaks, in the moonlight and the wash of a sunrise? Why had it felt like that to hold him, such a rush to have him hold her as well? What had he meant when he said her name?

It didn't matter. Feyi composed the scattered parts of herself and smiled back at him. "I like to think that we're becoming friends," she said smoothly. "It's been a while since I could talk to anyone about Jonah. I know I've only been your guest for a short while, but still. It means a lot to me."

He inclined his head. "And to me, to have you listen as I rambled on about Marisol and Devon."

Feyi started packing up their stuff, keeping her voice deliberately casual as Alim joined her. "I think I fell for someone, too, after Jonah died."

He hefted his backpack over his shoulder. "You did?"

Feyi made a face. "Yeah, my best friend, Joy. She's . . . amazing. We had a very brief thing about two years ago."

They both took one more look at the view before starting on the trail back. "But?" Alim prodded.

"I told myself she was self-destructive and not ready for a real relationship." Feyi shrugged. "It was easier to believe than the truth."

Alim held a branch out of her way. "What was the truth?"

"Ah, that she just didn't feel the same way about me." She glanced up at him. "At least Devon loved you back."

Alim scoffed. "That didn't end well for either of us. This Joy, she's still in your life?"

Feyi couldn't help smiling. "Yeah, we live together."

"You don't think she loves you?"

"I know she does. And that's something I've learned in the years since, that there are so many different types of love, so many ways someone can stay committed to you, stay in your life even if y'all aren't together, you know? And none of these ways are more important than the other."

Alim shot her a grin over his shoulder. "You're a wise friend. Joy is lucky to have you."

Feyi blushed a little. "Oh, please," she said.

"It's true. I might have had a different life if I learned that when I was your age."

She winced at the mention of their age gap, glad he couldn't see her face as she followed him down the mountain. Maybe he was just saying it to push distance between them after that hug, to remind them of their respective places in all this. She shook out her braids, tying them back in a ponytail. Well, she had said they were friends, and she meant it.

"Can I just say," she added, "that this is *the* most bisexual conversation I have had in a long time?"

Alim stopped in his tracks and burst out laughing, bending over with his hands on his knees. When he straightened up and looked at her, there were no storms in his creased eyes, no careful control, just laughter.

"You are a delight," he said, and Feyi beamed because he said it like they were cool, like they were homies, and so the air was easier between them as they walked back down the mountain.

Chapter Eleven

Feyi avoided Alim for the next few days. The rest of their walk back to the house hadn't been awkward, but once Feyi was alone in her room, under the beating pulse of her shower, she had burst into tears. It hurt, the way Alim had pulled away from her at the peak, closing himself off. She kept remembering how quickly he'd scrambled to his feet, like she was something he shouldn't have been touching, and even though that was technically true, it still made Feyi feel like shit.

She threw herself into her work instead, prepping for the group exhibit as Nasir drove her up and down the mountain. The show was opening soon, so Feyi stepped into her artist persona like a waiting and safe skin. She met the staff at the National Museum, sourced the materials she needed, and ran through the best ways to install her piece. Her name was now printed on all the promotional material for the show, under its title—*Haunted*. That theme had felt perfect for Feyi's work, the way it applied to so much of the personal as well as the wider emotions across Black Diaspora, as Rebecca had explained when they first spoke. The curator had been delighted to meet Feyi in person.

"I'm so glad Nasir brought you to our attention," she said, as they walked through the space. A small, mirrored room was being constructed for Feyi's piece, an eight-foot cube. "I very much look forward to seeing your work installed completely. You're sure two days is enough?"

"More than enough," Feyi replied. Rebecca was impressive, almost six feet tall with acacia skin and finger waves smooth on her skull. Feyi tried not to think about how good the woman would look next to Alim. Maybe they'd already hooked up once or twice, his body aubergine against Rebecca's flushed brown. The image sliced into her, and Feyi pushed it aside. It was foolish, careless even, to indulge in that kind of emotional cutting, over what? Some old man on a mountain? Nah, the work was the only thing that mattered. The work was the only thing that *could* matter. She was glad that the lunch with Rebecca that Alim had proposed when she first arrived never happened; she didn't think she could stand to see them together. Somehow, she just knew they had a wealth of laughter between them.

"Excellent." Rebecca stopped by the doors and smiled at Feyi. She was much warmer than Feyi had expected, even kind. "Let me know if you need anything. I'll see you at the walk-through before the private opening, okay?"

"Sure. And thank you so much, Rebecca. This—this means a lot to me."

"There's no need for thanks. You made the work. You earned your spot here." She left the room, fragrance wafting behind her, and Feyi turned to look at the exhibition space. They were staggering installs so none of the artists would be in each other's way, and several pieces were up already, draped for protection. It was nerve-racking to be showing on such short notice, and despite what Rebecca said, Feyi couldn't help but feel like she was here as a favor to Alim, not even a direct one but a secondhand one through Nasir at that. She'd tried talking through some of the shame with

Joy, but her best friend had shut her down.

"Get into the rooms you need to be in so your work can do what it needs to do," Joy had said. "Someone helped you, and so what? You know how many of these white kids are out here with art careers because their parents hooked them up? You better show up and show out, bitch. I can't believe I'm having to talk a Nigerian into this, of all people."

Joy had been right, of course, and now it was Sunday evening and the private opening was on Wednesday, the opening proper the day after. Feyi had all her outfits lined up, Nasir was being a fucking sweetheart, and everything should have felt perfect. She kept waiting for her feelings to click into their allotted places, but apart from the grim determination to show her piece as it should be, the only other thing Feyi could access was a twinge of sadness that she didn't have time to delve into. Too much dark water under thin ice, old currents. Jonah would've been so excited to be here. Her nails dug into her palm as she forced herself to breathe. He was always with her, but it wasn't suffocating her the way it had that first year or two. Now she had somewhere to channel the endless grief when it flared up. Now she could put it in her work.

That had to be enough.

. . .

When Nasir picked her up from the museum, Feyi was exhausted from whipping her thoughts into a neat line.

"You sure you don't want me to help?" Nasir asked as he started the drive back up the mountain. "You being hella secretive, even for you."

Feyi patted his forearm. "I want you to see it when it's all up. And it's only a few days now."

"Fine, I'll wait. Like everyone else, huh?"

She laughed. "I'm sure you'll survive."

His profile was caught in the evening sun, and Feyi felt a pang of guilt at how supportive he was being. "Thank you for driving me up and down for this," she added. "I'd rent a car, but this other-side-of-the-road shit is way over my head."

"No need to thank me," Nasir replied, turning his head to shoot her a smile. "Also, I was talking to Lorraine about your install. Why don't you crash with us tomorrow night at the family house? Just till your piece is up."

"See!" Feyi sank her face into her hands. "I knew you were tired of driving!"

"Nah, it's not even like that. I want you to see the house, that's all."

Feyi looked up and raised an eyebrow. "Lorraine's house?"

"It's not her house, it's the family house." For a moment, Nasir looked years younger. "It's the house I grew up in. Dad wanted to sell it once, but we wouldn't let him."

"Why not?"

Nasir shrugged. "Lorraine and I don't have a lot of memories of our mom. The house helps us remember."

Oh, shit. Feyi straightened up in the passenger seat and tried not to think about Alim. "Yeah, I'd love to see it, Nasir. You sure Lorraine's cool with it?"

He frowned. "You worried about Lorraine? What's good?"

"Nah, I just don't think she really fucks with me like that."

"Oh, that." Nasir shook his head as he made a turn. "She

can be spiky but fuck it. We'll have some drinks and y'all will be cool in no time. She just has to get to know you."

Feyi wasn't so sure, but she didn't say anything. Nerves wound a tight ball in her stomach at the thought of seeing the house where Alim and Marisol had loved each other, made a whole-ass family together. She forced herself to take a deep breath and let it go. Everyone had old lives. Somewhere in the blur of the past was a different Feyi—Jonah's wife, a walking ghost. And now she was here, watching thick green roll past the car window, on a strange island with a man driving her up a mountain to his father. The ocean licked the land below, and Feyi closed her eyes, living for a brief moment only in the salt of the breeze.

. . .

The next morning, Alim walked out into the driveway, barefoot and wearing a linen robe over his pajamas, as Feyi and Nasir were about to leave. Feyi tossed her backpack into the car and didn't look at him. They hadn't spoken since the day they watched the sunrise together, other than a few polite words that Feyi forced out in response to his greetings. She wondered if he was surprised by her new reticence, but he probably didn't even care. It was like he said, there were boundaries, and she was just keeping to them. Being a polite guest and whatnot.

"I hope you enjoy seeing the family house," Alim was saying to her, his espresso cup cradled in his palm.

"Nasir's told me a lot about it," Feyi replied, not letting her eyes drift up to his face. It was surprisingly easy to push

135

down the crush she had on him if she just avoided those eyes of his, the pigment of his lips, the half smile that pulled lines into his skin. All she had to do was not look. She climbed into the passenger seat as Nasir gave his father a hug.

"We'll see you tomorrow, yeah?" Nasir was saying.

Alim nodded and raised a graceful hand, watching them silently as Nasir started the car and pulled out of the compound. Feyi stole a look before Alim disappeared from view, and he was still standing there, the hem of his robe fluttering around his legs, his face turned up to the sky. Behind him, the albino peacock spread out its tail in a fan of brilliant white. The whole scene looked like something she could paint, if she let herself. Feyi tore her eyes away and checked her phone.

"What are we doing for breakfast?" she asked.

Nasir grimaced. "Lorraine said she'd cook."

"Okay . . . why you make that sound like a bad thing?"

"Shit, I've seen that girl burn a boiled egg. Hopefully Dad's given her some lessons since, or we might have to pick up some patties on the way to the museum." He slowed down to let an approaching car through a tight spot in the road. "I'm hype for you to see the house, though. It's not as fancy as Dad's place, but Lorraine and I had the best childhood there. At least, while we could." A thread of sadness snagged on his last few words, and Feyi watched the grief move in a slow wave through his eyes.

"Isn't it painful for Lorraine to live there?" she asked. "After Jonah, I couldn't even—I had to move out of our apartment."

Nasir looked thoughtful. "I mean, we had a lot of years there with Dad, so we got used to it, you know? And

Lorraine doesn't look it, but she's sentimental as hell. Dad says she's addicted to nostalgia. But yeah, no, she loves living there. Says the best thing was the two of us moving out so she could have the place to herself."

Feyi laughed. "That's cold."

"That's Lorraine for you. Brutal honesty whether you need it or not."

"Does she usually get along with the friends you bring down to visit? Like, eventually?"

Nasir's eyes flickered guiltily. "Well, yeah, but . . ."

"But what?"

He grimaced again. "They've all been guys."

It took a minute for it to click for Feyi. "Wait, wait, wait. You said your dad flies you and your friends down here all the time!"

"He does! You're just the first . . . girl I've invited."

Feyi smacked his arm. "Na*sir*! Why didn't you tell me?"

"Aw, man, I didn't want you thinking it was a whole thing."

"Well, is it a whole thing?"

He slid her a look that was unrepentant, hungry, and patient all at once. "Let's get through your show, then we'll talk," he said. "We're friends first, right?"

Feyi nodded, trying to figure out how the curling emotion his hunger called up in her had shifted from a mirrored desire to a sick unease in just a week or two. They weren't doing anything and still it felt too fast, like she was being smothered, like she needed to retreat.

"Yeah, we're friends," she replied, her tongue clumsy against her teeth. Would a friend feel the way she did about

137

Alim? Hug him in a private sunrise, hold his secrets from his son?

"So it's all good," he continued. "I just want you to kill it at this thing, blow all those bitches out the water."

"I mean, I'll give it my best shot."

Nasir glanced over and smiled at her. "Bet. They not ready."

His belief was sweet. They drove for a little while more before he turned into a compound filled with yellow and red hibiscus bushes, gravel rattling beneath their tires. A large bungalow sprawled in front of them, painted a pale green, with a porch swing on the veranda.

"Here we are," Nasir announced, turning off the engine. Feyi grabbed her backpack, and Nasir let them into the house with a brass key from his key chain. Feyi frowned at it.

"Don't you have that key when you're in New York, too?"

He grinned. "Yeah, I like to feel like there's a piece of home with me all the time."

"Damn, I didn't realize you were sappy like that."

"Oh, you got jokes, huh?" Nasir slipped off his shoes, and Feyi followed suit. The foyer of the green house was narrow, filled with potted plants and jute rugs layered on the floor. Nasir called out to his sister as they walked through the house, and Feyi tried to seize as much of the house in her eyes as she could. The parlor was a glimpse through a doorway—more plants and a large sectional couch, dark orange and splattered with bright cushions. Nasir led her down a corridor and into the kitchen, where a skylight stretched the ceiling open. Lorraine was flipping a pancake, dressed in a linen robe almost identical to the one Alim had been wearing. Her hair was tied up in a silk scarf, and to Feyi's surprise, she was wearing a pair of turquoise-rimmed glasses.

Lorraine pushed the glasses up and smiled at her brother. "Of course you're on time when there's food involved."

Nasir kissed her cheek and plopped down on a kitchen chair. "First of all, it's a miracle that there's actual food involved. I was low-key expecting cereal."

His sister rolled her eyes and gestured for Feyi to sit down. "Make yourself comfortable," she said. Feyi obeyed, wary at how much more relaxed Lorraine seemed, almost friendly even. Maybe it was because they were in her territory now, home turf, the place she'd lived all her life. Feyi looked around the kitchen, trying to imagine Alim in it, trying not to imagine him with Marisol. Copper pans hung above the massive stove, and open wooden shelves held stacks of plates and bowls and glasses. Herbs were growing in the windowsill, and French doors opened into a backyard with tall bamboo waving along the fence.

Nasir reached up to pull a picture frame off a shelf, then passed it to Feyi. "That's us with our mom," he said, pride coloring his voice.

Feyi took it from him, handling the carved bone of the frame gently. She was nervous looking at it, knowing she'd see another life there, another time, another version of Nasir and Alim that might be too real, too uncomfortable for the secrets she was holding. But Nasir was staring at her expectantly, so Feyi had no choice but to meet the faces in the photograph. She held her breath, but it still did nothing to soften the impact of Alim's face, years and years before the gray and the lines and the cratered sorrow. He was laughing in the picture, his arm around a woman with short bright red locs wrapped in copper wire and a gap between her front teeth, a yellow sundress whipped around her thighs. Marisol. She was smiling down at a toddler holding on to her leg and Alim was holding a little boy's hand.

"That's you?" she said to Nasir, and he nodded.

"Mad adorable, right?" The little boy was staring right at the camera with a glower, his shirt tucked into khaki shorts.

"You look like a troublemaker," Feyi replied, shaking her head.

"Like I said, mad adorable."

Feyi stared at the picture, the way Marisol's body was tilted toward Alim. "Your mom is gorgeous," she said. "You look a lot like her, Lorraine."

Lorraine threw a half smile over her shoulder. "Thanks," she said. "Daddy does say that, too." She came over and put plates of pancakes and grapefruit in front of Feyi and Nasir. "You want syrup or honey?"

Nasir grabbed a fork. "Both?"

Lorraine cut her eyes at him. "Wow, rot yuh teeth, why don't you?" She passed him both bottles anyway, then sat at the kitchen counter with her pancakes, her legs swinging off the stool. "Looking forward to your show, Feyi."

It was perhaps the first time she'd ever called Feyi by name, and it took Feyi aback. She coughed, then swallowed the bite of pancake she'd been eating and smiled. "Thanks, Lorraine. Your pancakes are bomb, by the way."

Nasir chimed in with his mouth full. "Yeah, when did you learn how to do this? I thought you were like Mom, couldn't cook if they put a gun to your head."

Lorraine made a face at him. "People can learn, you know!"

"Shit, has Dad tasted your food yet? He might cry in happiness just at the fact that it's not fucking burnt."

Lorraine grinned. "And why the hell I go tell him? So he could stop cooking for me? Yuh must be out your mind."

Nasir choked out a laugh. "Wow, my sister the scammer."

"Thank you, thank you."

Feyi listened to their banter as she ate her breakfast, the old family photo loud on the kitchen table beside her plate. She was choosing not to make more pictures in her head, of a pregnant Marisol padding across these worn ceramic tiles with bare feet, of Alim spinning a giggling baby under the skylight, of a time when he was happy and his family was complete. It would be ridiculous to be jealous of a ghost just because he'd loved her and touched her without recoiling. He'd also screamed over her cold body on a merciless beach, just like Feyi had screamed on that dark road. Those were moments that broke timelines, that cut them so deep and so bloody that they would never stitch back together again, that the life before the cut was as dead as the person who was lost. Just memories through a haze of hurt. Feyi knew better than to be selective about ghosts—for every happy echo of Alim and Marisol in the house, there was a broken man and two small children with no mother, years of grief navy blue in the air, sobs and nightmares and him rocking them against his chest, alone, alone, alone. There was nothing to be jealous of. Feyi ate her grapefruit and ignored the picture for the rest of breakfast.

The house had to be a stranger's house, because it was. The Alim she knew lived up the mountain, not in this pistachio bungalow. Feyi decided it was Lorraine's house, Lorraine's

141

decor, because it made no sense for it to be anyone else's, not after all the time. Nasir drove her to the museum after breakfast, and Feyi spent the day blessedly enveloped in the work, gold and mirrors, music thumping in her earbuds. The hours spilled by, evaporating like water, and she didn't leave until it was dark out and Denlis the security guard told her he had to lock up, for real this time. "Mi get a man at home, yuh know. He patient but he not *this* patient!"

Feyi had apologized and promised to buy him a drink, but Denlis waved her off. They'd been friendly since her first visit, and he was always smiling, with a full beard and a gold tooth. "I know yuh artists, it not ah problem to give yuh a likkle more time. Yuh leh me know if yuh want to start early tomorrow morning. Yuh have my number, oui?"

"Yeah, I will. Thanks, man."

"Yeah, yeah. Yuh boyfriend waiting outside fuh yuh."

Feyi rolled her eyes as they walked out. "I told you before, he's not my boyfriend."

"Mm-hmm." Denlis winked as she headed to Nasir's car. "Yuh keep telling yuhself that, sweetness."

Feyi slid into the passenger seat and hugged Nasir, ignoring the unease she felt, that there was a story between them that was fast becoming inevitable, like a noose tightening. She kept reminding herself that she had a choice, that she didn't have to end up with him. She didn't have to end up with anyone, no matter how pretty the picture looked to strangers.

Back at the bungalow, Lorraine had ordered takeout and Feyi curled up in a corner of the orange couch as they watched *BoJack Horseman* and ate jerk chicken with macaroni pie and plantains. When it was time for bed, Lorraine showed her to the guest room, pale blue walls and a cloud of a bed.

"Sleep well," she said, and Feyi was too exhausted to even marvel at Lorraine's new warmth or to wonder who this room had belonged to in another life. She pulled on a large T-shirt, crawled into the sheets, and fell asleep in minutes.

. . .

Feyi finished her install late the next evening, her hands aching from tying what felt like hundreds of knots with fine fishing wire, almost invisible to the eye but loud against her raw fingertips. The mirrored room felt like a contained madness, too many reflections, not enough space to escape, which meant she'd done it right. Feyi stepped out and took a few steps back to look at it from the main gallery space.

"All done," she whispered to herself. "Thank you, Jonah." With this work in particular, it felt like he'd been with her for each tedious hour, knot after knot, patiently watching. Feyi felt hollow, like she'd scooped fibrous chunks of herself out, like a pumpkin, and hung them up among the mirrors. She was still standing there, almost fixed in place, when Rebecca walked in and came up to her. The two women stood side by side for a moment, then Rebecca put a hand on Feyi's shoulder.

"It looks great," the curator said. "Go get some rest, you look exhausted. I'll see you tomorrow evening."

Feyi nodded and took a deep breath. "Thanks, Rebecca. I appreciate it."

She started heading out of the space, but Rebecca called after her.

"Feyi?"

"Yeah?" she answered, turning to look back.

Rebecca smiled at her. "Congratulations, dear."

Through all the fatigue, a tendril of warmth unfurled in Feyi's chest. She smiled back, then headed out to where Nasir was waiting for her in the car. He had some errands to run on the other side of town, so he played her Sizzla all the way up to Alim's house, then dropped her off and kissed her cheek before heading back down the mountain. Feyi let herself into the house and stripped off her clothes in her room, sprinkling some eucalyptus oil on the stone floor before she stepped into the shower, running the water for ages, scalding hot and steaming against the glass. She let the relief of having the work installed loosen her muscles and tried not to think about the opening that was coming up, all the people who would walk through the museum. Rebecca liked the piece, that was the important part. Feyi got dressed, slipping on a linen shift and buttoning it up in the front, then pulling her braids into a ponytail before leaving her room.

She wandered through the house without any particular direction, exploring the corridors and gazing at the art. When she found the library, she searched through the shelves before pulling some Helen Oyeyemi books and tucking them under her arm. The door slid quietly shut behind her, and Feyi resumed her wandering. A few minutes later, she came to the bottom of an unfamiliar staircase. Faint strains of music were dripping down, and Feyi hesitated before following the music, the soft percussion and piano. It was gentle, just a ghost of a sound from that distance, but it felt like a spell, like she was stepping through a portal.

Nasir hadn't shown her this part of the house, so Feyi was fairly sure that she was infringing on Alim's territory right now, even though she'd done such a good job of avoiding him since that sunrise. She kept going, though, because now there was a voice swelling in the air along with the music, raspy and rich, singing in Spanish with an ocean's worth of longing packed into the notes. Feyi paused at the top of the stairs, a cliff in her stomach. The lighting in this wing of the house was low and warm, simmering like embers, and she recognized that voice. *Concha Buika*. No one else had a voice like that, raw and strong, transforming the air it traveled through.

Feyi became aware of her senses—the linen she was wearing soft and textured against her hips and sides, the delicate touch of her braids brushing her shoulder blades. She knew she should turn back. No good could come of following a song like that when she knew who was waiting at the other end, but because Feyi was herself, and alive, she kept going, holding the books like a secret.

The music took her around a corner, and a set of double doors opened into a large kitchen soaked with light. Buika's voice rang through it like a cathedral, rhythmic clapping in the background and now a quick flamenco guitar. Across a wide swath of stainless steel, Alim was standing with a knife gleaming in his hand, roughly chopping up a hunk of palm sugar, his face tranquil and so beautiful it made Feyi stop in her tracks. The air was sweet and sticky, heavy with coffee, coconut, and nutmeg. Alim glanced up at her, and his hands stopped even as the music continued, climbing to a crescendo, now horns fast with the drums and guitar, and there was no room to talk. Feyi stared at him, sweat forming in the small of her back. Would he send her away? Should she just turn and leave? How invasive was this, walking into his private kitchen like she had a right to?

The song ended, and another began with soaring vocals. Alim smiled and resumed his knife work, tilting his head to gesture Feyi toward a stool on the other side of his table. She went over and sat down quickly, relieved to be welcomed, as Alim cleared the palm sugar into a bowl with the edge of his knife. Neither of them spoke a word; Buika took up all the air.

Alim reached for a glass carafe and poured a drink into a small tumbler, handing it to Feyi. She smiled her thanks and took a sip, then gasped as ginger effervesced down her throat, sparkling and sweet with passion fruit. Alim hid a smile and kept working, small bowls whirling around him, pans simmering on the stove behind him, endless spoons dipped in several sauces. He kept passing Feyi little morsels to taste—a small bowl of coffee bean granita, a piece of cassava pone with spiced chocolate ganache daubed on the plate, a spoonful of the coconut-lime sauce he had going on the stove, his hand cradled underneath. In between the tastes, Feyi leaned her elbow on the table and her chin in her scarred palm, watching him move and listening to Buika's voice.

Alim was liquid in that space, totally at ease, an ivory kitchen cloth slung over his shoulder. He walked over to a large refrigerator, his body reflecting warped on its surface, then pulled out a metal canister frosted with cold, shaking it before depressing its lever. A thick foam spurted out, deep and orange, splashing against the rim of the metal bowl on the counter. As Alim steadied the flow, Feyi smelled mango, sharp and sweet and tangy in the air. He put down the canister and tilted the bowl, then scooped some foam dripping off the rim with two fingers and held it out to her for a taste, his eyes still on the bowl as he tipped it back and forth with his other hand, gauging the consistency.

Buika's throat-tearing voice rang through the room as Feyi stared at Alim's fingers, a breath away from her mouth. It would have been easy to swipe the foam off his hand and onto hers, but somehow Feyi found herself steadying his wrist instead as she leaned forward and licked the sweet cloud off his fingertips, her tongue dragging against the fine ridges of his skin. She wasn't thinking. The bowl in Alim's other hand dropped to the table with a small clatter and Feyi's heart beat wildly against her ribs as the taste of mango detonated in her mouth. She felt like she was leaping off a waterfall, the rush of a river clamoring in her ears.

Alim raised his head and looked at her, his pupils dilated, ink filling his gray eyes into black, widening with a hunger that both terrified and elated Feyi, rippling up the fine hairs of her arm and the back of her neck.

There it was, open and exposed, *finally*.

Desire as deep as midnight, greedy as the ocean, changing his face, changing everything. Feyi released his hand, scraps of foam clinging to his damp fingers, and Buika kept singing as if nothing had happened.

Feyi wasn't sure how she was expecting Alim to react, but it took her wholly by surprise when he lifted his fingers to his mouth and tasted the rest of the foam, never taking his eyes off her. Blood rushed to her face, and she reached for her ginger drink, dropping her gaze. Had he done that on

147

purpose, to be suggestive? He was turning back to the stove, so casually, and Feyi took the time to stare at the back of his neck, the tapered cut of salt-and-pepper hair fading into his skin. She wanted to press her lips to it, and being on the other side of the table suddenly felt very lonely, like it was a canyon between them, a lifetime.

You always fall for the impossible, Jonah used to tell her. It hadn't mattered then because he believed in her so fiercely, everything had turned out to be possible anyway.

Feyi could feel the sharpness of tears threatening, foolishly and for no reason. What was she doing, playing make-believe in this man's world? She didn't belong here. Under the volume of Buika's music, she picked up the books she'd taken from the library and slid silently off the stool she'd been sitting on, her bare feet landing softly on the cool polished concrete. She was trying to be quiet, but Alim turned his head anyway, and Feyi smiled apologetically, raising a hand goodbye. There was a heartbeat of a pause, then Alim raised his hand goodbye as well.

Feyi left the kitchen quickly, trying not to think about how he'd looked standing there, surrounded by sweet things and so starkly alone.

Chapter Twelve

On the night of the opening, Feyi's pulse was a flock of birds going mad in her veins. Joy had approved her outfit, a silk dress in shimmering falls of dark red, scooped open at the back with a bateau neck. Feyi's gold braids were pinned into an updo, and small ruby studs shone in her ears, a graduation gift from her parents and the only jewelry she was wearing that night. The pouring column of her dress was enough, the way it left her wrists bare and pooled at her feet. She had a faint scarlet tint on her lips and black winged liner on her eyes, thick mascara lengthening her lashes.

"You look like you're about to assassinate someone," Joy had said. "You look perfect."

When Nasir saw her, he stared with a slack jaw for a few moments and that window was enough for everything he wanted to be blatantly clear in his eyes, a loud desire that Feyi wished she hadn't seen. By the time he caught himself and organized his face, it was too late to forget, but Feyi tried to push it away as they drove to the museum. Nasir was her friend, and that was it. They'd decided.

Still, it was a relief to have to mingle at the opening, to leave him behind in the crowd and walk with Rebecca, chatting to the other artists, many of whom she was secretly fangirling over. Katherine Agyemaa Agard was there, for one, wearing a floating indigo scarf and standing next to one of her paintings from her *Blue* series. The canvas towered over her, and a small crowd of people were gathered in front of it, staring up in awe. Katherine smiled at Feyi when Rebecca introduced them, and a piece of orange calcite fell out of her sleeve when they shook hands. Feyi fumbled over her words, trying desperately to play it cool, and Rebecca laughed a little when they stepped away.

"Breathe," she said to Feyi. "Your work is here, too, you know. These are your peers."

"Don't even say that." Feyi laughed. "Charmaine Bee's here, for God's sake. I've been following her work since she had that show in LA at Craft Contemporary."

"Everyone starts somewhere," Rebecca replied. "Don't sell yourself short." She raised her champagne flute to Feyi, then disappeared into the crowd.

Feyi took a sip of her cocktail and exhaled, then made her way back to her piece. There was always a nice little pocket of time when no one viewing it realized she was the artist and she could slip into the line of people making their way into the mirrored room like she was just another visitor, seeing it for the first time.

Four hundred and thirteen gold wedding rings hung suspended from the ceiling at varying heights, chiming softly as they rang against each other. Light reflected off them and the mirrors, breaking into pieces against the visitors in the room. It looked and sounded like rain, like wind chimes, like warning bells. It would be enchanting if you didn't know what it really was. Feyi walked through it slowly. The small room was silent, only three or four people could fit at a time, and everyone was trying not to disturb the rings too much. It was impossible, of course, but Feyi liked their discomfort, their disruption. It was some of the point. What most people tried to do was to stand in one place and look through the rings with their eyes, trying to find the epicenter, the ring that started it all. It was in her artist statement for this piece, but she never gave a map of where she'd hung it, the ring from the accident, splashed with old blood that Feyi was careful to never clean off. She always hung it and a few other rings out of reach, so they wouldn't brush against anyone's face or shoulders, and she always knew where it was, no matter how many rings she filled the room with.

Feyi glanced up quickly to check on it, and sure enough, there it was, spinning in a slight breeze, stained with brown. So small, but so heavy, so loud, so present in her heart. Showing work like this felt a little like screaming out loud in a public place, screaming and screaming until someone understood what the fuck had happened to her, until it drove them to silence because there was nothing, nothing any of them could say to make it better. Feyi dropped her gaze, and her eyes slammed unexpectedly into Alim's, knocking the air out of her lungs.

He was standing on the other side of the mirrored room, his eyes lined with kohl, shocked and wet as rings floated around his head. Feyi couldn't breathe. His face was raw among the gold, flayed open with feeling, and she knew he'd seen the blood-marked ring, that he knew what it meant that she'd kept it, that she was showing it like this, in a forest of forevers, the one that didn't happen. As Feyi stared at him, Alim's hand drifted to his neck, his fingers coal dark against his white tunic. Feyi knew what lay against his throat underneath, that silver ring. It was either his or Marisol's. She'd

151

never asked which, never said anything about it, really. It was too private, something like that. Unless you were Feyi, and alive, in which case you displayed it to strangers because something inside you had never stopped screaming.

She opened her mouth to say something to Alim, but then Rebecca poked her head into the room.

"Feyi, could I steal you for a minute?" The curator was wearing her official smile, which meant she was about to do another introduction. Feyi cast one last glance at Alim as she left the room, his inky eyes following her out. Rebecca looped an arm through hers, patting Feyi's hand. "I'd like to introduce you to Pooja Chatterjee, one of the museum's board of directors. Pooja, this is Feyi Adekola, the artist behind this stunning installation."

Pooja was a large gorgeous woman with gleaming black hair cut into a severe bob that framed her soft face. She wore a glittering sari, and her handshake was firm, her smile genuine, and her voice had the rushing power of a waterfall. "Ms. Adekola, I must tell you, I adore this piece. It is, in a word, unforgettable. What a memorial, what an ache! It is, I think, a devastation to look upon. How brilliant!"

Rebecca hid a smile as Feyi almost wilted under the force of Pooja's admiration. "I'll leave you two to it," the curator said, slipping away as Feyi shifted into her work face.

Pooja had questions about not just this piece, but the rest of her practice, where her studio was, how long she would be in town.

"I'm not sure yet," Feyi replied. "Perhaps another week?" Saying it out loud sent a twist through her chest. Another week and she'd have to return to New York, end things with

Nasir, never see Alim again. Feyi didn't dare look behind her to see if he was still standing there, shocked in the gold.

"Ah, you don't have a return booked?" Pooja was saying. "Perhaps I can interest you in a proposition, then."

Feyi snapped her attention back to the woman, curious now.

"If you would consider staying long enough for me to commission a work from you," Pooja continued, "I would be most honored. At my expense, of course, and if it would not be too disruptive to your life in New York."

Feyi stared at her, stunned, and Pooja let out a chuckle.

"It is a selfish offer on my part, make no mistake. As a collector, I am somewhat . . . determined. Impatient, as well. I would rather not chance the many interruptions life, New York, and a blossoming career such as yours will most likely bring if I were to wait."

Feyi was trying to come up with a reply when Pooja looked over her shoulder and broke into a wide smile.

"Alim!" she called, waving in the air. "Alim Blake, out in public, when did hell freeze over? Did I miss the memo?"

Feyi felt the air around her distort as Alim walked up next to her. "Pooja, my dear," he said, giving her a warm hug and kissing her cheek. "I should have known you'd be here, of course. Where's Sanjeet?"

"Ah, he's off with his mother on holiday in Tobago while I am working hard trying to entice the lovely Ms. Adekola here to stay longer on our island so I can commission some work from her. Perhaps you could support my worthy cause? Ms. Adekola, this is Alim Blake, one of the finest chefs this island and the world has to offer."

153

Feyi glanced up at Alim's face, now settled and amused, the corner of his mouth quirking up.

"Ms. Adekola is actually a guest at my home," he said, "and she is more than welcome to stay as long as she wishes." He held her gaze for a beat longer than she could stand, and Feyi dropped her eyes quickly, trying not to look as thrown as she felt.

Pooja clapped her hands in delight. "Well, that is just *perfect*! But if you ever get tired of the isolation up there, please say the word and we shall relocate you to the downtown Hilton in no time!" She slipped Feyi her card and smiled at both of them broadly. "I am off to make my rounds, but I shall see you both later, yes? At the dinner? And perhaps, Ms. Adekola, you might give my proposition some thought by then? It has been a pleasure!" She drifted away, humming to herself, and Feyi was left alone with Alim, who looked over at her with hooded eyes.

"You look . . . spectacular," he said, his voice low. He was in all white, a long embroidered tunic and narrow trousers, a touch of red on his bottom lip, the blackness encircling his eyes. Feyi wondered how they looked standing next to each other, deep blood and a long cloud, both adorned, both dark as two different nights.

"You look beautiful," she replied softly, and Alim's control slipped for just a second, strong feeling bolting through his face like lightning.

"Thank you." He cleared his throat and glanced back at her installation. "Your piece — "

Feyi stopped him by touching his wrist. "Not here," she said. "Sorry, I — I don't think I can talk about this here. Not

154

with you." She was terrified that she would actually cry, that the artist persona she wore around these people would crack once she remembered that the bloody ring was real, not just a symbol or an object standing in place for something else, like an everlasting grief.

Alim laid his fingers over hers. "I understand," he said. "It's a garden type of conversation."

Feyi gave him a quick relieved smile. "Yes, exactly." The warmth of his fingers on her skin was stronger than the champagne, making it hard to think, to remain the person she was supposed to be at events like this. "What dinner was Pooja talking about?" she asked, pulling her hand away from his.

Alim slid his hands into his pockets. "It was Nasir's idea," he said. "He wanted it to be a surprise."

Feyi narrowed her eyes. "He wanted *what* to be a surprise?"

Alim laughed. "Relax. It's just a celebratory dinner at the house."

"For me?"

He gave a look that was entirely too soft to be seen in public, and Feyi bit the inside of her cheek.

"Yes, for you. Rebecca must have invited Pooja—an excellent idea—and I believe some of the other artists are attending as well."

Feyi frowned, trying to fit all the pieces together. "Who's handling the dinner?"

Alim cut his eyes at her. "Feyi. You think I'm going to let someone else cook a dinner in my house?"

"Wait, wait. *You're* doing it? But—"

Alim raised an eyebrow. "But what?"

But you're Alim fucking Blake, she wanted to say, *and I'm just . . . me*. It felt like too much, but she didn't know how to turn it down. Everyone had already been invited, and Nasir had done this to be sweet, which made it even harder to think about what she had to tell him once they were back in the city.

"I wish y'all had asked me," she said. "It's bad enough that I've been crashing at your place, but come on, a Michelin-star chef making a dinner for some emerging artist no one's really heard of?"

"I think it's a wonderful publicity strategy," Alim replied. "They'll certainly know about you now, won't they?"

Feyi stared at him, briefly speechless, and Alim took that moment to lean in, his hand cupping her elbow.

"Congratulations," he murmured into her ear. "I'll see you at home."

With a wink and a waft of lemongrass, he was gone, leaving Feyi rattled. *Home*, he'd said, and God help her, but it had sounded so right, like she could belong on a mountain with this loving bruise of a man. Like anything was possible, even that.

. . .

The dinner turned out to be more like an after-party, as cars pulled up into the compound, spilling out breathless guests all delighted to be invited into Alim Blake's home. Nasir knocked on Feyi's door as she was changing her clothes.

"Courtyard in five!" he called. "We're toasting you, so you better be there!"

"Coming!" Feyi yelled back, wriggling her way into a fringed taffeta dress, short and pale pink, light as a breath. She'd barely had time to send Joy a voice note about how the opening went, but she'd promised to catch up with her as soon as she could. Feyi made sure her legs were oiled, then hurried down the stairs as she fastened long gold earrings to each earlobe. Her skin felt like it was buzzing, either from the success of the opening or the offer of a commission or the energy of the party, or a combination of everything. Nothing felt impossible. She could do this. She could be bright and brilliant and charming and act as if she belonged there, among these people, because weren't they all just people, after all?

Feyi caught a glimpse of her reflection in one of the windows and hissed out an annoyed breath—she'd forgotten her braids in the updo and it was totally the wrong look for this outfit. She stopped in front of the glass and started pulling out the pins holding it up, fluffing out the braids as they fell so they made a tangled gold cloud around her face. Alim came around the corner, and his eyes crinkled into a smile when he saw her.

"Just the person I was looking for," he said. "We're ready for you." He held out his hand to her, then dropped it awkwardly to his side.

Feyi wrapped the pins in her fist, feeling the metal press against her palm and the sting of a sudden hurt. What was she expecting—that they'd walk into the courtyard holding hands? Alim had reached out like it was instinct, or habit, and she'd almost taken his hand with equal ease.

As she followed him out, dropping the pins discreetly on a counter, Feyi wondered if it wouldn't be best to take up

Pooja on her offer of staying at the Hilton. That way Nasir could return to the city by himself, she'd be away from Alim and this house, and maybe that was better than staying here with whatever this was between them, something that couldn't afford to exist, something she wasn't entirely sure was even real.

Maybe she was imagining it. His voice at the sunrise, his eyes the other night in the kitchen. Maybe she was just seeing what she wanted to see. Feyi pasted a smile on her face as they walked into the courtyard and everyone there raised a champagne flute and cheered. Nasir was standing in the middle, wearing an ecru buttoned shirt, a wide grin on his face. Feyi could see Rebecca behind him in a bone-white suit, her mouth a vivid slash of purple. She and Alim looked like they'd coordinated their outfits, both tall and elegant in white. Feyi accepted a flute from a waiter, suddenly noticing the staff threading through the guests, holding trays of champagne and small bites. She wondered how much this all had cost. Nasir was now saying lovely things about her work, but his words sounded dull and muted to Feyi. What did he know? Could he even hear the screaming in the gold?

"To Feyi Adekola!" he concluded, and the sound of glasses clinking against each other rang through the courtyard like applause.

Feyi kept smiling and nodding, murmuring thanks as people she'd never seen before congratulated her. Over by the roses, she caught sight of Katherine Agyemaa Agard standing next to Charmaine Bee, their heads bent together in quiet conversation. What on earth were *they* doing here? Was she supposed to go over and talk to them, congratulate them on their pieces? She'd already fawned over their work at the museum, perhaps it would seem too heavy-handed now. Feyi took a sip of her champagne, then drained the glass. Fuck it. She wasn't going to deal with all this sober. If only Joy were here; she always had weed gummies in her purse. The thought dampened Feyi's buzz. If only Joy were here, *period*. Then Feyi wouldn't feel so lost, like she was just floating around alone, without anyone to keep her grounded, remind her what was real. She signaled a waiter over.

"Do you have anything stronger than this?" she asked.

"Of course," he replied. "It's an open bar. What would you like?"

"Tequila, neat."

He was back with the drink within three minutes, and Feyi took it like a shot, wincing as it burned down her throat. This was stupid—she knew the feeling only too well, how to try and chase away sadness with drink on top of drink, and she knew it wouldn't work, not in the end, but Feyi wasn't sure what else to do. She wanted Joy to be there. She wanted to be back in their living room in Brooklyn, eating pasta and watching a baking show. She wanted to be in Cambridge eating efo and pounded yam at her mother's kitchen table. She wanted to be someone she could recognize.

The guests were invited in for dinner, and Feyi decided to be someone else entirely, just for that night. It would be easier this way. She threw her shoulders back, asked the waiter for another tequila, and followed everyone into the dining room.

The slab table fit at least twenty people around it, and Feyi was seated between Nasir and Rebecca. Alim came in only to introduce each course as it was served, and Feyi tried not to look at him when he was there, but she missed his presence as soon as he left. The guests around her were chattering about Alim's art collection, the menu for the dinner, and the exhibit they'd just seen, which Feyi was grateful for because she could autopilot her way through most of it. The room hushed as Alim introduced the first course, and everyone cooed over their plates—fresh oysters in a pool of black squid ink bouillon, served on stark-white china with a sliver of pickled onion and a bright strip of shaved Scotch bonnet on top. There was a dash of the black bouillon inside the oyster shell and a rocket flower on the side, delicate and white. Feyi sipped at the accompanying drink, an expensive champagne with pomegranate seeds in it. Rebecca was talking to her about the show, and Feyi made whatever the appropriate responses were, her mask moving independent of her. The evening felt as surreal as a dream, and every bite she took just reinforced that feeling. She wasn't really here; she was living in someone else's fantasy, and to be fair, it was designed beautifully. It had Michelin-star food and gorgeous powerful people gathering at an exclusive celebrity's house on a tropical island.

It had the second course—poached shrimp with grilled jicama, mango, and red bell pepper, a pineapple vinaigrette and micro coriander leaves spotting green in the bowl. Feyi kept getting emotional as she tasted the food, trying not to think about if Alim had really made all this for her, his work in appreciation of hers. She told herself it was for his guests, for his reputation, but whenever his eyes met hers, it felt as if everyone else in the room had fallen off the earth. Feyi looked away and tossed down the aqua pearl cocktail that came with her shrimp. At this point, she knew damn well that the tequila from earlier had been a terrible idea, but Feyi had already decided to be someone else, someone decidedly not sober, and she was nothing if not committed.

When the third course came in, a lionfish ceviche in a coconut-and-lime sauce, garnished with toasted coconut and kaffir lime leaves, Alim glanced at Feyi as he introduced it.

"Since its introduction to our waters, the lionfish has posed an enormous ecological threat to our marine life," he was saying. "It preys on more than fifty different species of fish and has no native predators, so quite frankly, all murderous tendencies are deeply welcome when it comes to this fish."

His guests laughed, and Alim's eyes crinkled as he looked around the table. "Now, the lionfish reciprocates this sentiment by being severely venomous to humans."

Feyi flinched away from her plate and Nasir suppressed a laugh next to her.

"Don't worry," he whispered.

"However, the venom is only found in its spikes, none of which have made their way to your plates tonight."

Half the table sighed in relief, and amusement ghosted across Alim's face.

"The devastation the lionfish wreaks reminds me of grief," he said, his voice curling into Feyi's skin. "The way it destroys so much around us. The way it feels like a lifetime of venom, spikes piercing through us."

The table was silent now, almost reverent. Some of the guests seemed stunned at hearing Alim speaking so personally. When he looked directly at Feyi, this time she didn't lower her gaze because it was so brazenly clear that this *was* for her, about her.

161

Alim dipped his head in a small bow, and Feyi's breath caught at the public recognition.

"Tonight, we are celebrating Feyi and the art she makes, work that reminds me that grief can also be the softness when the spikes are removed, something that gives your palate joy, something that can fill your belly. And for that, Feyi, I thank you."

As the guests burst into gentle applause, Alim gave Feyi a smile that was both sweet and sad, tied to midnight gardens and their widowed hearts. She felt tears start in her eyes, and Nasir's hand at her elbow as he whispered more congratulations. Everyone was looking at her and saying lovely things as Alim left the room, and Feyi struggled to keep her composure. It was a low blow, him saying things like that in front of people, things that sounded so innocent if you didn't know about the peak of a mountain at sunrise or what sweetness tasted like on the pads of his fingers. She tried to eat her food, only to be hit with another wave of feeling when she realized the coconut-lime sauce was the same one Alim had been working on in his kitchen when Buika was playing.

"This margarita is phenomenal," Rebecca was saying as she tried the next drink. "You have to try it, Feyi, it's got coconut and jalapeno."

"I might need to slow down on the drinks," Feyi confessed. She was feeling more out of control every second, and with Nasir right beside her, she couldn't afford for him to get even a hint of what she was feeling for Alim. Anything could betray her—a glance held too long, a blush, a break in her voice.

"Perfect," Nasir was saying. "I'ma take yours, then." He grinned at her, and Feyi smiled back, scaffolding her mask as the rest of the courses came out, one after the other. Guava-stuffed chicken with caramelized mango and a spicy mango mojito sauce. Alim had ruined mango for her, but every time Feyi remembered how shocked and open his face looked with desire, she wasn't sure she minded. There was a lemon-grass-and-pineapple-glazed pork belly with Zanzibari spiced octopus, grilled jerk watermelon with couscous and a basil oil, and finally, a banana cream parfait with coconut short-bread alongside broiled pineapple with macadamia toffee, drizzled with rum caramel.

When the meal was over, everyone retired to the living room with fresh cocktails, and the music got louder, the air seemed warmer. Feyi found herself on a divan with Nasir, who was quietly feeding her gossip about the guests, a rum and Coke sloshing in his crystal tumbler.

"So apparently Chatterjee's husband has a lover in T&T. No one knows if she knows about it for sure, though, but I think she has to. It would be too fucking wild if she didn't, you feel me?" He tugged on one of Feyi's braids lightly. "You gonna take her up on that commission?"

She leaned her head against his shoulder, feeling full and a little drunk. "Dunno yet. Could take anything from a few weeks to a couple of months to finish a piece, depending on what she wants."

"What do *you* want to give her, that's the question. Fuck what she wants. You decide what you wanna make, and that's what she's gonna get."

Feyi giggled. "You'd make a great manager."

"Of course I would." Nasir grinned at her, and Feyi smiled back.

"I don't want to overstay my welcome here, though," she added. "Pooja offered to put me up in the Hilton." Reaching for Nasir's glass, she took a sip of his rum and Coke. "How much longer do you think you're going to stay here before you head back to the city?"

Nasir leaned back and ran a hand over his hair. "Shit, I forgot to tell you. Boss wants me to fly to Antigua tomorrow, handle some business there."

Feyi sat up, her head spinning a little. "You're leaving?"

"It's just for a week. We can hang out after I come back, I was thinking maybe another week or two before New York? Not sure if that's enough time for you to finish the commission."

"I could make it work." Three more weeks on the island, away from home and Joy. Three more weeks near Alim, before she never saw him again. Three more weeks pretending to Nasir that everything was the same as it'd been in Brooklyn. "Let me think about it?"

"No problem." He stretched his arms out along the back of the divan, and Feyi looked around the rest of the room. The music changed to a kompa and Rebecca whooped, getting up from her seat. She'd been drinking red wine steadily all evening, never spilling a drop on her white suit, and her purple mouth was wide and beautiful as she danced over to Feyi.

"Come, Feyi," she sang. "Do you know how to dance this?" She grabbed Feyi's hands, pulling her off the divan.

Feyi laughed. "Okay, show me," she said, smoothing down the skirt of her dress.

"Here." Rebecca slid her hand to the middle of Feyi's back,

and as the beat pulsated, she spun Feyi out to the middle of the floor. Feyi stifled a gasp—Rebecca might have been tipsy, but even so, she was dead steady on her feet and an excellent dancer. Feyi matched her two-step, their palms pressed against each other's, arms extended. It was strange to be this close to Rebecca, feel her hand strong and sure against her spine, guiding Feyi's movements.

As Feyi sank into the music, she let her eyes flutter half-shut, just enough to see her feet and make sure she didn't step on Rebecca while filtering out the rest of the room. She'd almost forgotten how much she loved this; it felt like ages since she and Joy had been out on a dance floor. There was something that settled in Feyi's chest when she reduced the world to just her body following Rebecca's, the drums and electric guitar, the song's vocals, the tingle in her veins from the alcohol. Rebecca was softly singing along in Creole, and Feyi made a mental note to ask her later how she'd gotten into kompa in the first place; it was a side to the curator she hadn't expected to see.

As the song wound down, Feyi extricated herself with an apologetic smile. "I'm going to grab a drink," she said, even though she very much didn't need one. Rebecca patted her hand and spun around, pointing to Nasir.

"You! Come, dance with me."

Feyi winked at Nasir as she slipped out of the living room and back into the courtyard. She sank down on a bench, and the waiter from before slipped her a glass of water with a knowing smile. "You dance well," he said.

Feyi blushed. She'd forgotten people were watching. "Thanks."

165

He nodded and walked off as Pooja came into the courtyard, exclaiming in delight when she saw Feyi. "There you are! I've been looking for you." She sat at the other end of the bench, the fabric from her sari pooling like a galaxy over the wood. "What have you decided about my proposition?"

Feyi tilted her head, her work mask clicking into place. "You know, I'm inclined to accept it, but I have to ask—what's your budget for the commission?" She wasn't sure if it was proper etiquette to discuss money so bluntly, but fuck it. It was a party, and she was drunk and alive.

Pooja tucked a piece of her dark hair behind her ear, revealing her lovely neck. "Well, as far as I know, no piece in any show Rebecca curates goes for under ten thousand, so why don't we say that?"

Feyi bit the inside of her cheek to stop her jaw from dropping open. If she had been sober, she probably wouldn't have said what she said next, but this whole world wasn't real anyway, so what did it matter?

"How about fifteen?" she countered, and Pooja clapped her hands, laughing out loud.

"I do love you Nigerians," she said, then held out a hand. "Fifteen it is."

Feyi shook her hand, and Pooja kept laughing as she stood up to return to the house. "I'll have my people be in touch. We'll have lunch and talk details soon. It's a pleasure doing business with you, Ms. Adekola."

"Likewise, Mrs. Chatterjee."

Feyi waited till she was out of the courtyard before kicking her feet and squealing in excitement. *Fifteen fucking thousand dollars?!* Was this all it took? To just be around the right people and they threw money at you? She patted her pockets looking for her phone so she could text Joy but came up empty. She must have left it on the divan with Nasir. Feyi chugged the rest of her water and skipped back to the house, forcing herself into a calm walk once she was inside.

As she walked through the living room, the kompa music was still playing. Feyi stopped in her tracks when she saw Rebecca and Alim locked together on the dance floor. Both of them had their eyes closed and their bodies flush against each other, hips circling slowly, with Alim's knee thrust between Rebecca's thighs. It was almost unbearably sensual, the way his temple rested on her forehead, his long fingers pressed between her shoulder blades, her arms wrapped around his neck. It made Feyi nauseous.

No one else seemed to notice. They were all chatting and drinking, a few nodding in time to the music. The painter Katherine was sitting cross-legged on a rug with a spread of tarot cards in front of her, dark hair tumbling across her face and Nasir watching intently as she spoke to him.

Feyi felt like she was the only one watching Alim and the curator sway together, as if they were alone in the dark. It didn't even look out of place; it just made sense. Alim with Rebecca, two people who matched, who had a real chance. Feyi took a deep breath and made her way around them. It was fine. She would have lunch with Pooja while Nasir was away and be set up in the Hilton by the time he got back. She could fly Joy down and they'd be together, and Feyi would make sense to herself again. Alim would be out of the way, and Feyi would tell Nasir to go back to New York, to not wait for her. Maybe she'd even tell him the truth, that she was dealing with irrational feelings for his father. That would be a surefire way to kill whatever he felt for her, end any chance of him trying to keep their friendship. A clean break.

Feyi dug down in the cushions of the divan and fished out her phone, then snuck out of the party and upstairs to her room. She'd meant to call Joy, but once the door was closed and she slipped out of the chiffon dress, Feyi found that what she really wanted to do was curl up in bed and cry. She wasn't sure what she was crying about: the sight of Alim wrapped up in Rebecca, the way everything had shifted so wonderfully when it came to the work but so horribly when it came to Nasir in just a few weeks, being away from Joy, hiding out upstairs while a party in her honor carried on downstairs, feeling so fucking alone. Feyi muffled her sobs in a pillow and fell into a haze, emerging only at the sound of someone knocking at her door.

The air felt quieter, the night heavier, like hours had passed. She wasn't sure if she'd fallen asleep. The knocking continued, and Feyi climbed out of bed.

"Who is it?" she called, swallowing back a yawn.

"Hey, it's Nasir. You awake?"

Feyi opened the door and gave him a look, her head throbbing. "No, I'm sleep-talking."

Nasir stumbled past her and flopped down on her bed. "You missed half your own party," he complained. "Come hang out with me."

Feyi got back into bed, and Nasir pulled himself up till his head was on the pillow next to hers. They lay on their sides, looking at each other, and Feyi giggled. "I don't think I've ever seen you actually drunk," she said.

Nasir raised his eyebrows even as his eyes were drifting shut. "I'm not drunk," he argued. "I'm just very . . . sleepy."

"Well, you can crash here if you want. I'm not sure you could find your way to your room right now."

"Mm . . . thanks. But hey, Feyi?"

"Yeah?"

"I'm fucking proud of you, yo. You did the damn thing."

Feyi smiled and stroked his forehead. "Thanks for everything, Nasir. For real."

He nodded and snuggled deeper into the pillow. "I'ma sleep now," he announced.

"Aight. Get some rest."

"Okay. Love you."

Feyi froze in place, praying that she hadn't heard what she just heard. When a few minutes passed and Nasir started snoring lightly, she cursed under her breath and hid her face in her hands, dread thickening around her heart.

Chapter Thirteen

"This is the worst fucking idea I've ever heard," Joy said, her voice crackling over the phone connection, her frown pixelated. It was early the next morning and Feyi was still in bed, chatting to Joy through her earphones. Nasir had rolled out of bed an hour before, yawning as he padded out of the room, and Feyi had pretended to still be asleep then.

"It's not *my* idea," she replied. "Nasir's the one traveling, and he has to because it's for work. Besides, it's only for a week."

"So go with him! Definitely don't stay in the same house alone with his sexy-ass father *whose fingers you licked mango foam off of*! I swear to God." Joy pinched her nose and shook her head. "This is exactly how incest porn starts."

"He didn't invite me! He asked if I'd be okay hanging out at the house alone for a week, and I said sure. I can start thinking about that commission, maybe even get some work done."

"Okay, boo, you're killing me here. One"—Joy counted off on her clear sparkly nails—"you're not alone in the house, Mr. Sexy Genius Daddy Chef is right fucking there, and two, you're not gonna be catching up on 'work,' you're going to be hooking up with his fa-ther!"

She punctuated the syllables of the last word with two claps, and waited for Feyi to argue back and claim innocence, but when Feyi just sighed and looked down, Joy's voice turned worried.

"Babe," she said, "talk to me."

"Look, I'm going to leave for the Hilton as soon as I can, but real talk, I don't wanna go with Nasir." Feyi's voice splintered by a fraction. She felt fragile and hungover. "What I really wanna do is stay here and make my work even though I know that means being around Alim, and I know this crush I have is stupid and wrong and five kinds of fucked-up, plus the man's literally old enough to be my father, but I—I like what it feels like being around him, and we're kind of friends, and yeah, I get that it can't ever be anything more than that. I get that he and Rebecca are a better fit, I get that none of this is real, it doesn't count as the real world, this is just some mountain paradise he's built for himself, but it's been nice to be in it, you know? Apart from all the crush bullshit, it feels better than I've felt in a while, now I have another friend I can talk to about Jonah—"

"Whoa, hold up. You talked to his dad about Jonah?"

Feyi shrugged. "He lost someone, too, he knows what it's like." She wiped her eyes roughly. "Look, I know you don't approve, and maybe you don't get what it's like to be alone in a particular way, when the person you thought you'd spend the rest of your life with is gone, like gone forever. But I always feel alone, Joy, and I know Alim does, too, and when I'm here it's like . . . it's like I found someone to be alone next to, even just for a little bit. I'm not tryna do anything with him. I just wanna enjoy the last few days or however long before I leave and literally never see him again." She pressed her hands against her face. "Okay, you can yell at me now, I know this is crazy."

"First of all, bitch, that's ableist, don't say that." Feyi laughed and dropped her hands to see Joy smiling at her.

"Second of all, that makes complete sense, and I'm never here to judge you, babe. You made a new friend, and yeah, you have a pretty disastrous crush on him and it will probably tear apart his family if anything happens between y'all, so that's some pretty tragic unrequited shit, but that's still a friend who knows a little bit about what you're going through. So, fuck it. Live your life, boo." Joy shrugged and popped her gum. "No one's gonna die, shit."

"You bring up a fair point."

Feyi didn't tell her what Nasir had whispered before he fell asleep the night before, or even that he had stayed over in her room. There was no point. After he left, she'd decided that he meant it as a friend, that's all. Joy would turn it into something it wasn't.

"You're lucky to have me," she was saying. "Voice of reason and perspective. When's Nasir heading out?"

Feyi pulled off her bonnet. "Late this evening, I think."

"Damn, that's quick! I guess you wouldn't even have had time to tag along."

"Yeah, it sounded like some last-minute emergency shit, but it's a short flight to Antigua, so . . ."

"So you could technically still jump on that plane with him?"

Feyi cut her eyes at her best friend, and Joy raised her hands, backing off.

"Fine, fine. I'm just tryna add some friction to what looks like a slippery-ass slope."

Feyi grinned. "That's what she said."

"Girl, bye." Joy rolled her eyes. "And congrats on that motherfucking commission! FaceTime me later!"

She ended the call and Feyi rolled off her bed to go help Nasir pack. If she kept moving, then there wouldn't be enough time to think, and if she stayed in the work, then it would be even better. Nothing had to be as complicated as Joy was making it out to be. It was a huge house, there was no reason she had to be around Alim more than was absolutely necessary. Everything was going to be fine.

The door to Nasir's room was cracked open, and Feyi knocked gently before pushing it wider. To her surprise, Nasir was dressed already, a packed duffel bag in his hand. "Hey!" he said. "I was just about to come find you."

"I thought your flight wasn't till later," she replied, frowning as he gave her a hug with his free arm.

"Boss shot me a text at like five this morning asking if I could get in any earlier." Nasir rolled his eyes. "Annoying as fuck. I'm about to head into town." He paused and took her hand. "You sure you gon' be aight while I'm gone?"

"Yeah, don't even worry about me. I'm going into full work mode to come up with something for that commission."

He whistled. "Oh, shit. I forgot about that. Yesterday was wild!"

"Tell me about it." She didn't mention him coming to her room. There were some things that needed to stay and die in last night.

"You feeling good, though? Everyone thought your piece was sick, yo. And Rebecca loves you. Clearly."

Feyi grinned at him. "I'm, like, buzzing to make work. It's the best feeling."

"All right, then. I'ma kill it over there and you kill it over here, and we'll pick up this vacation when I get back. Deal?"

173

"Bet." She followed him down the stairs and out to where the cars were parked by the bougainvillea, wincing at the sunlight. Nasir tossed his bag into the trunk of his car.

"I gotta go find Dad. I think he's out on the grounds today." He held out his arms to her. "Come here, you."

Feyi stepped into his embrace, and Nasir hugged her tightly.

"I know it's just a week, but I'm gonna miss you. I hope this trip has been everything you wanted."

Feyi hugged him back, trying to swallow down guilt. "It's been more than I could've expected," she managed to say. "But you talking like it's over, damn!"

Nasir laughed and let her go. "Nah, we still got time. Go chill out, I'ma text you from the plane, okay?"

She nodded and waved goodbye as he set off to find Alim, then Feyi turned back into the house, which was now roaring with emptiness, stunning in its solitude. Feyi stood for a few minutes in the light pouring into the living room with her eyes closed, trying to feel the aloneness of being there without anyone else in the house. She was interrupted by a voice breaking into the silence.

"Everything good?"

Feyi snapped her eyes open to see Lorraine staring at her with a quizzical look. "Oh! I didn't know you were here," Feyi said, startled.

Lorraine tilted her head. "It my father's house, yuh know." It was as if she couldn't help but be bitchy as soon as they were up the mountain, like something about this house changed her.

"Of course, I just meant—" Feyi shook her head. "Never mind. Good morning."

"Morning." Lorraine looked past Feyi's shoulder. "Where's Nasir? He tried knocking on my door at some rassclat early hour of the morning."

"He's looking for Alim—for your dad. His flight got moved up."

"Oh, so he going into town now? Perfect." Lorraine grabbed her purse from a side table. "Tell my dad I'll call him later, and that I getting a drop back to town with Nasir." She tossed a cool smile at Feyi and was out of the house in a whirl of lavender, slamming the door behind her.

. . .

Feyi went back to bed after chugging what felt like a gallon of water, but when she woke up around midday, her head wasn't pounding anymore. She threw on a bikini and went for a swim, floating and staring up at the sky for a long time. The water lapped cool and constant around her face, and the mountain was nothing but birds and sunshine and trees, the view extending like a universe. There was an undercurrent of anticipation boiling under her skin—what if Alim came up on her while she was half-naked in the water, wearing nothing but these scraps of sunshine yellow that Joy had convinced her counted as a bikini? What if he pulled off his shirt and got into the pool with her? She could still see his face in her gold rings, gazing at her in the middle of dinner, and having just a few days left before never seeing him again was starting to sound like an argument in favor of something popping off. Feyi growled at herself and dispelled the image, irritated. His knee had been rubbing all up in Rebecca's thighs. She was better off just minding her business before heading back to New York, instead of imagining unnecessary things.

Feyi climbed out of the pool and went back to her room, taking a quick shower before changing clothes and heading down to the kitchen. She grabbed a large guava from the fruit bowl as she settled into the breakfast nook with her sketchbook. The sun was hanging bright and high above the mountains when Alim walked in, his presence pushing its way into the room, bending the air. Feyi paused her doodling to glance up at him, and the moment their eyes met, she became terribly aware of how alone they were up on that mountain, with no one to interrupt them for days, no one to hear any of the sounds he could pull from her so easily.

Fuck, she thought. *Joy was right.*

She composed her face back into order. "Hi," she said. "I thought you were out on the grounds today."

Alim slid his hands into his pockets. "I finished early," he said.

"Oh, cool. Did you get to see Nasir before he left? He was looking for you."

"Yes, he found me out in the orchard. You seen Lorraine?"

Feyi sketched a few lines to avoid the swamp of his eyes. "She caught a ride with Nasir back to town already. Said she'd give you a call later."

Alim shook his head. "She really can't stand to be up here without him, that child. Always rushing back to town." He sat down across the table from her. "How has your insomnia been? I haven't seen you in the garden since that night." He said it like he'd missed her.

Feyi definitely didn't dare to look at him now that he was

176

this close, just in case he saw everything she wanted leaking out from her eyes. It was too dangerous, just like that damn garden, and she had no idea why he was bringing it up now. It all fell into the category of the peak and the sunrise, moments they'd shared that she was trying very hard to forget.

"I've been sleeping okay," she answered, closing her sketchbook. It would look rude to keep drawing pointless lines while he was sitting there trying to talk to her. Feyi could smell his skin, that goddamn lemongrass again.

"Have you eaten?" he asked.

She brandished the core of the guava, pink with dotted seeds. "I had some fruit, but I could make something, if you like." As soon as she said it, Feyi blushed furiously. *You don't cook, and the man has two Michelin stars*, she scolded herself. *God, you're such an idiot.* She hadn't been thinking, it had just popped out because she felt like she should contribute more, now that Nasir wasn't there to buffer, now she was directly his guest.

Alim raised an eyebrow. "If you wanted to get me out of the way, there are other options," he drawled. "Food poisoning seems a little drastic."

Feyi gasped and tossed her sketchbook on the table in fake outrage. "How dare you."

He laughed, and she cursed silently as it sent a thrill through her. Last night was supposed to have put this to rest, but here she was, fighting the urge to touch his face, just once. Just so she could know what his skin felt like under her palm, maybe see his eyes soften as he leaned into her hand. Or maybe he'd pull back? No, she couldn't pretend that evening in his kitchen with the mango foam hadn't happened. Feyi knew what desire

177

looked like and it had been loud in his eyes, soaking the air between them. That, and the way her exhibit had stripped something from his face, that naked look she'd caught and hadn't been able to put down. It had been so much easier to resist him when she thought he didn't want her, when she felt pathetic and alone in the crush, but now? Now there was *real* possibility, and it was sitting across from her; it was trapped alone with her in this irrational dream of a house.

"How about I make some food?" Alim was saying, standing up from the table. "One guava doesn't count as a meal."

Feyi swung her legs down from the bench. "Only if you let me help." He cut his eyes at her, and she laughed. "Come on! I can't chop up some shit?"

Alim made a disbelieving face. "*Can* you?"

"Oh, you got jokes." Feyi followed him into the kitchen and leaned against the zellige-tiled counter. "What happened to you teaching me?"

"Ah." He opened the fridge and looked around in it. "You make a good point."

"See?" Feyi folded her arms. "Teach me, then."

When Alim stilled with his back to her, Feyi wondered if she'd made the challenge sound as suggestive as it had felt coming out of her mouth. There were so many lessons she'd love to learn from his hands. A taut moment passed before he pulled out some peeled and cleaned carrots and Swiss chard from the fridge, handing them over to her with a root of ginger.

"We'll start simple," he said. "Peel the ginger, then try slicing the carrots for me."

"Yes!" Feyi grabbed a cutting board and made dramatic swoops with her arms. "*Iron Chef*, here I come!"

178

"Good Lord." Alim laughed as he handed her a spoon. "Take it easy." He was pulling spices as well as quail eggs, then put a pan on the stove and poured caraway seeds into it, back in the flow she now associated with him whenever he was in a kitchen, easy and smooth.

"Um . . . what do I do with this?" Feyi asked, holding the spoon up in confusion.

Alim laughed softly. "Use it to scrape the skin off the ginger, sweetness."

Oh God, he'd called her *sweetness*. One casual endearment and Feyi was already wet, for fuck's sake. She took a deep breath and turned to her task at hand, trying to focus. The ginger's bright yellow revealed itself as she pulled the spoon over it, brown skin curling aside in scraps. Alim shook the pan as the seeds toasted and the air turned all nutty and spicy. Feyi put aside the ginger and reached for the carrots. They were slim and bright orange against the bamboo board, much prettier than anything she would've found in a grocery store in New York. There was a click as Alim turned off the stove, and Feyi tried not to check him out too obviously as he moved around the kitchen. A ray of sunlight struck his jaw, spilling across his mouth, and Feyi bit her lip against another tug of desire.

This was getting ridiculous. She started chopping the carrots with a little more enthusiasm than they needed, then stopped, uncertain.

"Wait, am I doing this right?"

Alim was cracking quail eggs into a bowl, the delicate shells coming apart between his long fingers. "Just give them a quick julienne," he replied.

179

Feyi stared at him. "Bruh. I don't even know what that *means*."

Alim burst out laughing, putting the eggs aside. He came over and shook his head at the slices she'd cut already. "I leave you unsupervised for two minutes and you butcher my poor vegetables," he said. "Here, let me show you."

He stepped behind her and brought his arms around, lightly placing his hands over hers. "So you cut them this way first, then hold your knife like this . . . yes, just so. It's about a millimeter or two, that probably means nothing to you Americans, but look . . . just this thin . . . and the knife like so . . ."

Feyi tried to listen, but Alim was entirely too close, and she couldn't *believe* he had put himself in such hazardous proximity to her, as if it was nothing. It wasn't just his voice against her ear, but his breath, his body almost pressed behind hers. Whatever vibe they'd been trying to cultivate with this little cooking lesson evaporated as the air in Feyi's chest turned sticky and troublesome. She jerked her hands away from his with almost too much force, and the knife clattered on the cutting board, the sound echoing through the room.

Alim's voice clipped off into silence, and he stood still, dropping his hands to the counter, oval fingernails on emerald tile, her body still trapped in the frame of his.

Feyi couldn't speak. She was barely even breathing. His mouth was so close to her skin, his slow exhale fanning her left ear. Time decelerated to a crawl as Alim lifted a hand to push Feyi's braids behind her ear, exposing the side of her neck. Electricity buzzed down her spine and Feyi dragged in a trembling breath, feeling the smooth coolness of a stray carrot slice under her hand. She was transfixed, spelled into place, surely hallucinating as Alim's breath drew closer and closer. This couldn't be happening.

An unhurried lifetime passed before she felt his lips graze her neck, and Feyi couldn't help the whimper that escaped her, so loud in the quiet kitchen, so ragged with want. Alim drew in a sharp breath before pressing the full heat of his mouth to her skin, and fire exploded through her. Feyi stepped back into him, her hands falling off the counter, carrot slices tumbling to the floor as Alim slid an arm across her stomach and pulled her flush against his body, his teeth scoring into her neck. He moaned into her skin, and Feyi dropped her head back against his shoulder, opening her throat to him. Alim spun her around, one hand holding up her jaw so he could kiss her collarbone, her throat, and then he was kissing her mouth and Feyi stopped caring about anything except how he felt, how it felt now that he was finally touching her, now that her fingers were in his hair, gripping his head, and she was kissing him back, at last, at last. He tasted like sin and coffee."

Dimly, in the back of her head, alarm bells were clamoring, but she didn't care. To hell with what trouble this would bring, she was alive. She was fucking *alive*, and Feyi knew that in that moment, she would burn anything, everything, a whole world just to hold on to that feeling.

The air had gone from slow molasses to frantic whitewater in barely seconds. Feyi's tongue was sliding against Alim's, desperate whimpers digging in the back of her throat. He was pushing everything aside on the counter, cutting board and knife clattering into the sink, a blue bowl crashing and breaking open on the floor, spilling out carrot slices in bright neon

181

discs. Alim ignored it all, reaching behind Feyi's thighs and lifting her up onto the counter, his hips pushing between her opened legs as she wrapped them around him. She was wearing a cotton romper, and it rode up her hips as he slid his hands against her skin, pulling her closer till she could feel how hard he was against her inner thigh. Feyi gasped and pulled away, breaking their kiss as reality slammed back into sharp focus.

"Alim," she said, her breath half-gone. "Alim, slow down."

He stopped immediately, his breath ragged and quick, his eyes searching hers as his brain caught up with what they were doing.

"Ah, fuck, Feyi, I'm sorry." He rested his forehead against hers and closed his eyes. "I'm so sorry, sweetness, I—I shouldn't have done this."

Feyi tightened her legs around him in case he got the terrible idea of pulling away. Her chest was cramping up—he'd called her *sweetness* again, and God help her, there was nothing casual about it this time. It sounded so right in his mouth.

"I didn't say stop," she said, "just slow down."

Alim looked back up at her, his face all kinds of soft and confused and wanting and guilty. Feyi brought her hands down to his shirt and pulled him closer so she could kiss him, slowly, deliberately, with a world of choosing in it.

"Don't stop," she whispered against his mouth.

"Feyi . . ."

"We can talk later . . . unless"—she jerked back—"unless you *want* to stop? Oh my God, I'm so sorry, I—"

"No." Alim slid a hand behind her head, her braids tangling in his fingers, and pulled her mouth back to his. "I don't want to stop."

Chapter Fourteen

It was like a wildfire, the way he felt against her, the way it spread and consumed, and even—as the ignored alarms in Feyi's brain reminded her—the way it was going to destroy. But this thing between them didn't leave space for thinking beyond what she wanted, and so Feyi reached down for the hem of Alim's shirt, pulling it over his head and flinging it aside, her hands finding his chest, his arms, his back, as he kissed her face and mouth and neck. This time, he was the one who pulled away, panting.

"Feyi, I—" Alim laughed, a wild and scattered sound. "Oh, fucking hell."

She'd never heard him curse this much. It sounded delicious. "You okay?" she asked, her mind scattered and screaming with want.

"I'm perfect, sweetness. I'm just—I'm trying really hard not to tear this little one piece you're wearing into several other pieces and I'm thinking, perhaps not in the kitchen? There are knives here, and I'm fairly sure we broke something." They both looked down at the shattered bowl, then at each other for a moment, and burst out laughing.

"Oh my God," gasped Feyi, "this is so on brand. I can't believe I'm making out with you in your kitchen."

"Don't distract me," he scolded. "I'm trying to focus on relocation. Here, put your arms around my neck . . . good." Alim slipped one arm under her knees and another around her back and lifted her off the counter, picking his way through the blue shards on the floor till they got to the doorway.

"All clear," Feyi said. "You can put me down now."

"Mm, not yet." He lowered his head and kissed the tip of her nose. "A little trip first."

She squealed as he turned and started up the staircase. "Where are you taking me?"

"Just to my room," he answered.

Feyi's pulse skipped. "You sure?"

Alim smiled down at her, looking a thousand times calmer than she felt. "Feyi, with the things I want to do with you, it really doesn't matter where we are in the house."

"You do have a little hang-up about the kitchen," she teased, trying to mask how nervous she was.

"Knife play is only allowed in controlled situations. That was not one of them."

Feyi smothered a smile at that, hiding her face in his shoulder. He smelled so good with his skin bare and warm against her. If she could've talked to Joy, if Alim was any other guy, she'd be blowing up her friend's phone from the bathroom with text messages—*Bitch, he's kinky!* And Joy would shriek because, honestly, jackpot.

Alim kicked open the door to his bedroom and strode across a rug, depositing Feyi on the massive bed in the center of the floor. Feyi laughed as she hit the duvet, drowning in a cloud of white, then emerged to look around the room. She'd been wondering what his space would be like since she got there.

It was stark and soft at the same time—monochrome bedding, a large television spilling black glass across a wall, metal sculptures. The far wall was entirely glass looking out into the mountain, nothing but trees and jungle stretching to the horizon. It was—like most views in his house—magnificent, and Feyi swung her legs out of the bed to go take a closer look, crossing the cool floor and pressing her hand against the glass. "This is gorgeous," she said, glancing back at Alim.

He was looking at her with an odd expression on his face, still shirtless, his arms corded, his torso carved.

"What?" she asked. "You're staring."

Alim ducked his head and cleared his throat. "I'm just—I was just having a moment."

He walked over to her and slid his arms around her waist. Feyi hugged him back, marveling that she could hold him, that she was holding him.

"You don't know how many times I lay in that bed," he said, his voice muffled by her braids, "wondering what you would look like standing right where you're standing."

Feyi turned her face into his neck and inhaled, citrus and earth and him.

"I can't believe you're *here*," he said, and something chipped off his voice on the last word, a fragment breaking apart.

Feyi squeezed her arms tighter around him, blinking back unexpected tears. She knew exactly what he meant. *Here* as in his arms, his room, with him, without the careful distance they'd been trying to build since that first night they'd been alone in the garden. He sounded like she felt, so full of wonder that it hurt a little.

When he pulled away, he wouldn't look at her for a moment. "Maybe we should talk now."

Feyi didn't know what to do with her hands once they were separate from him. She shoved one into the pocket of her romper and tried not to stare at his back or imagine her teeth in his shoulder. Before she had time to worry about if he was pulling away, Alim turned back to her and took her free hand, tugging her down to sit with him on the bed.

"So," he said. "That just happened."

A laugh leaked out of her, even though she was starting to panic a little. They weren't supposed to be talking or thinking. This was entirely too dangerous.

"Yeah, I'm sorry," she said. "I know I shouldn't have—"

"Don't apologize," he said, lifting her hand to his mouth and kissing her palm. His mouth on her scar sent a wave of anxiety through her, like a ghost of Nasir had just passed through the room. "You've done nothing wrong. Besides, I kissed you first."

This was coming down to earth too fast, starting to smell like regrets and mistakes. "Do you wish you hadn't?"

"Hmm." Alim stroked a thumb over the inside of her wrist and smiled at Feyi, his eyes wrinkling. "I don't know if I should have, but at the same time, a part of me wishes I had done it sooner." Her pulse stumbled at that. "The morning we watched the sunrise, maybe," he continued.

"Did you want to then?" It was hard to imagine that he'd been thinking about the same things she had, that they'd walked side by side with silent mirrored wants drumming inside them.

"Very badly," Alim replied, his voice soft. "You were so beautiful in that light, and when you held me, I thought I was going to break."

186

"You pulled away." She couldn't help reminding him. Even the memory of it still stung.

His smile twisted. "Sweetness, I couldn't—I'd been trying so hard. I don't want to hurt Na—"

Feyi covered Alim's mouth with her hand before he could finish the sentence. "Not yet," she whispered, feeling like she might cry. It was too soon to break this dream apart. "Just a few minutes more."

She'd never gotten to see his face this close, to look as openly as she wanted, for as long as she liked. She could reach up and touch the salt-and-pepper stubble along his jaw, calling back how it had felt scraping along her throat, and so she did, running her hand along his face. If it was just the two of them, then nothing and no one else had to be real, had to interfere.

"Careful," Alim warned, his eyes smoky. "We're not going to get around to talking if you keep looking at me like that."

Feyi laughed and hid her face in his shoulder. "I'm scared," she admitted. She was two breaths away from panicking, to be honest, but she didn't think it would be helpful to share that information. "Can't we just skip the talking part?"

Alim kissed the top of her head. "I know, sweetness. But it's always going to be there, isn't it?"

"Ugh, fine." She sat up and nudged his arm. "But you're starting, not me."

It was almost heartbreaking to see his eyes sober up. "Let me put on a shirt," he said.

Feyi watched him walk into his closet and interlocked her fingers, squeezing them tightly to control her nerves. Alim pulled on a gray cotton T-shirt, then came back and sat next to her.

"So," he said. "We need to talk about Nasir."

Even though Feyi knew this was where they were going, where they had to go, her stomach dropped into a free fall. She wasn't supposed to have gotten this involved, she'd had a whole plan to get out unscathed.

"It was just a kiss," she said, too quickly. "Do you *want* to tell him?"

Alim frowned. "*Was* it just a kiss?" he asked, and something in his voice had gone tense. "Maybe we should be clear about that first."

Feyi twisted her hands nervously in her lap, not sure what he wanted to hear. It could be just a kiss if that's what he wanted it to be, but right now, she didn't know what it was, or what it could've been if she hadn't asked him to slow down, if she hadn't gotten distracted by his room, if she'd pulled him down on top of her instead and given neither of them time to think. She should have listened to Joy. She should have gone with Nasir. She should have asked Pooja to put her up in the Hilton immediately, come up with some excuse.

"Feyi?"

She dragged her eyes up to meet his. "I don't know, Alim. What do you want it to be?"

"You're evading. Was it just a kiss for you?" When she started to answer, he held up a hand to forestall her. "And please, I only ask one thing—don't lie to me. I will hold anything you tell me with care, just let it be the truth. Please."

Feyi nodded. "Okay," she said. "I just need a minute."

"Of course."

Feyi stood up and walked to the window, wrapping her arms around herself. If she pushed aside the fear, she already knew the answer—she'd known it since the conversation with Joy, when it hit her that she wanted to stay here, with Alim, even if his world was an escape. It was why she'd wanted to get out of it, before the spell sucked her all the way in, before she made the mistake of thinking an escape could be a real life. Maybe the whole appeal of it was *precisely* that it was an escape, which it would quickly stop being if they kept going down this road they'd started on.

Shit would hit the fan if Nasir and Lorraine found out there was anything going on between her and their father. How long would the fantasy last then? Even if they could deal with that, how long could they keep this going, whatever this was? Till she left the island? How would she tell her parents she was dating Alim? Did Alim even want to *date* her? It was a tower of questions, and Feyi knew the only way through it was to tackle them one at a time. She turned around, and Alim was watching her from the bed, his hands clasped loosely between his knees.

It took a while for her to arrange her words. All her sentences felt like they were kneecapped by hopelessness before they left her mouth. She thought of Jonah, of how the world with him always felt both like a dream and like the most real thing she'd ever known, at the same time. She thought of who he'd taught her to be.

"Everything I want seems impossible," Feyi finally said, "and I don't know what to do about it, so I told myself I couldn't have it. I don't know *how* to say what I want because it sounds mad. It sounds absolutely wild and like a thousand people are yelling at me in my head telling me how stupid and reckless and fucked-up it all is."

189

"I know," Alim said quietly.

She threw up her hands. "He's your fucking *son*, Alim."

A deep sorrow filled his gray eyes and spilled into the murky whites. "I know," he said, and his voice was a thousand pieces of sharp glass stitched together.

"I mean, we're not dating, me and Nasir, and we've never slept together, and I don't—I don't feel the same way that he feels about me."

Alim's eyes didn't waver from hers. "I know."

Feyi paced by the window. "Fuck. I tried so hard to avoid this, you know? I was so close." She shook her head and pressed her hands to her face. "I've felt so wrong the whole time for feeling like this and even worse because I can't stop, and now I'm terrified that I'm gonna say something and you're gonna look at me like I'm out of my fucking mind, like how could I even think that, let alone say it out loud, and I'll be horribly wrong about everything and feel like absolute shit."

"Me too," he said. "I'm with you."

Feyi paused, surprised by the admission. Alim hadn't moved, hadn't looked away, and seeing how he looked at her made her want to burst into tears. She wasn't even sure they'd be happy ones. It was as if what had just happened had broken a timeline and there was no way Feyi from the old timeline could handle this, so she had to become Feyi from the new timeline. Feyi who had kissed Alim Blake in his kitchen and shattered carrots over his floor. Feyi who he'd held as if he'd almost lost her. Feyi who he was gazing at like he was just a man, just a man at her mercy.

"Okay, so fuck it," she said, throwing care and sense and any form of rightness to the wind. "It *wasn't* just a kiss. It's not 'just' anything. I haven't felt this way about anyone since . . . since Jonah. I know it's just been a few weeks. I know there's a situation I need to handle with Nasir, and I really *really* don't have any answers or solutions whatsoever, but I was talking to Joy this morning, which seems like a whole different fucking life, by the way, and I was telling her how much I love being here. With you. Like even if I still felt alone, at least I felt like I was alone next to your alone, like our alones could walk together. And you"—Feyi ran a hand over her face—"ah, fuck. You feel like the first time in a long time I can even wonder about a possibility of not feeling alone." She folded her arms, panic still threatening steadily inside her. "So. Your turn."

Alim was staring up at her, and Feyi couldn't read his expression anymore.

"Was it just a kiss?" she pressed, making her voice harsh because that was the only way she could keep being brave. "What do you *want* from all this? Is it worth blowing up your whole fucking family? Because, just so you know, that's absolutely what's going to happen."

Alim rolled back his shoulders and stood up from the bed. "It could never be just a kiss with you, Feyi." He took a step toward her, and then another. "And even if we hadn't stopped, it could never be just that, or just one night, or just one week, or one month."

All Feyi's bravery melted into nothing as he came closer and closer to her.

"A lot of people have come up this mountain," he was saying. "You're the first one I don't want to let back down."

"I have to go home at *some* point."

191

Alim's eyes crinkled. "I'd go with you."

"Your restaurant is here," Feyi answered, falling back on automatic logic to avoid the full weight of what he'd just said.

Alim shrugged. "I'm me. I can cook anywhere in the world I want." He stopped in front of her and smiled, full and radiant. "I'd cook anywhere in the world for you."

He was making it sound too easy, too sweet. It didn't make sense. This couldn't be happening. "Why today?" she asked. "What made you not care about hurting Nasir today?" It wasn't a fair question, but they were blood and she wasn't.

Alim didn't flinch, but the sorrow returned to his eyes. "I don't want to hurt my son," he answered, after a pause.

"You're going to. *We're* going to. Fuck, Alim, we already have."

He sighed and reached out to cup her face in his hands. Feyi tried her best not to feel despair clutching at her ankles and calling from deep water.

"I didn't plan it," he said, and Feyi wrapped her fingers around his wrists, feeling the gathered bones, the soft tissue pulsing in between, her eyes searching the depths of his.

"I didn't, either," she said. "I was going to leave, you know? I was going to have Pooja put me up in a hotel, so I could be out of both your lives before he even came back." Now she definitely felt like crying. "Why did you have to kiss me?"

Alim's mouth curved into a shadow of a smile. "I made a choice," he admitted. "You were standing in my arms, in my home, and I have been fighting this for weeks, Feyi. Badly, perhaps, but fighting it nonetheless." He stroked the pads of his thumbs across her cheekbones. "I was here minding my business, you know, a successful recluse, and then this loud and beautiful woman comes into my home, into my garden, comes with me to the sunrise, and utterly blindsides me. You are so generous with your heart. You were like light. I couldn't help but to turn my face to you if I wanted to keep living."

It was hard to catch a full breath. "What was the choice?" she asked. "What made you decide today was different?"

Alim released her face and took her hands in his. "A moment of clarity," he said, "with you so close to me." He exhaled a deep breath. "When I lost Marisol—when we lost Marisol, I made sure I was everything for Nasir and Lorraine." He glanced down at her, and Feyi saw old and new griefs weaving together on his face. "For twenty years, I've given them everything I had, put them before everything else. All my work has been to carve a place in the world for them. I don't regret a second of it, they're my beloveds, pieces of Marisol and me out in the world. But now . . ."

Feyi felt goose bumps race up her arms and thighs as Alim slid a hand into her braids, his palm against the back of her head as he looked intently at her.

"God forgive me for this selfishness," he said, his voice rough. "I know it will break Nasir's heart. But I've seen the way you look at me—"

"I did lick mango foam off your finger."

Alim barked out a laugh. "You broke me. I'd wondered before then, but I wasn't sure."

Feyi blushed. "Still can't believe I did that," she muttered.

He smiled at her. "I'm glad you did. And then today, I blinked, and you were in my arms, and all I could think was that I've spent a significant amount of time trying to change what I feel into something else, and I can't. I am so tired of denying myself, Feyi. Not even for my children. Not after giving up Devon. There's not enough life to keep living like that, so yes, it will hurt my son, but I want you. I want you for myself, and that, *that* is why I kissed you."

Feyi felt like she was back to hallucinating all this. "First of all," she said, trying to pump the brakes. "You don't really know me. I don't really know you, so what are we even talking about?"

"We never really know anyone," Alim replied with an easy shrug. "And I want to spend an obscene amount of time discovering you. It's honestly half the fun."

She didn't laugh. "Alim . . . this is not going to be fun. They're going to hate us."

The sorrow was like a weight he kept trying to throw off, but it kept coming back, marking lines in his face.

"I know," he said. "It's going to be hard and difficult and possibly some of the most painful conversations I've ever had with my children since their mother died. But you know what, Feyi?"

It was ridiculous how much she loved to watch him smile, even through the heaviness he was carrying.

"I think it could be worth it, even just the attempt."

She wasn't sure she believed him. "Even if this goes nowhere?"

"I don't think that's possible." Alim dropped a kiss on her cheek. "I'm saying you make me feel not alone, Feyi. I don't think you understand how hard I'll fight for that, how long it's been since I had that."

"Twenty years, four months, three weeks?"

He raised an eyebrow. "Oh, it's like that?"

Feyi shrugged, trying to keep her voice light. "Quick maths."

Alim pulled her closer to him. "I'm all in, sweetness. As long as you're here with me, as long as you want this, too."

Feyi slid her arms around his neck, lacing her hands behind his head. God, touching him felt so good, so complete. It would be so easy to believe him.

"Does everything you want still feel impossible?" he asked.

"Not as much," she admitted. Only if she believed him.

He nodded, his eyes searching hers. "We're doing this?"

"What, setting our lives on fire?" A corner of her mouth quirked up. "Sounds fantastic."

Alim wrapped his arms around her. "I'll burn with you," he murmured, and Feyi held him as tight as she could. The mountains laughed green beyond the glass, a new world intact and fragile, for now.

Chapter Fifteen

When Feyi woke up in the morning, light was pouring in through the windows and Alim's back was next to her, a ridged expanse of dark skin. Feyi blinked and fought the urge to touch him, rest her cheek on his shoulder blade, kiss his spine. Instead, she stared down at his body, watching his rib cage rise and fall. The night before, Alim had gone back down to the kitchen and made them breakfast for dinner—a Swiss chard and culantro shakshuka—then brought it back up to his room.

Talking about Nasir and the tangled layers of their situation had amputated what they'd started over the carrot slices, but in its place was something new and tender. Deciding to move forward meant that their feelings ran deep enough to uproot lives, and that was already enough to sit with. Neither of them particularly wanted to talk or process more—it felt enough to just be close. Alim had given Feyi one of his T-shirts and a pair of striped pajama pants, and they'd cuddled in bed while watching *Bob's Burgers* till she fell asleep. When she woke up briefly in the middle of the night, Alim was asleep with his arm thrown over her stomach, his mouth slightly open. Feyi had traced his hair and watched him sleep for a while before it overtook her as well.

"I can feel you staring, you know." Alim rolled over and squinted at her, his voice rasping. "How come you're awake?"

Feyi could feel the warmth radiating from his body. The hair on his chest was shot through with silver, curled against his skin. She tried to ignore how close he was. "How do you even sleep when it's this bright?" she complained. "I should've brought my eye mask from my room."

Alim stretched, feline in the sunlight, and sat up in the bed. "I'm sorry," he said. "I can get it so you can sleep in more."

"Nah, I was just teasing." Feyi pushed her braids out of her face. "I mean, I genuinely have no idea how the fuck you sleep with this much light, but I'm also good. I slept enough."

She smiled at him to show that she meant it, suddenly awkward as she realized that she was in *his* bed, wearing *his* clothes. Alim fucking Blake. Joy was going to kill her, but still, it was unbelievable—literally unbelievable—that the last evening had been real, that he was shirtless *in bed* next to her. And the things they'd said to each other! Were they out of their minds? Had he just been carried away? Had she? Because surely, they couldn't have agreed to this just for the possibility of a relationship. They didn't even have the excuse of being committed to each other, because that would be ridiculous, but they were going to wreck his family just so they could *date*? And see where it goes? Feyi's throat was suddenly dry and terrified. It was a mistake. It had to be a mistake. This was Nasir's *father*.

"Hey." Alim leaned toward her, concerned. "Feyi, you okay? Where did you go?"

She was in bed next to Nasir's *father*. And he was shirtless. And she'd kissed him in the kitchen, felt him against her inner thigh, pushing close. What if they hadn't stopped? What if they'd kept going when he brought her upstairs? What the *fuck* was she going to tell Nasir?

"Feyi." Alim reached out and his fingers held her chin, turning her face to his. "Look at me, sweetness."

She almost flinched at the endearment. He didn't know her. She wasn't worth the trouble she was bringing to his house; she'd just been fucking around, first with Milan and then with Nasir, none of it was supposed to get this serious. He was going to look for something in her worth the twenty years he'd been alone, and all he was going to find was a broken widow marking her grief in blood over and over and over again. It wasn't going to be enough, there was no way she could make it enough. Feyi felt the back of her nose begin to sting with tears.

"Look at me," Alim was saying, but she couldn't, not into those stained eyes of his. That's how all this had started in the first place. Looking in places she shouldn't have been looking, wanting what she had no business wanting.

She stared at the white bedding until it began to blur, her body heavy and unmoving. Alim pulled her into his arms and tried to hold her.

"I've got you," he whispered. "You're okay."

But it wasn't true, it couldn't be true, none of this was okay. They hadn't done anything, they'd done too much, and even as guilty as she felt, Feyi still couldn't stop the raw thrill that sped through her skin from being close to his. She still wanted to kiss him, feel the heat of his tongue again, his hands gripping her head, her throat, her legs.

Feyi wrenched away and slid off the bed, the cool floor hitting the soles of her feet like the only real thing in the room. She looked up at Alim just in time to see a flash of hurt skitter across his face. He pulled himself back together so quickly that she was tempted to pretend it hadn't happened, but her guilt was burgeoning in every direction.

"I'm sorry," she said, even as she backed away from the bed, from the gorgeous man kneeling amid white rumpled clouds, from the horrifying and lovely things he'd told her. That he would go anywhere with her, that she was light, all of it was lyrics. It wasn't real.

"I'm sorry," she said again. "I just—" Feyi threw up her hands, then let them fall, smacking loosely against her thighs, as helpless as she felt. "What the *fuck* are we doing, Alim?"

A veil of emotion she couldn't read cloaked his face, but Feyi could feel the effect almost instantly in the air. Something cool and distant drifted in between them.

Alim got out of the bed and pulled on a linen robe, belting it closed. "I thought we talked about this yesterday," he said. His voice was low and level, but he wouldn't quite look at her. "I thought you were in."

"Me?" Feyi stared at him in disbelief. "Don't worry about *me*, you're the one whose family is going to implode over this! It's not—I'm not worth it. They're all you have left."

Alim sat down in a leather armchair and crossed his legs at the knee. His toenails were painted red as oxygenated blood. "You're not worth it?" he echoed, finally meeting her eyes. "Do you mean that?"

Feyi paused, confused. "What?"

He drifted a hand through the air, looking tired. "Do you mean that? If you're telling me you're not worth it, I'll listen to you, Feyi. I have no interest in replacing who you know yourself to be with my imagination of you. It's not sustainable in the long term, so if you're telling me who you are now, telling me not to bother, then be clear."

Stung, she stared at him for a few seconds, wondering if she should feel insulted or if she had just insulted herself. Alim sighed at her expression and uncrossed his legs, leaning forward with his elbows on his knees.

"I don't mean it badly," he explained, his hands opening in front of him. "But I cannot coax you into this, Feyi. I won't. It has to be your choice, entered willingly, you know?"

She shook her head at him. "Bruh, do *you* know what you're entering?"

A muscle spasmed in Alim's jaw. "What do you *think*, Feyi?" he bit out, his voice sharpening. She flinched, and he sat back in the chair, passing his hands over his face.

"I'm sorry," he said, his voice muffled. "I just don't understand what changed between yesterday and right now. I feel like I'm not talking to the same person." Alim dropped his hands and looked at her, his face bruised with confused hurt. "Did you change your mind? You can just tell me. We can stop this if you want to. Just say the word."

The offer sent cold water down Feyi's back. He'd said it so casually, like they could take the last eighteen hours out back and slit its throat, watch it drain into the grass, clogging the soil with short memories. And then what, they'd go back to what they were before? Polite and distant and longing?

Feyi looked at Alim, and her heart wrenched. He had kissed her. He'd put his mouth to her neck and broken the distance between them, made a choice and now she was throwing it back in his face like he didn't know what he'd

200

done, or what it would cost him. He had touched her, and wanted her, and now he didn't know if she wanted him after all, now he was swearing it would be fine if they stopped everything, rewound and erased everything, because it looked like that's what she wanted, or wanted for him. *You fucking idiot*, she thought to herself. *Put your big-girl panties on.* She took hold of her fear and dragged it under control. Alim was looking at her, waiting for an answer, soft distress in the lines of his face. Feyi let out a deep breath and sank to the floor, sitting cross-legged and resting her hands on her ankles. She took a couple more breaths before she spoke.

"Aren't you afraid?" she asked, looking up at Alim.

He stood up from the chair to sit on the floor across from her, mirroring her pose. "Feyi, I'm ashamed to admit this, but I'm fucking terrified."

A knot in her chest eased up a little. "Of what?"

Alim gave a short laugh that sounded more sad than anything. "Breaking my son's heart. You deciding this is too much to bother with, or that you got . . . carried away, perhaps. This turning out to not be real."

He had no business being as fine as he was gentle. It made it hard for Feyi to think about a rest of the world outside this and him.

"How do we know if it's real?" she said, her voice folding. "I'm scared that you'll wake up from this and look at me like, *What the fuck was I doing*, you know? I'm scared you'll wake up and I'll still be in it."

"Oh, Feyi." Alim's eyes had gone impossibly liquid. "Tell me when you're afraid. Tell me whatever you're feeling. I'll take whatever it is over you pushing me away."

"It just—it seems too much. Like, there's messy, but this is some next-level shit."

Alim laughed a little and looked out the window. A parrot wheeled past, red and blue feathers fanned out in the air. "You know, last night I thought about what Marisol would say."

"Yikes. How would that go?"

"Oh, she'd be furious with me. Incandescently annoyed. Not for how I feel about you, but for how I went about it." Alim looked back at Feyi, and the corner of his mouth tugged up. "I moved more recklessly than I should have. Marisol always called me impetuous; she was the careful one."

"Wouldn't she be on Nasir's side?"

Alim wrinkled his nose. "Marisol wasn't the type of person to take sides, not in that way. Not when it's this complicated. She . . . she wanted people to be as kind as possible, even making difficult choices." He sighed and shook his head. "The kindest way to go about this situation would probably have been to talk to you first, then talk things through with Nasir before moving forward."

"I mean . . . that does sound extremely responsible."

"What would Jonah have thought?"

The question shouldn't have felt as unexpected as it did, with the strangeness of Jonah's name coming from Alim's mouth. Feyi could see Jonah's face as easily as ever, his eyes tightening as he burst into laughter, his locs falling around his shoulders. Missing him felt like a fist swallowing her heart. She blinked back tears.

"He would've thought it was hilarious," she said. "He loved people being messy as fuck—he said it was one of the best things about being human, how we could make such disasters and recover from them enough to make them into stories later." Feyi bit her lip, feeling the odd mix of anger and love that sometimes came up when she thought of Jonah. "I was so mad after he died because I knew he would think it was just going to become part of my story, a disaster I'd recover from, and it made me so angry because I didn't *want* to recover. I didn't want to keep having a story. I wanted our stories to run together and stop at the same time, so neither of us would have to be alone. I got married thinking that's what would happen, and then he literally fucking died before our first anniversary." Feyi dashed tears from her eyes with the back of her hand. "So yeah, he would think this was funny, me having feelings for someone else, and now I'm actually mad about it."

Alim untangled his legs and moved to be closer to her, within reaching range but giving her enough space to be sitting alone, his gray eyes fixed on her face, the sun carving out the deep charcoal of his skin. "What made you keep going?" he asked.

"Ugh." Feyi threw her head back and blinked the rest of the tears away. "Honestly, for a long time, I don't think I kept going. I think I just . . . stopped. It was—" She hissed out a hard breath. "I don't want to go back there. It feels like a place that could eat me up if I stopped by, even for a little bit, just by talking about it."

"I know the place." Alim was looking at her with a sober and sad smile. "If I didn't have the kids, I would never have come out. Never. I would've ended up right in that water looking for Marisol's current to take me as well."

"Yeah . . . I couldn't drive after the accident, I still don't. For too long it was like, maybe if it happens again, maybe if I try again, I won't be the mistake left behind this time."

Alim ran a hand over his hair, letting out a deep breath. "I can't remember how many years I spent looking at Nasir and Lorraine and thinking that those two lost the wrong parent."

Feyi looked over at him. "We can wait, you know? If that's the better way to do it."

Alim frowned and she kept going.

"Like how you were saying the best way would've been to talk to Nasir first? We can pause everything and do that if you like, if it'll make things easier between you two."

Alim gave a short, strangled laugh. "Sweetness, nothing is going to make this easier at this point. You should see the way my boy looks at you when you're not noticing. I'm not sure he'll be able to find a way to forgive me for what I've already done, even if we did stop now." There wasn't much humor in his laugh or his words—he sounded like they were damned.

"You make this sound so bad." Feyi groaned, hiding her face in her hands. "Remind me again how any of this isn't totally fucked?" She kept her face covered as Alim slid in next to her, his arm coming around her shoulders.

"Tell me how you feel about me," he said in her ear, and his breath sent goose bumps across her skin.

Feyi dropped her hands, and Alim's face was inches from hers, the strong angle of his nose, his slurried eyes, his deliciously wide mouth. It was surreal to see him this close, the same man who warped the air in front of the airport when she first saw him, now looking at her with a gentle mischief, old black pigment smudged at the corners of his eyes.

"You just wanna hear nice shit about yourself," Feyi retorted, because if she didn't joke about it, she would just get overwhelmed all over again. "You don't think we should stop? Wait to sort it out with Nasir? That's cold-blooded, man." She kept her voice light, but at the same time she was curious—wasn't he worried about how that would go with his son?

Alim didn't move his arm from around her. "I think a conversation needs to be had before this goes much further, yes, but what does stopping mean to you? What do the boundaries look like?"

Feyi sighed. "I don't wanna sound like I keep rubbing this in, but he's *your* son, Alim. I want to know what you're comfortable with and how you're thinking about it. My relationship with Nasir is new, it's nowhere near as important as what you have with him, and quite frankly, if he's going to feel betrayed by anyone, it's going to be you way more than me, you feel me?"

He took his arm off her shoulders but didn't move away. The sun was rising higher in the sky and outside the glass of the windows, everything sounded as beautiful as it always had, a pristine world untouched by this particular bout of human messiness. Feyi felt like she was sitting in a glass box and all their feelings were locked in there with the two of them, weighing on the polished floor, pressing up against the wood ceiling, out against the stretching glass. Was this what the world was made up of? Millions of boxes filled with people and feelings? Alim pulled his knees up and draped his arms over them, speaking slowly as he chose his words.

"I don't think things will be sorted out with Nasir anytime soon, so stitching the timeline of us to the timeline of his heart seems . . . unwise. I think there is a pace to be found, but I very much want to respect your heart in this, too, which is why I'm asking about which boundaries feel comfortable for you. Was spending the night in my bed too much? What if I kissed you again?"

The very thought of it sped Feyi's pulse into a gallop, but she kept her face steady as she listened to him speak. Alim was looking at his hands, twisting his fingers together and pulling them apart slowly.

"When I think about the ways I want to touch you, there's no space for anything else. I am consumed, utterly. When we were alone in my kitchen and you did the thing with the foam, I was sure I had lost my mind. It took everything I had not to kiss you then, and it's taking almost everything to not kiss you now."

He tilted his head to look at her, and Feyi found that her breath had caught somewhere in her chest and wasn't moving.

"But you're asking about how I fit Nasir into this, if we should stop, and terrible as it might sound, when it is between you and me . . . I *don't* fit my son into it. What we decide to do is ours, if you want it to be. I will come to terms with you, not with Nasir, because it will be simple for him— are we involved or are we not? The degrees won't matter, the specificity, and besides, how could that be measured?"

"He'd care if we fucked," Feyi blurted out. "I fucked his friend Milan before Nasir and I went on a date, and we were supposed to be taking it slow. What's it going to look like if I fuck his dad so quickly, you know?"

Alim's eyes darkened as his pupils dilated. "You talking about fucking me is going to end this conversation much faster than we planned, Feyi."

She shoved him and laughed, but he wasn't wrong. It would be too easy to lean in and stop talking, kiss him again, take that damn robe off and step out of these pajamas, into his bed, into his skin, into his mouth. Alim was staring at her, his gaze dropping to her lips, and the air had gone syrupy. Feyi pulled back and scrambled off the floor, her throat dry as she stepped to the window. They couldn't just topple back into all that; there was still too much to figure out.

"I know there's nothing we can do that wouldn't hurt Nasir except not do this at all," she said, keeping her gaze on the mountains, their dark rolling green. "But I think we can try to not make it any worse than it has to be, at least for now." Out of the corner of her eye, she saw Alim stand up and stretch his arms over his head, then fold his body over to brush his fingers against his toes.

"I agree," he said, knifing back upright. "Perhaps we hold off on making plans with each other until we've had a chance to talk to him?"

Feyi turned around, relief filling her voice. "Real talk, that would make me feel so much better. Like, I know he and I weren't dating, but I don't want to start, like, dating you behind his back, you know?" She heard herself, and a flash of worry flared inside her—what if she was being presumptuous? Sure, Alim had talked about being with her, but he'd never said the word *dating*, and somehow that made it sound real, official, not the blurred vagueness of whatever she'd been doing with Nasir. Maybe she should've let Alim be the one to label it first. "I mean, not that I'm saying we'd be dating, I guess it depends . . ."

Feyi trailed off her backtracking as Alim broke out into a sharp grin. "I love the sound of you dating me even more than the sound of you fucking me," he said, taking a step toward her. "Is there anything else you'd like to hold off on?"

He was moving honey-slow, a smile tucked in the corner of his mouth, and as he stopped in front of her, Feyi flashed to all the little moments they'd shared, from that first night in the garden when their hands had touched to the sunrise, his black-rimmed eyes looking at her through a forest of gold circles, and she wasn't the girl who had pulled Milan into a bathroom or negotiated with Nasir. She was the one who'd sat under moonlight with an old grief and a dead husband, next to this stranger who had an even older grief and a drowned wife, and something that had been welded shut in Feyi since that dark road was cracking open by a sliver, just enough to terrify her.

She put a hand on Alim's chest and waited for his heart to beat through the linen, reassuring and steady. "I can't move quickly," she said, her voice sober. "I mean, I could, but it would backfire, and I don't want that. Not with this . . . not with us."

He covered her hand with his, turning immediately serious. "I was only joking, Feyi. I want us to take our time, to believe that we *have* time to take." Alim leaned down to press his forehead against hers. "Sweetness, you have me for as long as you want, however much or little you want. I'm not going anywhere."

Feyi forced back a hiccuping sob. "We're not supposed to be making plans with each other."

"It's not a plan. It's a promise." He pulled her to his chest, and Feyi slid her arms around him. "You will learn this about me with time, but I keep all my promises. So you don't have to believe me now, but I will be here. With you."

"How can you say that?" she said, her voice muffled against him.

"Well, first of all." Alim dropped a kiss on her braids. "You fill me with light till I feel like I'm about to splinter apart from it, so there's that. It's a feeling I'd like to keep around."

"Convenient. What was second?" His palms were splayed across her back and Feyi felt him rest his chin lightly on her head.

"Come on, you haven't figured it out by now?" he teased.

She tried to tilt her face up. "What?"

Alim pulled back a little so he could see her better. "You're my friend," he said, as if it was obvious, and as Feyi looked into his eyes, she was horrified to find that not only did she believe him but it also felt so much more true than the number of times Nasir had said it to her, because while he was trying to be friends with the hot girl he'd met at the bar, Alim had slid all the way into her chest and found someone she'd been storing for years, someone she thought she'd never see again after the road with all that glass.

You are recovering from disaster, she thought, but it came in Jonah's voice, and Feyi got mad all over again at the thought of how pleased he would be to see her being this self with someone else, specifically someone this gentle, someone who could see her in all her crushed and dazzling pieces. It made her tear up, and Feyi ducked her head to wipe at her eyes.

"You're annoying," she complained, and she didn't even know if she was talking to the man in front of her or the one who'd left her too early. Feyi leaned her body into Alim's as they stood in the morning light, a whole new day rolling out before them.

"Yes." He laughed and kissed her head again. "I know."

Chapter Sixteen

Feyi watched Alim whisk eggs and pull out some cheese—Boursin pepper, he'd said—as he put together an omelet. He'd made her a blood orange, grapefruit, and basil juice, which she was cradling in her hands, the deep red lapping against the sides of her glass. The memory of him dancing with Rebecca the other night floated back to the surface of her mind, and Feyi spoke without thinking.

"Did you ever fuck Rebecca?"

Alim stopped, staring at her in surprise. "What?"

Feyi shrugged. "It's a simple question."

She didn't think it was an unreasonable ask—Nasir had said Rebecca had a crush on his dad and the two of them had been basically dry-humping in front of everyone at the party.

Alim put down his whisk and leaned his hip against the counter. There was a sliver of amusement in his expression. "Would it matter if I had?"

Something sour boiled up in Feyi's chest. So he *had* fucked her. "You're grinding up on her one night, kissing me the next, then asking me if it matters?" The sourness was pushing at the back of her throat. How could he be flippant about this? Had he slept with Rebecca after the party, in that bed of his? Were those the same sheets she'd slept in?

Feyi stood up. "I need a minute."

Alim came around the counter, wiping his hands on his

211

apron. "Feyi. Sweetness. I've never done anything with Rebecca. I would have told you."

Feyi stared at him, the sourness muddling into uncertainty. "Then why didn't you just answer the question?"

"I was being silly." He gave her a lopsided smile. "Rebecca only sleeps with women, you know. She insists on being called a lesbian, not queer or anything else. Lorraine tells me that's old-school, but what do I know?"

Feyi's mouth fell open. "But Nasir said she has a crush on you!"

Alim rolled his eyes. "Nasir has a hard time processing platonic affection. If anything, Feyi, you were the one she wanted that night. Not me."

"But the way you were dancing . . ." Feyi felt like she was scrambling to keep up.

"It's kompa," Alim said, as if that explained everything. "It's nice to dance it with someone who you're safe with. When it can just be dancing."

"Oh." Feyi winced. *Yikes.* "I might have overreacted. I'm sorry."

"Ah, I am learning not to tease you." Alim tipped his head forward and rested his forehead against hers. "That feeling you just had, I know it well. It happened with Devon and me more times than I cared for. I don't want you to feel like that if I can help it."

Feyi exhaled at the pressure of his skin against hers. "Thank you," she said. The sourness was receding, fading away into her body.

Alim grinned at her. "Kiss me," he whispered. "I miss your mouth."

The ease with which he said it made her heart flutter slightly. A day ago, she wouldn't have been able to do this, to touch his face and pull his mouth down to hers, feel the restrained force of his lips, his tongue, hear him moan at the back of his throat as she pressed her body against his. So much could change in such a short slice of time.

Alim broke off the kiss, his breath ragged. "Are you certain you want this omelet?" he asked. "Because I could wash my hands and do other things with them, if you'd rather."

Feyi laughed and pushed him gently back to the counter. "I'm starving," she said.

Alim's eyes licked up and down her body. "Yes," he replied. "That's what I'm trying to tell you—so am I." He laughed at how hard Feyi blushed in response and relented. "Fine, I'll feed you first."

Feyi settled into the breakfast nook as he returned to his cooking. This new world they'd fallen into so quickly was still terrifying, but on the other hand, this wasn't the first time Feyi's life had changed at a breakneck pace, so the uncertainty was both familiar and uncomfortable.

Back in New York, she'd just been settling into a life that she could call her own. It had taken years to find a rhythm that didn't include Jonah's stride in lockstep with hers, that didn't include her stumbling with grief every time she realized he was gone. What was going to happen now, if this thing with Alim was real? They'd been so worried about him and his children, Feyi hadn't even thought about how *her* life would change.

Would they date long-distance, across a stretch of seawater? Oh God, her mother was going to be furious. An

213

older man with kids was nothing like what she wanted for Feyi. What if Alim wanted more children? Feyi had assumed not, but they hadn't even talked about it. She didn't have any siblings, so did this mean that her parents were never going to become grandparents? She knew they'd been looking forward to her and Jonah adopting, even though they would have preferred a biological child, and they hadn't had the heart to bring it up to her after he died, but Alim's presence would resurrect conversations Feyi had hoped to never have again. Jesus, neither of them had even talked about if they *wanted* to get married again. Fuck, imagine if she ended up being Nasir and Lorraine's *stepmother*? A panicked giggle tore through Feyi, and she clapped her hand over her mouth to stifle it.

Alim looked up. "You okay?"

"Mm-hmm. It smells amazing." She wasn't about to bring any of this up with Alim. Not yet. "I gotta catch up with Joy for a while after breakfast," she added. "Is there anything you'd prefer I not tell her?"

Alim came up behind her with a buttery-yellow omelet folded on a plate, a drizzle of bright orange on top of it. Feyi could smell the mango and Scotch bonnet from the sauce. He tucked a stray braid behind her ear as he slid the plate in front of her. "You can tell her whatever you like, sweetness."

Feyi tilted her head back to look at him. "You sure? I don't wanna, like, invade your privacy."

"Please. I understand the intimacy you have with her. Don't worry about it." He went back to the stove to flip his omelet in a second pan. "If you like, you could tell her that I'm generously endowed. Apart from the money, that is."

Feyi choked on her juice and reached for a napkin, spluttering. "What?!"

Alim's laugh was rich with a mischief that seemed much younger than his age. "From what I've heard of Joy, the odds of her asking you that were already quite high."

He was absolutely right, but still. "You know they say if a guy claims he's packing, then he usually isn't, right?" It was such a distracting visual! Feyi found herself wondering if she'd be able to wrap her palm around him, if her fingers would touch. She drove the thought away, even as she flashed back to the kitchen counter the night before, the pressure of his body against hers. "You're supposed to wait for me to find out on my own!"

"We are in extenuating circumstances, Feyi. Trust me, you would have found out for yourself otherwise." He threw her a sharp grin over his shoulder, then changed the subject, much to her relief. "I have to run some errands this afternoon anyway, but I'll see you in the evening. Is there anything you need from town?"

"Nah, I think I'm good. I'll talk to Joy, probably take a swim, and then start thinking about the piece for Pooja."

"You know she'll be delighted with whatever you make her, right?"

For a moment, Alim sounded unnervingly like Nasir, and Feyi fought the pang of guilt that it set off in her. Nasir wasn't here. Nasir could wait. She hadn't checked her phone in hours, though, and she was going to have to keep texting him as if everything was okay. Did that count as lying? She forced her head clear as Alim brought his plates over to the table to join her, smiling at her like both their

215

lives weren't on a flashing fuse. It was easier, then, looking into his eyes, for Feyi to believe that everything was going to be all right.

· · ·

The conversation with Joy was hard, there was no other way to put it. It was one thing for this to be just her and Alim, but saying what had happened out loud to someone else made Feyi feel like she was losing her entire mind. She couldn't even bring herself to joke about it.

"I haven't talked to Nasir yet, but yeah, that's what's been going on." Feyi glanced at the phone screen, bracing herself.

Joy had both hands pressed to her mouth, her eyes wide with shock. "Are you fucking serious right now? Like, you're messing with me. You gotta be messing with me."

Feyi glared at her, feeling frayed. "Do I *look* like I'm fucking around?"

"I mean, bitch, you *gotta* be fucking around because there's no way you're telling me that you and Nasir's father are making some plan to ride off into the sunset together. It's been what, twenty-four hours?!"

"I know it sounds ridiculous—"

"I'm not even saying that. I'm just trying to understand. You've been there for a couple of weeks, I thought you just had a crush on him. When did all the rest of this happen?"

"I don't—I don't know how to explain it, Joy. We've been talking, that's all. About real shit. I guess it happened somewhere in there?"

Joy ran a hand over her face, dragging down the skin. "Are you okay, though? Like, this is a lot, babe. How are you going to tell Nasir? *What* are you going to tell Nasir?"

"I have no fucking idea."

The two girls stared at each other through their screens for a moment, then Joy leaned in. "You know you can always just come home, right? Like fuck it, hop on a flight and be here in a few hours. Let them figure their shit out without you in the middle of it. I don't think that Pooja woman would mind if you rescheduled the commission, not if she's willing to drop that much money on it." Her eyes were filled with worry. "You can just come back, Feyi. If Alim is serious, he'll come after you. You don't have to stay there and stick around for the fallout."

It was tempting, and Joy was right. Feyi could bail and be back in the brownstone the same day, even. She didn't have to stay for Nasir or for Alim; she didn't have to stay at all. It seemed too easy when Joy put it like that, to tap out and return to the world she knew. But still, like Joy said, it had also been only twenty-four hours.

"Let me sleep on it," she said. "At the very least, I know my feelings for Alim are real, you know?"

Joy frowned. "Can you say the same about his feelings for you?"

Feyi hadn't even considered that. "You think he's lying?"

"I'm not saying that. I'm just—" Joy sighed. "I just don't want you to get hurt, Feyi. This is the first real thing since Jonah, and it seems to be coming with a lot of stakes. Like a *lot* of really high stakes. Shit, I just—I wanted something less complicated for you."

"I mean, weren't you the one telling me to take a chance on something new, something real?"

"Bitch, I also very clearly told you not to get with Nasir's dad from day one, don't even play with me right now."

"Come on. It's Alim Blake, though." Feyi grinned at her best friend.

Joy cut her eyes at Feyi. "I can't with you."

"*The* Alim Blake."

"What, you want a cookie for bagging a two-Michelin-star nigga?"

"Actually, yeah. I *would* like a fucking cookie. What were the fucking odds?"

Joy glared for a few seconds, then gave up, dissolving into laughter. "Bitch, you messy as fuck, and I can't believe I'm actually here for it. Nigga rich, he got a mansion, he famous, *and* he 'bout to blow up his whole family for some pussy he ain't even eaten yet? Sheeeit." She reached for a lighter and lit up the joint she'd been rolling while they talked. "I love you, but pass me the motherfucking popcorn, 'cause this is about to be a *shitshow*."

Feyi groaned. "Tell me about it."

Joy blew out a cloud of smoke and regarded Feyi through it. "Maybe that's why you wanna stay," she suggested.

"Because it's going to be a shitshow?"

"Yeah. What's that shit Jonah used to say about people and their messiness? And your thing of wanting to remember you're alive? What's more alive than this?"

Feyi paused for a moment. "Remember when we did the Grace Jones memoir for book club?"

"Of course. That shit was life-changing."

"It's more like that. Like when you look back over a whole life, you realize the things you panicked about before stop mattering in, like, thirty years. I think that's why I'm nervous about this, but at the same time, I think it might all work out okay in the end. I didn't think I would survive losing Jonah, not ever, but here we are, and yeah, I guess messy and alive is a good way to put it." She shook her head and smiled, even though it didn't feel funny. "None of this shit really matters, you know?"

Joy sighed. "Damn, when you get all existential like that, it really doesn't. You might as well fuck a rich nigga and piss off his kids."

Feyi exploded into laughter, and Joy joined in, and for a few minutes, everything really felt like it always had, like they'd be good as long as they had each other.

. . .

By the time Alim got back, Feyi had just gotten out of the pool and showered. She was sitting at the edge of her bed with her door open, clipping her toenails when he knocked and stuck his head in.

"Hey, gorgeous," he said. "Would you like to go for a walk?"

Feyi looked up at him and smiled. "I'd love to. As long as it's not up the mountain to watch a sunset or some shit."

Alim laughed, and the evening light glinted off his teeth. "It's not far. I have something to show you." He reached his hand out to her like he had the night of the party, in the corridor, and this time Feyi took it because she could, because he didn't pull it back, because there was no one there to see or stop them.

Hand in hand, they left the house as Alim led them down a path that curved past his citrus orchard, through an edible garden Feyi hadn't even seen before, and up to a small wood-and-glass house with French doors and hibiscus lined up against the walls.

Feyi looked at Alim. "What's this?"

He went up to the doors and pulled them open, standing aside so she could enter. "It's a studio. *Your* studio, if you want it."

She glanced at him as she stepped into the large bright room, taking in the slab worktable, the shelves, the daybed arranged under looming birds of paradise. Cool air whirled around her, and Feyi pushed her braids out of her face. "What d'you mean, my studio?"

Alim raised his hands. "Only if you want it. I know things just got immensely complicated and to make work on top of all this might be excessive. I wouldn't blame you if you still wanted to leave." He took a few steps toward her, and Feyi wondered when the sight of his face would stop piercing her the way it always did. "Know that my feelings for you will not change, whether you stay or leave. But if you did choose to stay, I wanted you to have a space that was just yours, where you could make your work."

Feyi spun around slowly, taking it all in. "You didn't just build this, right?"

"No." He laughed. "It was here before. We just cleared it out and set it up for you."

"Wait, is that what you were doing all day?"

Alim shrugged. "I wanted you to feel welcome."

"You turned this space into a studio in what, an afternoon? That's impressive."

A corner of his mouth tugged down. "It's really not. You'd be amazed how many things become simple once you throw enough money at them." There was an undercurrent in his voice, but Alim slipped it off and turned his brilliant smile to Feyi. "Do you like it, though?"

She walked up to him and held his face in her hands. "Alim, it's perfect. It's the sweetest thing."

Relief shot through his eyes and he leaned his jaw into her palm, gazing softly at her. "I want you to stay." His voice was close, soft and intimate. "I also want you to choose what's best for you, but if you were wondering where I stood on it, or what I wanted, it's you. Here, with me."

Feyi stroked her thumb across his stubble. "For how long?" she teased. "I still have a life in New York, you know."

"All right, I take it back. I just want you, wherever you want to be."

He was so beautiful; it made no sense. "What if I want to be here? At least for now."

Alim slid his arms around her. "Are you sure?"

Feyi nodded and dropped her hands to his chest, feeling his heart beat under the bone. The sun was setting outside, and the room was turning into gold. "Thank you for this," she said, looking around.

He pulled her close, tucking her head under his chin and hugging her tightly. "For you, Feyi? Anything."

Feyi wished she could replay that moment for Joy, the way the light wrapped around them, the way their bodies fit together, the easy assurance in Alim's voice. *His feelings are real*, she'd tell Joy, *you should have heard him. You could build a house on how sure his voice was; you could build a house that would never fall down.* And Joy would laugh, but it would be true, Feyi knew it would be true.

Chapter Seventeen

As it turns out, she did tell Joy, a few days later while curled up in the library's window seat, but Joy had other more pressing questions. "What I wanna know is, have y'all fucked yet?"

"I already told you I was going to wait!"

"Yeah, yeah, I know what you *said*, but nigga's been cooking you Michelin meals, set you up with a whole-ass studio—" Joy broke off and gasped. "Oh my God, bitch, you got a sugar daddy!"

"He is *not* my sugar daddy!"

"I mean, if it walks like a duck, talks like a duck, I'm just tryna find out if it fucks like a duck."

Feyi burst out laughing. "That doesn't even make sense!"

"It doesn't need to make sense. It just needs to blow your back out." Joy grinned at her. "But for real, though, y'all cuddling every night but no one's tried to slip some dick in? What's up with that? You not feeling him or what?"

Feyi pulled her knees into her chest. "I just don't wanna go there yet. There's too much up in the air. Plus, it's nice to just talk."

"So y'all . . . talk about fucking but don't actually fuck?"

"We talk about other shit! You know . . . extended family, art, medical histories—"

"Oh, that sounds *fascinating*."

"It's part of getting to know someone if you're serious.

Last night he was telling me about when he got a vasectomy—"

"Wait, he's had a vasectomy?" Joy narrowed her eyes at Feyi. "Y'all nasty."

"I really want to know how you got there from a medical history."

"Oh, you think I forgot about you and Milan in the bathroom? A vasectomy is like a go-all-the-way-to-raw-sex card. Do not pass go, do not collect two hundred."

Feyi blushed at the thought of doing that with Alim, the look on his face when he'd slide into her. "It's not even like that."

Joy scoffed. "Whatever, girl. Let me know how the barebacking goes. Nasty ass."

"I'm done with you. What's happening with your married woman? Justina, right?"

Joy's face clouded over. "Ah. She came out to her husband. It . . . didn't go well."

"Aw, babe. I'm sorry." Feyi could see Joy folding up the hurt, getting ready to tuck it away like she always did, in a box full of aching. "Are y'all still talking?"

"Nah, she blocked me."

"What? Why?!"

Joy shrugged. "She didn't say. Just left me a voice note crying about how badly the conversation went, and by the time I tried to reply when I woke up, she'd blocked me."

"That fucking sucks, man."

"It is what it is." Joy forced a smile. "I'll get over it."

Feyi bit her tongue. She wanted to tell Joy that it didn't have to keep being like this, that she didn't have to keep choosing unavailable people, but it would sound too much like a lecture and Joy didn't need that on top of her hurt. Also, it wasn't like Feyi was in a position to scold anyone about their romantic choices, not with this mess she'd put herself in. There were a thousand things Joy could've said, things that Feyi told herself every day, but she hadn't, she'd been supportive and the least Feyi could do was be supportive back.

"I'm here if you wanna talk, babe."

"It's cool. Yo, did I tell you I ran into Milan last week? At some karaoke bar in the Village."

"Oh, shit. How is he?"

"He seemed cool. I was *dying* to ask him how he felt about you and Nasir 'cause he brought up that y'all had traveled together, but I figured that was crossing a line."

Feyi heard the faint click of a door opening in the house and turned her head slightly. Alim had gone out for a run, but he usually took longer with them. Maybe he'd cut his route short. "Yeah, definitely a good call not to ask him that," she said. There was another click as the door closed. "Hold on, I think Alim's back from his run."

"Already? Damn, old man."

"I know, right? Lemme call you back."

"Okay, cool. Love you."

"Love you." Feyi hung up and dropped the phone on the window seat, swinging her legs off it and heading for the corridor. "Alim?" she said, opening the library door. "You back already?" She stepped into the corridor just as Nasir came around the corner.

They both stopped, and Feyi felt a wave of panicked terror wash through her.

"Nasir . . . what are you doing here?"

Nasir's face was calm, and his voice controlled. "I live here, Feyi," he said, cool and unflustered. "Did you forget already?"

"No, of course, I meant—when did you get back? I didn't see your car pull up."

"I came up the back road . . . job ended early." He tilted his head, his eyes like black pearls fixed on her. "Aren't you going to come say hi? Kiss me hello?"

Alarm bells were clamoring in Feyi's head. There was something wrong, terribly wrong about how he was looking at and talking to her. As if he knew, but he couldn't—there was no way he could know.

"Is everything okay?" she asked, taking an imperceptible step backward, away from the strangeness radiating off him.

"You look scared," he said. "What for? I've never done anything to hurt you, have I? I've never been anything but patient, and I've tried—God knows I've tried to care for you the way you needed. Right?"

He knew. She didn't know how, but he *knew*.

"Right, Feyi?" He took a step toward her and Feyi instinctively backed away. Nasir froze, hurt passing over his face like a storm, disrupting the still mask he'd been wearing. "Wow," he said. "That's fucked-up."

"I'm sorry, Nasir, I—I don't understand what's going on—"

"You're backing away like I'm the bad guy? Like I'm going to do something to you?"

"Nasir—"

"Where's my father?" She could feel what was coming off

him in hot waves now—rage. Cold, blinding rage. "You were calling for him just now, weren't you?"

"He—he went for a run."

"Mm. So it's just you and me, then."

Feyi didn't remember the last time she'd felt so scared. Nasir looked like a different person. As she watched, his left hand tightened and relaxed, making an intermittent fist.

Oh God, Alim, please come back, she thought. "Nasir, tell me what's going on."

His jaw flexed, muscle jumping under dark skin. "Is it true?"

Feyi felt the cool plaster of the wall behind her, the back of her legs knocking against a potted plant. "Is what true?"

"You know what?" Nasir's voice turned light, conversational. "Let me tell you a story."

Feyi's pulse continued racing, not fooled by this new mask he'd put on. She watched as he leaned against the wall opposite her, folding his arms.

"I get in early, right? I figure I'll spend a night or two in town, hang out with Lorraine, come up here and surprise you. I've been thinking about you for days, impatient to get back to you. Feyi, stuck up there on the mountain, waiting for me to get back." He laughed, a short and empty sound. "So anyway, I'm at Lorraine's, and Mr. Phillip stops by."

Nasir paused. "Do you know Mr. Phillip? Nah, I don't think so. Okay, so Mr. Phillip's, like, this heavyweight badass horticulture motherfucker. He designed Dad's gardens here and grafts trees and does all that shit. Lorraine's been trying to see how many fruits she can graft onto some citrus tree back at the family house, and she needed a pomelo cutting. Now, the best pomelo grows, guess where?" He snapped his fingers and pointed outside. "Right here, on the mountain, in Dad's orchard."

Feyi put her hand over her stomach, like that would stop it from sinking as quickly as it was. Nasir's eyes were a sharpening blade, getting ready to cut into her.

"So Mr. Phillip comes up, he doesn't live too far from here, and he decides to swing by and say hi to Dad. Comes up the back, and then, what the fuck does he see but my father in the garden with some young lady." Nasir's lips curled back into a warped smile. "That's how Mr. Phillip said it when he told me and Lorraine. *Your father out there with some young lady, kissing up on her.* He thought it was funny, you know? That my dad had some secret lover he didn't know about. He never met you. He didn't know you were at the house. He just wanted to know who the 'young thing' Dad had picked up was. They've been friends for decades."

Feyi didn't dare look away from Nasir, from the way he was pinning her to the wall with his words, like a butterfly.

"I thought it was someone else, at first. Like, it had to be. There's no way. So we asked Mr. Phillip what she looked like." Nasir shook his head, blinking back furious tears. "And you know what he said, Feyi? He said she was beautiful. That she had braids like gold, glittering under the sun. The kind of deep, black skin that always looks perfect, like a goddess, he said. Alim's a lucky man, he said, to find a sexy little thing like that." Nasir dragged his eyes up and down Feyi, and her skin crawled. "I can't quite decide which parts he's right about."

Feyi tried to say something, but the words withered in her

throat, under his condemning look. There was nothing to say, she realized. He hadn't come to ask her if it was true; he already knew. Her vision blurred with tears, and she wiped them away hurriedly.

"Oh, you're crying now? That's rich, Feyi. That's fucking hilarious." Nasir pushed off the wall and leaned in over her, his palm on the wall behind her head. "What the *fuck* did you think you were doing? You went and fucked my dad behind my back? My fucking *father*?"

"I—"

"Shut up." The venom in his voice amputated her words, and Feyi stared at him with wide eyes as Nasir slipped back into the light and chatty mask that was so obviously a lie. "You know what it made me think of? The first time I ever saw you. 'Cause it wasn't at that bar, did you know? Nah, it was at the rooftop party, when you met Milan. You didn't even notice me then. You just left the roof with him and you know, I never asked him what happened. Figured it wasn't my business. But now I can't help but wonder, Feyi, what *did* you do with him that first night? Did you suck him off in a corner of a bedroom? Is that how you got my dad? Like some signature move I didn't get the chance to experience 'cause I was the dumbass talking about let's take it slow?"

"Nasir—"

"Nah, don't even say my name. Keep that shit out of your mouth." He lowered his head and spoke directly into her ear, his voice poisonous. "You're fucking trash, you hear me? I wish I'd never fucking met you." Nasir slammed his palm against the wall, and Feyi flinched, cowering away from him, covering her mouth to choke back the sobs. He stepped back

229

and stared at her, his face cold. "Go get your shit and get the fuck out of my home."

Feyi's mind was a blur of blind panic. *Beg him*, her fear told her. *Maybe he'll back off then.* "Nasir, please stop. You're scaring me."

Nasir growled at her. "Feyi, I swear to God. If you don't get the fuck out, I'm gonna throw you out myself."

Feyi sagged against the wall, one hand digging into the planter as she held herself up, her fingers sinking into the moist soil. She couldn't move, she couldn't stop crying, even though she knew it was making him angrier. "I'm sorry, Nasir. I didn't mean for any of this to happen."

He sucked at his teeth. "You know what. Fuck this shit." He turned and walked away, heading up the staircase.

Feyi pulled herself together and ran after him as soon as she realized he was heading for her room, catching his sleeve on the staircase. "Nasir, wait!"

He shook her off and strode up the rest of the stairs, flinging her door open. Feyi tried to pull him back, and Nasir turned on her, his teeth bared. "Get your fucking hands off me," he snarled. She flinched and backed off, and he raked his eyes around her room, then threw open her closet doors and pulled out her suitcase.

"Nasir, please don't do this. Please, just listen."

He ripped her clothes off the hangers and threw them into the suitcase. "Listen to what, Feyi?" Her shoes landed on top of the clothes and he swept everything off her bedside table, bottles of perfume and earrings scattering over the suitcase and floor. "I treated you well, you know? I knew you came with baggage, I knew you were all fucked-up, but

I didn't care. I thought you were *special*." He paused and stepped into the bathroom, then gathered her things from the counter and threw them toward the suitcase. Feyi gasped and jumped back as a bottle broke, spewing oil and glass all over the floor.

Broken glass, a dark road, the sounds of shattering. Feyi snapped out of the spell and looked at Nasir, really looked at him. "What the fuck are you doing?" she yelled, her panic burning away into hot swirls of something else.

"Taking out the trash." He gestured at the suitcase. "Zip up your shit and get it out of here."

"Nah, fuck you, Nasir." She was still crying, but enough was *fucking* enough. "I'm not doing this with you."

"Fuck me? Fuck *me*?" He took a step toward her, and Feyi glared back at him.

"I don't deserve this shit," she hissed, her voice wound wire-tight.

Nasir put his face close to hers, his breath skimming her skin. "You deserve every fucking bit of this," he whispered. "Don't ever get it twisted."

A door slammed, and Alim's voice rang out from downstairs. "Feyi? Nasir? Is that your car outside?"

Nasir's face contorted. "Oh, look," he said. "Daddy's home."

He grabbed the handle of Feyi's suitcase and started to drag it out of the room.

She grabbed the other handle and tried to pull it back from him, her clothes spilling out to the floor. "Stop this shit right now, Nasir!"

Nasir gave the suitcase a sharp yank, tearing it away from

231

Feyi's hands, spinning it out into the hallway, shoes and more clothes flying out. He stepped out of the room to kick it, and Feyi pulled at his arm.

"I said, stop it!"

Nasir whirled around and came at her so fast that Feyi tripped backing up into the room and stumbled as she scrambled away from his rage. "You don't get to say anything!" he yelled. "You fucked my *father*, Feyi! Get your shit and *get out*!"

His face was close to hers, spit flying from his mouth, his eyes burning and his face wet, then Alim's arm was across his chest, pulling him back. Nasir struggled as Alim forced him out of the room. "Don't fucking touch me!"

"That's enough, Nasir. Wait outside."

"I'm not gonna—"

"I said, *wait outside*." Alim's voice was like a whip, the edge of it slicing through the air. Nasir fell silent, his eyes red and resentful. Alim came up to Feyi, his hands gentle as he touched her face, looking her over. "Are you okay?" he asked, his voice soft. "Did he hurt you?"

Feyi shook her head, her throat raw. "I'm fine," she said.

Alim was quickly examining her arms, her hands, her neck.

"I'm fine, Alim."

He looked around the room.

"There's glass."

"I know. A bottle broke." Feyi felt precarious, like she'd been stretched whisper-thin and even the smallest thing would snap her into a thousand sharp pieces.

She could feel Alim's concern like tendrils of care around her, shielding and soothing, and it made her want to cry. His shirt was damp with sweat, and he smelled like grass and sun, but Nasir was standing right outside the doorway, his face thundering in silence. Alim needed to stop touching her. He was going to make Nasir even more angry. Feyi could see the way Nasir's eyes were flickering, absorbing every moment his father's hands brushed Feyi's skin, the easy intimacy. She could see the way his mouth was beginning to curl, and Feyi wanted to pull away from Alim, but he was wiping the salt water off her face, his thumbs firm against her cheekbones.

"I'm so sorry for this, sweetness," he said. "I really am. This"—he looked around the room and his face glitched in anger—"this should never have happened."

Feyi shook her head, holding on to his wrists as she pulled his hands off her. "It's not your fault," she whispered. "But, Alim, you need to back up a bit. It's going to make things worse. He's watching. Please."

His mouth twitched and he dropped his hands. "Give me a minute with him," he said.

Feyi nodded, and Alim turned to the door, to his storm of a son standing outside.

"Downstairs," he ordered.

Nasir looked at him, full of bitterness and betrayal. "Are you fucking serious?"

Alim took his elbow and steered him toward the staircase. "Downstairs. Now."

Nasir shook him off angrily but obeyed, his back ramrod straight with fury. Alim followed behind, and Feyi came out of the room and sank to the floor in the corridor, her back against the wall, her suitcase scattered beside her. Her room was a ransacked disaster, and Nasir's voice kept replaying in her head, telling her to get the fuck out, full of biting hate. A sharp pain wrenched at her heart, the fresh memory replaying over and over. Feyi put her face in her hands and sobbed quietly, her body shaking as she tried to muffle the sounds. Nasir's and Alim's voices drifted up the walls, faint but distinct.

"You can't behave like this, Nasir. It's not acceptable. Not now, not ever."

"Dad . . ." For a second, Nasir sounded like a child again, unsure and unmoored. "Why? Why did you do it?"

Alim paused. "I hear you, and we're going to talk about that, I swear. But first we need to address what just happened. You don't ever, and I mean, *ever*, raise your voice like that or treat someone that way. Jesus, Nasir, I know I raised you better than that."

Nasir gave a hollow laugh. "Are you really lecturing me about how I talk to the girl you basically just stole from me? Really, Dad?"

"Nasir. Her clothes are on the floor. I walk in and there's broken glass everywhere, the girl is weeping, and you look like you're *this* close to catching a domestic violence charge. It's unacceptable. I don't care what your provocation is, you don't behave like that, and you know better. What would you have done if I hadn't walked in? Dragged her out by her hair?"

"I don't want her in this house, Dad. She can't stay here. She can't fucking stay here."

"Language."

"*Fuck* language! I *brought* her here! I invited her into my home, and the minute my back is turned, she fucks *you*?"

234

Nasir's voice rang against the glass of the house, warped and ugly. "Nah, fuck that shit, Dad, I'm kicking her out."

Alim's voice cooled to slick ice, like a stranger was speaking out of his mouth. "Boy, this is *my* house."

There was a stunned silence from Nasir and the tension curled like a thick root through the air. When he spoke again, his voice was tight. "Gotcha. I'll be going, then."

"Nasir—" Alim's voice cut off as the door slammed.

There was a pause before Feyi heard Alim walking back up the stairs. She frantically wiped the tears off her face and went on her hands and knees, picking up her stuff and shoving it into the suitcase. Alim turned the corner at the top of the stairs and clicked his tongue when he saw her.

"Feyi, leave it." He crouched by her, pulling her up by her shoulders. "I'll get it later, just leave it."

Feyi twisted away from him. "No, it's fine. It's all my stuff. I can put it away." Her hands trembled as she picked up a shirt and folded it clumsily. "It's all my stuff; he threw out all my stuff."

Her voice caught, then broke as she said it, and the pieces of herself she'd been trying so hard to hold together since Nasir walked into the house all fell apart. He'd treated her the way he now saw her, like trash, like someone who didn't matter in all the worst ways. He used to be her friend. Feyi splintered into tears as the shirt fell out of her hands.

"He threw out all my stuff," she sobbed, and Alim pulled her into his arms.

"I know," he murmured into her hair, his voice thick. "I'm so sorry, sweetness. I'm so sorry I wasn't here."

Feyi clutched at his shirt, hoarse sobs ripping their way

out of her throat, tears and snot puddling against his chest. Alim gathered her to him and rocked her, both of them on the polished floor, her fragments of life strewn around them.

Chapter Eighteen

Alim insisted that Feyi stay in his room while he cleaned up the mess Nasir had made. She tried to sleep, hoping that she could reset that way, slip out of the feelings she was in like they were clothes, wake up wearing something else. Alim's sheets smelled like sweet orange, cool against her skin, his pillows like clouds seizing her head. She didn't belong there. She was an interloper, and maybe Nasir was right, maybe Joy had been right, too, that she should just go home. It wasn't supposed to go down like this. Feyi closed her eyes and pulled the sheets over her head, making a cocoon until the oxygen gave out and she had to come back up for air.

Alim was just returning to the room, still in his running clothes. He sat on the bed and leaned toward her, his torso in a graceful swoop as he propped himself up on his elbow. "How are you feeling, sweetness?"

Feyi wanted to smile to reassure him, but she couldn't quite pull it off. "A little better," she said. "You really didn't have to clean all that up, I could've done it."

Alim stroked her cheek, a gesture that was quickly becoming familiar to her, and it made her heart tighten with a confusion of feelings. It felt unreal that he was here, right here, touching her and looking at her with those eyes of his. What was he seeing, and how could it be so far away from what Nasir now saw her as? Wasn't she both those people, whoever Alim was falling for, the woman Nasir now hated?

She was guilty of everything. Just thinking about it had her fighting back tears.

"Hey, hey." Alim tilted up her chin as she dropped her head, trying to hide her face. "Talk to me."

Feyi shook her head, pulling away and hugging her knees to her chest.

Alim hesitated. "Do you . . . do you want to go home?"

To her surprise, there was a fraction of uncertainty in his voice. She looked up at him through wet eyes, but Alim's face was shifting between emotions too quickly for her to trace.

"After today," he said, "I would understand if you changed your mind, if you wanted to leave. Or if you didn't want to do this anymore. It was . . . unconscionable what happened."

A corner of her mouth quirked. "I think a lot of people would disagree with you. In fact, I think a lot more would say I had it coming."

"Feyi . . ."

"Are you sure you *want* me here?" She kept her voice clipped, so it wouldn't show the fear hiding under her tongue. "And I need you to think about that, for real. Because this is serious, Alim. Nasir wasn't supposed to find out about us like this, it's literally the worst possible way this could have gone, and things are gonna get much worse." She'd explained to him how Mr. Phillip had been the one to break the news to his kids.

Alim's eyebrows drew together. "I've been serious about this from the start, Feyi. We've talked about this."

"I'm just saying." Feyi didn't know why she was being so spiky to him. He hadn't done anything, other than set his life on fire for her, which she hadn't asked him to do.

"I want you here. But I want you to be okay more than anything, Feyi. Tell me what you need."

"It's not me!" she shouted, and somehow, she was crying again. "You're the one acting like this isn't a big deal, like me being here is a good idea, and now you keep shoving this option of me leaving down my throat, like what, so it can be my choice? You can just ask me to go, it's fine! I get it."

Alim climbed on the bed to get closer to her. "Feyi, what on earth are you talking about?"

She shook her head, wiping the tears off her face. "It's fine. You don't have to keep pretending."

"I'm not pretending, I'm—" He took her shoulders, asking her to look at him. "I'm *here*, Feyi. I'm here. Why are you trying to make me go away?"

"Why do you keep asking me if I want to leave?"

"Because I don't know if you'll want to stay, if you'll still feel comfortable here. My son was—was violent to you today." Alim's face glitched with pain and shame as he said the words. "I wasn't here to stop him. I couldn't protect you, and, sweetness, I never want you to feel unsafe. I'm trying to ask you how you feel, and yes, I thought there was a chance you might want to leave."

"Do you want me to leave?"

"*No.*" Alim ran a hand through his hair, agitated. "I don't. I want you here, I want *you*. I want to fall asleep with your skin against mine. I want to do everything I can to make sure no one ever hurts you again. I want to wake up and see your face in the sunrise."

Any other time, Feyi would have been swayed by his words, but this time she wouldn't even look at him. Why would Alim want someone who brought this much drama into his life? How much of what Nasir said was true?

Alim sat back on his heels, deflating a little. "But I've been very clear about this, and that's not the real problem, is it?"

Feyi wanted so badly to glance over at him, but she was too scared of the ball she'd started rolling.

"You don't believe me," he said, and there was a stirring of pain and surprise in his voice. "You don't believe I'm telling the truth."

"I believe you *think* you're telling the truth," she said, her voice small but stubborn. "Like maybe that's how you feel now. But when this shit with Nasir continues, because it's not going anywhere anytime soon, I don't know if you'll feel the same."

Alim exhaled. "I don't even—" He broke off and got up from the bed. "I can't force you to believe me, Feyi. That's a step you have to make off the cliff yourself." He looked at the time and plucked his shirt away from his skin. "I need to take a shower. But I'm here, and I'm listening."

He waited a beat for her to respond, then started heading for the bathroom when she didn't, pulling his shirt off over his head. Feyi watched him from beneath her eyelashes, the way his shoulder blades shifted under his skin as he lifted his arms, the valley of his spine, his ribs, the skin stretching over all of it, scarred at his hands and forearms from a life in the kitchen. Alim tossed his shirt on an armchair and each movement was just casual grace spilling all over the place, his long legs as he walked, the lazy flick of his arm, the way his neck turned.

"Wait," she said, before he went into the bathroom.

Alim stopped and looked at her. Feyi could tell he was up-set, but leashing it, controlling his feelings like he always did, like he'd done with Nasir just earlier. She leaned forward in the bed and took him in slowly, saying nothing at first. Alim stood easily, his weight on one leg, his arms relaxed, watching her as she watched him.

"Take those off," she said, nodding at his running shorts.

Alim hooked his thumb into the elastic of the waistband, then paused. Feyi stared at him, her face blank, the air between them both uncertain and sure. He pulled them off, his spine curving forward as he bent to tug them away from his feet, tossing them to one side, then standing naked in front of her. Feyi examined him from across the room, the cut of his hips, the soft skin at the tip of his uncircumcised penis, the trimmed hair above it, the small whorl of his navel. Alim studied her curiously, saying nothing.

Feyi climbed out of the bed and walked over to him, the T-shirt he'd given her hanging halfway down her thighs. Alim looked at her and tugged on one of the curled braids falling over her shoulders. Feyi kept her face neutral as she raked a finger down his sternum, along one rib, tracing it under his arm to his back and into his spine as she walked around his body. He let out a jagged breath as she stood behind him and slid her arms around him, splaying her hands over his chest and pressing herself to his back, her cheek flattened between his shoulder blades.

"What will you do when you get tired of me?" she asked, her voice spilling on his skin. Alim put his hands over hers.

"You're a whole world to me, Feyi. I could spend the rest of my life learning you and I'd never get tired." He let out a

241

brief chuckle. "I should be asking you why you feel this way about some old man."

"Don't be ridiculous. You know exactly how exceptional you are."

"Ah, sweetness." He shook his head and squeezed her hands. "Sometimes I count the decades I might have with you, if I'm lucky?"

"Don't say that." She pressed a kiss against his spine, sweat and salt dry on his skin. They weren't supposed to be talking about plans or the rest of their lives. It was supposed to wait until later, but perhaps now was later, now that Nasir knew, now that their secret was flayed open and exposed.

"No, but it's true," Alim was saying. "I think about how many years you'll have left when I'm gone, how it feels inevitable that I will abandon you." He turned around so he could look at her. "And I'm selfish, so selfish that even with that, I can't bring myself to not try to give you the best of every year I have left."

Feyi looked up at him. "No plans," she reminded him, if only to stop the flood of words he was giving her, to stop the way it made her feel. "This is already almost impossible."

"Do you truly believe that?" he asked, frowning a little.

"Not really," she admitted. "But literally everyone else will."

Alim shrugged. He was even more relaxed naked than he was with clothes on. "I only care what you think."

"I think—" Feyi broke off and took a deep breath, her arms still wrapped around him. None of this mattered, except the parts that did. "I want to be with you. I feel clear about that, even when I'm terrified that you'll change your mind about wanting to be with me. This feels . . . right. It feels like living in another world, one that's just off to the side from the one everyone else is in, but it feels right."

Alim nodded. "It's ours. And just because it's just us in it right now doesn't mean it's not real. You're real, so am I, so are our feelings. I'm not running away, Feyi, but you're so afraid I will that *you're* the one running, or trying to."

She grimaced. "I know. I'm sorry."

He kissed her cheek and stepped out of her arms. "I'm going to jump in the shower, feel free to join me. Or watch."

"I think I'll take you up on that," Feyi replied. "But just the watching part."

Alim shook his head. "Little voyeur." He grabbed a towel and flicked it at her, and Feyi followed him into the bathroom, laughing.

. . .

Jonah.

They're pulling her to safety, and someone's shouting that the car's about to blow. She's trying to find her voice, to pull it out of her bruised throat, but it's taking too long. She's struggling against the people trying to help her, she's not the one who needs help—he is. He's still in there, and they've turned to go and get him, but she knows why they helped her first, she saw when they took his pulse and shook their heads, except they need to pull him out, they need to try. They take a step, and the air goes whoomp *as the car blooms into an orange flower. She's screaming, her voice is back, she's screaming his name.*

Jonah. Jonah. Jonah.

Feyi jerked up in the bed, his name mangled in her mouth, the car still aflame before her.

Alim snapped awake beside her, sitting up. "Feyi?"

She swung her head toward his voice, her eyes wide and unseeing.

"You're dreaming, Feyi. Wake up."

Feyi looked up at him, her eyes focusing, then she gasped in a massive breath and doubled over, pain knifing through her. "Oh God." She wrapped her arms around her stomach. "Oh God."

It hurt like it had just happened, like the years between then and now had collapsed into nothing and this was normal, Feyi's old therapist had reassured her of that, but it still came unexpected and hard and fast and the boy she'd loved for so long was gone, with his terrible puns and almond eyes, with his burnt-sugar hair and thick eyebrows.

"Can I hold you?" Alim was asking, and Feyi managed to nod through her sobs. Alim climbed over the pillows and sat behind her, pulling her back flush against his chest, wrapping his arms around her ribs and resting his chin on her shoulder.

"Breathe with me," he said, and Feyi followed along as he coached her through the inhales and exhales.

She leaned into his body and the way it curved around her, like a whole shield, a bracing. When her chest was steady again, Alim didn't let her go. Instead, he began to tell her stories about Marisol, about the nightmares he'd had the first couple of years, of drowning, of not drowning, of saving her and then being wrong. He told her about how the years after that dulled some things and sharpened others. The ways his memory betrayed him, the ways it saved him. When there

244

was a lull in his storytelling, Feyi told him about Jonah. About the last look he'd given her as the car was spinning out of control, like he knew what was about to happen, the way he'd reached for her hand before the impact stole their consciousness.

Feyi and Alim sat like that for a long time, swapping memories of their lost loves, until the night ran out of darkness and fell into morning.

Chapter Nineteen

The next time Feyi went into town, it was to have lunch with Pooja Chatterjee and sort out the details of the commission. Alim dropped her off downtown at the restaurant Pooja had picked, not far from the museum. "Make sure you order the sea bass," he said. "Lyle is one of the best seafood chefs I know."

Feyi leaned through the window for a goodbye kiss. "I will," she said. "Text you when I'm done?"

"Sounds good. I'm going to drop by Phillip's house and say hello."

"Oof." She stood back on the sidewalk. "Have y'all talked since—?"

"Yes, yes. He called me once he realized what had happened. Was so full of apologies." Alim chuckled dryly and shook his head. "He doesn't quite know how to look Nasir in the face now."

"Well, yeah. That sounds awkward as fuck."

"It'll be fine. I have a nice rum from Antigua for him." Alim put on his sunglasses and flashed her a smile. "See you soon, sweetness."

Feyi waved as he pulled away, then went into the restaurant. Pooja was impossible to miss—she was flirting loudly with all the staff, who were clustered around her table, but broke off as soon as she saw Feyi.

"Well, ladies, so sorry to end this, but my lovely date is here."

Feyi raised an eyebrow as Pooja stood to exchange air-kisses with her. "What would your husband think of that?"

"He'd probably be jealous I didn't invite him along," Pooja said blithely, sitting back down and gesturing to a server to pour Feyi some wine. "But then again, Sanjeet is amused by my diligence in seeking out new artists."

"That's a shame." Feyi sat down and unfolded her napkin, draping it on her lap.

"Not at all! I get to constantly prove that my taste is superior." Pooja leaned in and mock whispered. "I rather think he's into it, to be honest. He likes when I remind him how much smarter than him I am."

Feyi laughed and accepted the menu the waiter was handing her. "Alim recommended the sea bass," she said, as she read through it. "What would you suggest?"

"Oh, I'm not about to disagree with Alim Blake." Pooja put down her menu and took a sip of her wine. "That's insider information that I will gratefully accept."

They made small talk as they put in their orders, trying out warm pieces of the freshly baked bread the restaurant made, paired with a spicy olive oil and an aged balsamic. It wasn't until they were halfway through their sea bass that Pooja brought up the commission.

"Administrative logistics bore me to tears, but my accountant wanted me to tell you the first half of the payment should be in your account shortly." Her eyes took on a sharp gleam. "I looked up more of your earlier work, Ms. Adekola. You have quite the range."

"Thank you." Feyi laid her fork down next to her plate. "May I be blunt with you, Mrs. Chatterjee?"

Pooja looked positively delighted at the concept. "Yes, of course!"

"You've gone to quite some trouble to secure this commission from me, and I guess I'm just wondering—why? What is it about my work that resonates with you? I just—I get the feeling that you're looking for more than just a piece to collect as an investment."

"Ah." Pooja dabbed at her lips delicately with her napkin, then sighed as she laid it back down. When she looked up, Feyi was surprised to see that her face had gone somber; it seemed so at odds with the irrepressibly cheerful woman she'd observed so far. Pooja was silent for a few moments, gathering her words, then she squared her shoulders and smiled directly at Feyi. "Sanjeet and I once had a daughter. Keya. We were living in T&T then. She was very young when she passed away from leukemia and . . . I can still feel the shape of the hole that is left in my heart, how sharp the edges are. We spread her ashes in Tobago."

"I'm so sorry," Feyi said, knowing how useless the words were as she offered them. "I had no idea."

Pooja dismissed it with a wave of her jeweled hand. "There is no need," she said. "When I saw your work, I looked you up before I had Rebecca introduce us, and I realized that you *understood*, Ms. Adekola. You understood that . . . madness. The way it never really leaves you, even if you learn how to hide it from everyone else. I want a piece of that, in whatever form it comes to you. I believe in that, perhaps more than I believe in a lot of other things in this world."

Feyi nodded slowly. Madness was exactly right. "Okay," she said. "Do you have a preference as to size?"

Pooja shrugged a silken shoulder. "Nothing too small. I like things to take up space." She gave Feyi a dazzling smile, the somber look in her eyes dissolving into light. "I try my best to live by that, in fact."

Feyi glanced around at how half the restaurant kept sneaking adoring looks at Pooja. "I think you're killing at that, Mrs. Chatterjee."

Pooja's laugh was like a crystal bell breaking through the room. She cut a piece of her sea bass and waved her knife at Feyi. "Do you have any more questions for me?"

"Um, yes. I work in blood a lot, and it's quite a fugitive pigment. Is that a concern for you?"

"Not at all." Pooja gestured for more wine, and three people scrambled into action. "I loved what you said in your artist talk with Yagazie Emezi about decay and the ephemerality of the work. I think it keeps it from being . . . static. To have a natural process viewed as a corruption of the work seems so controlling, don't you think?"

"I think people desire permanence," Feyi replied. This wasn't the conversation she'd expected to have with Pooja, but it was a delightfully pleasant surprise. "An archive that lasts."

"Well, we know all too well how futile such a desire can be, don't we?" Pooja laughed, a sharp shadow slinking under her words, and for a moment, Feyi genuinely wondered what kind of man Sanjeet Chatterjee was, to love a woman who was this brilliant and furious and alive.

Pooja leaned forward, her dark hair swinging sharp at her jawline. There was a darkness in her eyes that ran fathoms deep, and Feyi couldn't understand how she had missed it before.

"Give me an archive of madness that *rots*, Ms. Adekola. I wouldn't mind it one bit."

The waiter appeared with their wine, and Pooja sat back in her chair, smiling as she finished off the last of her sea bass. Feyi picked up her fork and started thinking about what she could make for this woman who had a dead little girl seeding madness in the hollow of her heart.

. . .

After their lunch, Feyi decided to go check out a bookstore around the corner, thinking she'd sit and do some writing about where she wanted to go with Pooja's commission. She had just spotted it down the block when her phone rang.

"Denlis!" she answered. "How's it going? I'm just in town."

The security guard's voice boomed through her earbuds. "Good, because I was about to tell yuh to come down here. It's your boyfriend."

It took Feyi a minute. "Nasir? What's he doing there?" She listened to Denlis as he explained what was going on, then Feyi nodded even though he couldn't see it, anger pulling the back of her neck tight. "I'll be right there," she said, turning to head in the opposite direction. The museum was only a few blocks away. She called Alim as she was walking and had to fight to keep her voice level when he picked up.

"I have to handle something at the exhibit," she said immediately. "Could you wait for me at the bookstore when you're done with Mr. Phillip?"

"Of course. Is everything all right, Feyi? I could pick you up from the museum."

"No, no." She debated for a quick second whether to tell him or not. "It's Nasir," she said. He might as well know. "The security guard called me—apparently he showed up and is making some kind of scene there."

"*What?*" Tension sang like a naked wire through Alim's voice. "I'm coming down there, Feyi."

"No, let me handle this."

"Feyi—"

"It's *my* work he's fucking with." The anger was hot under her skin. "This is between me and Nasir, Alim. Let me handle it."

Alim took a breath, and she could tell he was fighting not to get involved, but Feyi wasn't in the mood to wait for him to listen to her.

"Do *not* come down here," she ordered. "I will text you when I'm back at the bookstore." She hung up the phone as she jogged up the stairs to the museum, hanging a left at the lobby and down the corridor to Denlis's office. He opened the door as soon as she knocked, then let her in, shaking his head.

"Ei, he real upset, bwoy."

Nasir was sitting on a metal chair on the other side of the room, his head in his hands and his elbows resting on his knees. Feyi looked down at him and then back up at Denlis.

"Did he do anything to the piece?"

"Nah, I think I got him in time."

"I wasn't going to fucking touch your work," Nasir snapped, not looking up at her. "The program said they were doing artist walkthroughs—I just wanted to see if you were here so I didn't have to go up the fucking mountain."

Denlis put a hand on his belt and frowned down at Nasir. "Doh yuh live up that mountain? Why yuh can't go there?"

Nasir coughed out an ugly laugh. "My father lives there, not me," he said, then threw a baleful glare at Feyi. "Ask her."

Feyi turned to Denlis and put a hand on his arm. "Thank you for calling me. Can you give me a minute with him?"

"Hmph." Denlis gave Nasir a suspicious look. "Leave the door crack open and call if yuh need me, you hear?"

"I will." She smiled reassuringly until he left the room, then pulled up another chair and sat in front of Nasir, leaning forward. "What the *fuck* do you think you're doing?"

He looked at her, and his eyes were bloodshot. Feyi grabbed his chin and tilted his head up to get a better look at his face in the dim light of the office.

"Are you fucking drunk?"

Nasir jerked his face away from her hand. "I *wish* I was fucking drunk. Maybe that would make this shit easier to deal with. Maybe I should try that."

"What were you doing here, Nasir?"

"I told you! I wanted to see if you were here, so we could, you know, *talk*." He spat out the last word and gave her a sickly smile. "And look, Denlis so nicely called you for me. How did you get here so fast?"

"I was already in town."

"Ah, I'm guessing Dad is your chauffeur now. It must be nice, having a Blake man around all the time to help you with shit. When one doesn't work out, fuck it, just go for the other one." He chuckled bitterly. "At least you didn't have time to get around to Lorraine."

"She's not my type," Feyi shot back. "Denlis said you were making a scene in the gallery. Right by my piece."

Nasir waved a hand. "I may have said some things, but hey, none of them were lies. You all into excavating yourself for these people's money, don't you want them to know the truth about who you are? Shit, I helped you get this show, I figured I'd help a little more."

Feyi's fingernails bit into her palm as her hands curled into fists. She wanted to hit him, to knock that smirk off his face, choke the shit he was saying till it rotted in his throat. The anger was boiling so white-hot inside her, she was surprised he was still intact across from her, not burning and crackling in a melted black. Denlis had said Nasir kept calling for her, asking people where she was hiding, saying she didn't have to hide from him. He'd walked through her piece, pushing the gold rings aside roughly, as if she was crouched in a corner of the mirrors, trying to avoid him. Denlis had recognized Nasir from all the pickups, so he'd jumped in quickly and gotten him out of there, but not before Nasir had yelled to some of the people that they wouldn't be so impressed if they knew what he knew about the artist. Feyi couldn't even look at him without the rage calling itself up from her bones, where it was always sleeping, where it had been simmering for years, since the dark road and the broken glass and the utter outrage of Jonah's absence from his own body. And now Nasir had the unmitigated fucking nerve to sit across from her with a challenge in his eyes, as if he had punished her, as if he had done something.

What he didn't understand was that it had taken years for Feyi to become the girl he'd screamed at in his father's house, someone he could intimidate because she had *chosen* to be soft, chosen to care, chosen to allow her heart to shed the deep rot-dark scales it grew on that road. Men like Nasir didn't see the other parts, the fork in the road, the thing she was before she decided to live again. He didn't respect her, he thought she had no power because she had wept under the onslaught of his words, and so he felt brave enough, safe enough, to *fuck* with her work. The rage unfurled like a bonfire and Feyi let it wash over her, wash away the soft girl, coat her in the widow who would gladly burn the whole fucking world down. Some of the challenge drained out of Nasir's face as he watched the steel form under her skin, the liquid iron pool in her eyes.

Feyi's hand lashed out and seized his face, pulling it toward her, her fingers digging into the flesh on the sides of his mouth and pressing painfully against his teeth. Nasir was too shocked to react. She leaned close to him till her breath was raking across his face and her eyes skewered him in place.

"Listen well, because I'm only going to say this shit once, Nasir. Don't you ever, *ever* in your fucking life try to fuck with my work or my career again. I don't give a fuck how you feel when it comes to this. I don't give a fuck if I sucked Alim's dick in front of you and Lorraine or if I fucked him in front of all your friends. Nothing and I mean *nothing* gives you the right to come to my exhibit and pull this shit."

Nasir tried to pull his face away, but Feyi tightened her grip.

"Oh, I'm dead-ass about this, my nigga. I don't give a fuck about anything other than my work. You touch that, you try to come for that, and I will fuck you up so thoroughly that you will never remember a time when you were anywhere close to okay." She let go of his face, shoving him away roughly and leaning back in her seat. "You think you're the only person who can come and make noise?"

Nasir rubbed his face and looked at her, opening his mouth to say something, but Feyi interrupted him before he could even start.

"And you wonder why I didn't want to be with you? When at the end of the day you can come and try to scatter my fucking *work*? My *wedding ring* is in that install, Nasir, and you know what's on it?"

A shadow of shame passed over his face and Nasir looked away to the side.

"Nah, you probably read the artist statement while you were out there acting like a fucking fool, so tell me what's on it. Go ahead."

Nasir looked up at her from under his lashes, his head still bent. "Feyi—"

"*Blood*, Nasir. Mine and Jonah's. You wanna walk in there and fuck with something like that? Are you kidding me right now?" The rage had reached her lungs now, burning her air, expanding her with heat. "Do you know what it was like when I retrieved that from our effects? Of course not. You have no *fucking* idea what it's like to exchange rings with someone, look into their eyes as they promise to love you forever, then wear that ring every day of your life together, until you have to fish it out of a fucking plastic bag of bloodstained shit!"

In the back of her head, Feyi realized that she would be crying while saying this, while remembering this, if she was still the soft girl. But she wasn't, so her eyes stayed dry and

255

hot as they burned into Nasir, who was shifting uncomfortably in his chair.

"*That's* what my fucking work is about." Feyi stood up because being in the same room as him was making her skin crawl. "You think about that next time you try to fuck with me."

"I'm sorry." Nasir looked up and his jaw was locked tight, like it physically hurt him to say the words, but he got them out anyway. "You right, and I'm sorry. I shouldn't have come here, and it won't happen again."

Feyi stared at him, then nodded once. "Okay," she said.

"Don't think this means we're cool, 'cause we're fucking not," he replied, his eyes flashing with resentment.

A corner of Feyi's mouth curled down. "No," she agreed. "We're fucking not." She turned and left Nasir in the room, slamming the door as she walked out.

Chapter Twenty

When Lorraine's black Jeep came up the driveway, Feyi was making toast in the breakfast nook. She heard the crunch of gravel under the tires and went to look out of the window, cursing softly when she saw who it was. Lorraine hadn't been up to the house since the news broke—she hadn't come up that horrible day with Nasir, she wouldn't answer Alim's calls, nothing. If she was here, it couldn't be for anything good. Feyi dropped her plate and left the nook, alarm beating wings in her back.

"Alim!" she called.

He was already coming down the curved staircase, pulling a shirt on and buttoning it, his face drawn and anxious. "I saw her car," he said, as Feyi met him on the stairs. "Can you—"

"I'll go upstairs," she said quickly, "don't worry."

Alim let out a breath, standing close to her as he finished the last button. "I'm sorry. I just—"

"Don't be." Feyi kissed his cheek. "It's better if I'm out of the way."

He tucked a braid behind her ear and gave her a small smile. "Thank you."

"Go, go." She shooed him off and took the remaining stairs two at a time, going into the first room, the one she still thought of as hers even though she spent most nights in Alim's bed now. All her things were still here, restored after

Nasir had thrown them about. Feyi locked the door, a pang of sadness clicking along with it. Was this really what it had come down to? Being so afraid she was barricading herself in this guest room? Did she really think Lorraine was going to attack her the way Nasir had?

Alim wouldn't allow it.

Feyi had to believe that Alim wouldn't allow it.

She unlocked the door, then backed away from it and sat on the bed. There was something shameful about hiding like this, like crawling into a closet or under a bed. It wasn't like she wanted to be there for whatever conversation Lorraine and Alim were having, but there was a difference between being out of the way and hiding like this, which, she realized, was something *she* was choosing. Alim hadn't asked her to go lock herself in her room and pretend like she wasn't in the house, Feyi was the one pressing herself into this corner.

"Stop acting like a small girl," she said, forcing herself to her feet and out of the room. The house was quiet, other than the sound of wind and trees and birds. Feyi walked back to the top of the staircase and stood listening for a minute. She could hear faint ghosts of sound coming from the library, and she knew she should stay upstairs like she'd told Alim she would, but she also knew the conversation in there was about her. With Nasir, it had been straightforward, he'd told her what he thought of her directly, to her face. Lorraine wouldn't, and Alim probably wouldn't tell her the worst of what his daughter had said.

Feyi walked down the stairs as quietly as she could, keeping close to the wall and barely breathing. There was a large Wangechi Mutu piece on the wall next to the library, and she made sure not to touch it as she inched closer to the door. They hadn't closed it properly behind them, and so their voices slipped through, Alim's low and patient, Lorraine's heated and spiked.

"Yuh have any idea what yuh doing to Nasir?" she was saying. "Forget about me, but God, man, think about him, just for a moment! That's if you can even stop thinking about *her*."

"Lorraine, you are my children," Alim replied. "I think about you both constantly."

She scoffed. "How yuh could even fix yuh mouth to say that? Yuh stole his girl!"

"I didn't steal anyone, Lorraine. Feyi and I, we . . . we found each other. I'm trying to explain this to your brother, and I know it's difficult—"

"Explain? What's there to explain? Yuh let a damn groupie into our house—"

"Lorraine, that's—"

"Nah, Daddy, Nasir tell me the whole story already. From the moment she find out who yuh are, that yuh rich, yuh famous, yuh on TV. Come nah, man. Yuh don't think she put two and two together? Once she see this house? Please. Yuh not that fucking stupid."

Alim's voice took on an edge. "Watch your language."

"Or what? You'll kick me out the house like yuh did to Nasir? I not scared of you like that. I don't give a fuck how much bass yuh does put in yuh voice."

"I didn't kick Nasir out of the house!" Alim raised his voice slightly and Feyi could hear the hurt under his words. "I would never ask either of you to leave."

Lorraine scoffed. "Daddy, come on. He ask her to leave, and yuh tell him this *your* house? It come down to yuh son and this girl and yuh choose *her*? Wow. She pussy *must* be fire, bwoy."

Even from outside the room, Feyi felt Alim's rage, heard him hiss a sharp intake of air. There was a terrifying moment of silence before Lorraine spoke again, her voice betraying only the tiniest sliver of fear.

"I wish yuh could see how yuh looked at me just now, Daddy." She let out a small scared laugh that sounded like she was about to cry. "She really does have her hooks in yuh, oui?"

"Lorraine." Alim's voice was raw, scraped down. "Please. I'm not trying to hurt you."

His daughter laughed again, and this time it ended in a sob. "It too late for that, Daddy."

"Baby, please. I need you to try and listen to me."

"Yuh cyah say nothing, Daddy! Yuh have any idea how everyone in town is talking? What kind of humiliation yuh putting us through? Our whole family, we the fucking scandal of the week. Your little wutless girlfriend, she know what that means? What that's going to be like, when she all up in the gossip section of the papers? Or maybe that's what she come here for—any kinda fame, any attention. And yuh here giving it to her. Yuh was *that* lonely, to fall for this bullshit?"

Feyi stifled a gasp, covering her mouth with both hands, her heart wrenching as she listened to the barbs Lorraine was throwing. Didn't she know how cruel she was being, couldn't she hear herself?

Alim's voice cracked. "I'm glad your mother isn't here to hear you say that to me."

"Don't bring Mummy into this. Not when yuh fucking that girl."

"You were always so angry when you were in pain, even when you were little. My sea urchin, my spiky one." There was warmth in his words, pain and love all wound tightly together. "I know worlds more about my loneliness than you ever will, and I like to think your mother does, too."

"Yuh think she would be okay with any of this? You sleeping with a girl young enough to be yuh daughter, destroying the family, breaking Nasir's heart? *This* is what yuh think Mummy would want?"

Alim gave a short, dry laugh and sighed. "Your mother would be furious, but she knew me, Lorraine. She knew that I can be impetuous, fast, that I could bruise things when I'm making other things. But, baby girl, I'm not trying to break what I have with you and your brother. I know I've stretched it, I know I've hurt it, frayed it, but I am here, fighting to keep it, keep us together. I'm here to have the difficult conversations, I'm here to take whatever spikes you throw at me, always, forever. I will never love you any less. I am so grateful you came here to talk. Thank you."

Feyi heard Lorraine sniffle and take a deep breath. "Why can't yuh just send her away, Daddy? Please? We could try and fix everything, the three of us, we could get through this and forgive you and put it behind us. It's what I want, it's what Nasir wants. Please?"

"Baby girl . . ." Alim's voice was thick with tears. "I can't do that. I know you real vex with me right now, but I can't do the ultimatums. I'm so sorry."

"*Why?* Why can't yuh just *stop this*?" Lorraine's voice was raised and shaking. "Why is she worth all this to you? She worth losing yuh kids?! She worth the scandal, the gossip, losing face in front of the whole fucking island? Yuh know how many people look up to you here? They eh care when the tabloids say all that shit about you, they eh care about how you dress, how you does present yuhself. Because you're Alim Blake, yuh a champion. And now what? Yuh want to be some old man who fucking his son's girl? Fuh real?"

"This isn't about Feyi—"

Lorraine steamrolled over his words, her voice tumbling frantic and angry. "Nasir and I, we trying our damn best to fix this, and yuh keep saying yuh want to, but yuh refusing to *do* anything, to *change* anything. Yuh just want us to fall in line with this bullshit!" She slammed into a pause, and a note of incredulity slid into her voice. "Oh my God. Yuh not sorry . . . yuh don't even think yuh done anything wrong."

Alim hesitated.

"Wow, Daddy, really? *Really?*"

He sighed. "I made a choice. It might be hurtful and hard and difficult, but that doesn't make it *wrong*. I thought I had taught you that by now."

Lorraine scoffed, contempt dripping from her words. "Yuh could try all the loopholes yuh want, but it cyah change how fucked-up this is, and the fact that yuh refusing to see that is madness. I don't even know why I bothering to talk to you."

Alim exhaled a slow breath, and there was silence for a while. Feyi swallowed hard but didn't dare move until they started talking again, when she could leave without being heard. She'd already stayed for too long, listened to too much.

"I wish you could see me," he finally said, and there was grief packed in his words, a stone sinking into blackness. "I'm trying to explain to you and Nasir why I'm choosing myself in this, how that doesn't mean I'm choosing Feyi over you two, or that I'm not choosing you as well. How it doesn't have to be these binaries, these ultimatums."

"Daddy, we—"

"No." His voice was heavy. "No, let me talk. You've said so much already, and I hear you. I hear that you want me to end things with Feyi, to do what you and your brother want, what would make it easier for this family. I hear you. I feel with you and for you, this pain I've caused by seeking out a relationship like this. I wish it had been another way, that I had met her somewhere else, that she had come to the mountain some other way, but I can't change the circumstances that brought her to me, and with her, the possibility that my life could go in a direction I thought was closed off. And for this, this possibility? You're so young, baby girl, your whole life is still nothing but possibilities. You can't possibly know what it's like to lose it, and how much even a chance of its return is worth to me."

"Daddy . . ." Lorraine's voice was full of pity. "None of this is real, don't yuh see? If yuh going to do alla this, do it for something real, not for a groupie. All she does want is a fling with a man who rich and famous. She trying to take advantage of you. Nasir and I just trying to protect you."

Feyi couldn't bear to listen anymore. She started edging

263

away from the door, but their voices still spilled into the corridor.

"I appreciate your concern, baby girl, but let me take care of myself, okay? This is not how I want things to be between us."

"We eh want this, either, Daddy. But Nasir and I cyah pretend like we think this is okay, not while she still here, while all this still going on."

"Lorraine, this is your home, too. That hasn't changed."

"Nah. It eh feel like home right now."

"Lorraine—"

"I gotta go, Daddy. Call us if yuh decide to come to yuh senses."

Feyi slipped into a side room just as Lorraine left the library, her heels clacking against the marble tiles, her ponytail shiny as it bounced down her back. She was dabbing at her eyes as she hurried out of the house, and soon the engine of her car roared to life, and the wheels spun gravel along the driveway as she sped back down the mountain.

Feyi stood with her forehead against the door, her heart pounding. This was worse than she'd imagined, somehow even worse than Nasir's rage, this cold stating of terms, the way she'd laid it out for Alim. Feyi, or his kids. His family, or this attempt they were foolish enough to think they could make. The thought of Nasir deciding that she was a gold-digging groupie cut Feyi deeply. He'd known her. He'd held her while she slept, kissed her forehead in the morning, made her breakfast. That was the Nasir she knew, the patient and sweet man, not the swirling rage that had barged into her room, not this revisionist storyteller making her into a lie.

This one was a stranger. And the things Lorraine had said to Alim! He must be devastated.

Feyi opened the door quietly and went back toward the library. "Alim?"

She stepped into the room, pushing the door ajar. He was standing by the French doors, his shoulders curved in as he watched his daughter's car recede and get swallowed by the greenery.

"Is everything all right?" she asked. She wanted to go up to him and touch him, take his hand, hold him, but she wasn't sure if that would be welcome.

"I'm sorry if you heard any of that," he said, still looking out. "I'm not sure how loud we were."

"I came downstairs," she confessed. "Heard some of it."

"Hmm." He just kept staring out through the glass and for a moment, Feyi wanted to disappear because it felt like he didn't even notice or care that she was there.

"Do you want me to leave? Like, do you need a minute?" She hated herself for letting the insecurity show in her voice, the slight plaintiveness that colored her questions.

Alim looked at her and frowned. "No, I don't want you to leave." He reached out a hand. "Come here."

Feyi stepped forward and slid her hand into his, feeling some tension loosen as soon as she was touching him, close to him again. Alim pulled her against his body and Feyi laid her cheek against the crisp white cotton of his shirt. Her head fit under his chin and she held him as tight as she could.

"I'm sorry," she whispered, not sure what she was apologizing for, other than the pain she could feel knotted up in him.

"Don't," he said, his voice winding among her braids. "You're perfect."

Tears stung at the back of her eyes. How could he say that?

Feyi felt a wave of guilt pull up through her. "I'm sorry," she said, "this is all my fault. I don't want to drive a wedge between you and your daughter, it's already bad enough with Nasir . . ." She dropped his hand and took a step back. "Maybe I should go, Alim, just for a bit. Just till they calm down. It might be—"

"Feyi." Alim's voice was low and tight, but it cut through the fog of her worry, and she looked up at him. He had closed his eyes. "Don't do that," he said.

She twisted her hands together. "Do what?"

"Don't make it—and I mean this in the gentlest way possible—don't make this about you." He ran a hand over his face and didn't quite look at her. "If you're going to leave, then leave for yourself. Don't make it sound like you're leaving for me. I've already told you what I want."

Feyi wanted to object, but his read was too accurate, and so she stood there, speechless. Alim glanced over at her, and his eyes were shuttered windows. He looked so tired.

"I'm going to go for a run, okay?" He kissed her cheek lightly and left the room.

Feyi looked around the library, then sank down on a chair, dropping her face into her hands. After a few minutes, she pulled out her phone and texted her therapist, asking if she had time for a session in the next day or two. They had an arrangement built over the years since Jonah died, that Feyi could reach out any time and ask to talk, even after they discontinued their weekly appointments. It had carried Feyi through the dark years before she decided to live, and she knew it was important to recognize old faces, the moment the anxiety became louder than a background hum, when it jumped in front of your face and instead of seeing the people you cared about, all you could see was the thrumming noise, the fear, the voice seizing everything around you to confirm that you weren't wanted, that you were the problem.

This wasn't something she could keep expecting Alim to hold. He had enough of his own and this was hers, her monster to fight and slay and skin, dry it in the sun, hang it on her wall as a reminder that she was more than what the voices in her head tried to tell her.

Feyi waited in the chair until her phone pinged with available slots from her therapist, then she sat back, relieved. It was time to shift some things.

. . .

The session wasn't until the next day, but just having it scheduled settled Feyi's stress considerably. She went out into the courtyard and did some meditative stretches to re-center herself in the thick heat, techniques she'd had to learn after the dark road. In the back of her mind, ideas for Pooja's commission were swirling around.

What did survival mean? Madness, certainly. Guilt, but she didn't want to lean into that. It leaned into you hard enough already, it didn't need encouragement. Feyi could feel it even now, trying to replay the conversation she'd just had with Alim before he walked out. The guilt whispered that she was a burden, a child who couldn't control her feelings, that he would get tired of reassuring her if he wasn't tired already and the rift with his children would be her fault if things didn't work out.

Feyi extended her arms above her head and tilted her neck back, brash sunlight falling on her face. The guilt was a liar—she had to remember that. It was possible that Alim could get tired of reassuring her, but it was Feyi's job to reassure herself, too. That was work she had to do with her therapist, to take responsibility for her own feelings. She was grown, and so was Alim. They would both live with their choices and be the ones accountable for them. It would be messy, but so was surviving.

So, madness and mess. Something that took up space. Something that felt furiously alive, because survival could be so very, very angry. Feyi had seen a glimpse of it in Pooja during their lunch, had felt it in herself while confronting Nasir at the museum. Madness and mess, anger and life, but the anger was *specific*, a fire fueled by grief. Heart-rending, cloth-rending grief, but it couldn't return to that place she and Alim had talked about, the place you might never get out of. You weren't alive in that place.

Feyi stopped her stretches and went into the kitchen because her left temple was throbbing slightly. She was dehydrated and probably needed to eat as well. There was a jug of cucumber-infused water in the fridge, and Feyi stared at the rest of the shelved contents as she drank down a glass. She wanted to make Alim something for when he got back from his run. It obviously wouldn't be as amazing as anything he made himself, but he was always the one doing the cooking, the reassuring, the caretaking, and as much as it was easy to fall into that because, my God, it felt amazing to have someone care for you like that, Feyi knew it wasn't healthy to leave it that imbalanced. He needed to know he was safe with her as well, not ambushed by her anxiety, unseen by her fear, and all that.

Feyi already knew there was no way she could cook something fancy from scratch, but what she could do was jazz up a simple recipe. She pulled out her phone and looked up grilled cheese recipes, then hit shuffle on one of her favorite playlists, letting the music bounce around the kitchen as she started cooking. Feyi heated up a skillet and added some butter and olive oil, then roughly chopped up fresh thyme and rosemary from the herb corner, swirling that in the fat with salt and pepper. So far, so good. The recipe she was attempting called for caramelized onions, so she diced a white onion and added it to the pan, stirring until the onions started to soften and brown, then shook in some brown sugar. It felt counterintuitive to add sugar to a grilled cheese recipe, but if there was anything Feyi had learned from watching multiple seasons of *Nailed It!*, it was to follow the damn recipe and not fuck around. She slid the onions out onto a plate; a few of them seemed a little crispy, but Feyi figured that charred could be a flavor. Technically.

More butter, more rosemary in the skillet, then she pulled out two slices of pumpernickel bread and here was the truth—of course Feyi had cooked before. Her mother would have been appalled to hear her say that she didn't know how to, but a life was a complicated thing, and Jonah had loved cooking, so he'd done most of it and between him and her mother; Feyi got by for years without having to cook. After

Jonah died, she hadn't picked it back up. What was the point in learning how to scale down, how to make things in single portions? What was the point in cooking in bulk, freezing Tupperware as if you believed in a consistent future enough to plan meals for it?

As she spread mayonnaise on the slices of bread and slid them into the sizzling rosemary butter, something tight eased up a little in Feyi's chest. She was alone, just with herself, remembering the creeping peace of putting something together on a flame, the sounds of bread turning gold, the rhythm of grating Gruyere cheese and layering it, then watching it soften and melt. Feyi spread the onions on the cheese, then sandwiched the pieces of bread together, turning the stovetop down to its lowest setting. She was watching it so closely to make sure the bread didn't burn while the rest of the cheese melted that she didn't hear Alim come into the kitchen or see the slow smile as he took in the sight of her.

"I thought you didn't cook?" he said.

Feyi looked up from the skillet, startled, then blushed when she saw him. "Ah, I still can't." She laughed. "But I wanted to make you something."

Alim poured himself a glass of water, then sat at the kitchen counter, his shirt slick to his chest with sweat. "This looks like more than a little something."

"It's just a sandwich." Feyi flipped it over in the skillet and tried not to feel too self-conscious that he was watching her. "It's no big deal." She lifted the sandwich out once all the cheese was melted and plated it. "How do you like your halves?"

"Diagonal tastes better, don't you think?"

"Facts." Feyi cut the sandwich and slid it in front of Alim, not quite meeting his eyes. This was all suddenly so juvenile, making a fucking grilled cheese sandwich because that was the only thing she could think of, the best thing she could come up with. Feyi was turning back to clean up and wipe away any evidence that she'd had this terrible idea when Alim reached out and grabbed her arm.

"Hey," he said, and Feyi had to look at him then.

The tension that had been in his face before he left was gone now, worked out somewhere during his run. "Thank you for this," he told her.

"You haven't even tasted it."

"You know that's not what I mean."

Feyi sighed and leaned on the counter across from him. "I just wanted you to know that I care, Alim. Even if I'm shit at showing it sometimes."

Alim picked up half the sandwich and bit into it, Feyi watching as he chewed. It was fine if the sandwich sucked, she decided. It had been more of a gesture anyway. Still, when he looked up at her with genuine pleasure in his eyes, Feyi exhaled in relief.

"It's not trash?"

"It's really good, Feyi." He tilted the sandwich and examined it. "Caramelized onions?"

Feyi beamed. "Yeah, I found this recipe online."

Alim shook his head and took another bite. "What's amazing is that you've gotten away with me doing the cooking all this time." He shot her a look. "Were you pretending to not know how to slice carrots the other day just to seduce me into helping you?"

271

She flicked a tea towel at him, laughing as she started to clean up. "No! I just wanted to know how thinly you wanted them sliced. Nobody asked you to come put your arms around me—you did all that on your own."

Alim chuckled. "That's fair," he said.

"Do you have a therapist?" she asked, wiping down the stove so she didn't have to see his reaction. There was a surprised pause before he replied, but Alim didn't sound too thrown that she'd asked.

"I do," he answered. "We talk a few times a year at this point, but I've been with them for a long time now. Why do you ask?"

Feyi put down the tea towel and came around the counter to sit next to Alim. "I've made an appointment with mine, and I think you should talk to yours, too. This is . . . a lot going on, and I have Joy, but I legit don't see you talking to anyone about all this. Like, where are your friends? Who are the people in your support circle?"

Alim's eyes creased as he smiled. "I think that's a fantastic idea," he said. "Thank you for looking out for me."

Feyi touched his knee. "Of course."

"As for the friendships, I'm not so much of a loner to not have any," he teased. "I'd say Phillip and Rebecca, but I haven't told her about this yet. I'm thinking of how to phrase it without sounding like I seduced one of her artists."

"Didn't you?"

Alim finished off the last bite of the sandwich. "I wasn't the one licking mango foam off fingers, Feyi." He smirked as the memory flushed through her, then stood up and cupped her face in his hands. "Thank you for that, for waking me up," he said.

Feyi leaned into his palm, a trace of oiled rosemary wafting off his skin.

"We're going to be okay," she said. "One way or another. We'll figure this out."

Alim looked unexpectedly vulnerable. "Do you really think so?"

She thought of Jonah and Marisol and hungry graves and mad grief. "We're alive," she reminded him, sliding her hands under his shirt and up his back. "We have time."

Chapter Twenty-One

The next several days dripped past in the steady trickle of a new routine. Alim woke up and went for a run each morning as Feyi slept in, then they'd have breakfast together before she left for her studio and he vanished into his test kitchen. Feyi invited Pooja up the mountain and handed her reams of soft chiffon.

"You said you wanted a piece of the madness," Feyi told her. "I want a piece of yours in this. I'll do it with you."

Standing in the center of the studio, they screamed together, tearing the fabric apart with their bare hands, soaking it with anger and grief and all the terrible feelings that came with being alive. Pooja committed to it immediately, without hesitation, like she'd been waiting for a place to put all this. When it was over, Pooja dropped to her knees and wept, holding scraps of white chiffon to her face as her tears soaked into them. After she left, Feyi delicately lifted the fragments and added them to the painting, tears and blood and red paint, layers and layers of it. When she was alone, she sat with strips of linen in her arms and went as far back to that dark place as she could bear, all the missing of Jonah coming out in salt, caught in the linen, seized in the painting. Pooja came back twice, and the second time, she brought a small lace square.

"I cannot tear this," she told Feyi, "but it belonged to Keya." Her hands trembled as she offered it, and Feyi took the lace from her as if it were made of ash, like it could fall apart with a breath.

"Thank you," she said, because there were no other words.

Pooja nodded and left without saying anything else.

When Feyi had dinner with Alim later, like they did every evening, she told him about the lace and the rending and the layers of resentful life she was putting into the painting. He looked at her the way he had at her exhibit, with something stunned scraping raw through his eyes.

"Would you like to see Marisol's headstone one of these days?" he asked, and the question floated out over the table, thick and heavy.

Feyi wasn't sure why the painting had made him think of that. "I'd love to," she answered. "If you're sure."

Alim smiled at her and melancholy hung around his mouth. "I'm always sure," he said.

The next morning, he asked if he could stop by her studio to drop off something. "I can look away from the painting if you'd rather keep it unseen until it's complete," he offered, but Feyi waved him off.

"You can see it in any stage it's in," she said. "I don't care. I like showing myself to you."

There was a tinge of something new in the air between them, as if they both understood without having to say it that once the painting was complete, Feyi would leave the island.

She'd known this as soon as the painting started making itself into a tangible thing under her hands, and even though she hadn't told Alim, he seemed to know as well. Neither of them brought it up, but full silences started to follow them around, settling in their skins when they held each other at night, a ghost they weren't ready to make real. Nasir and Lorraine were absolutely refusing to speak to Alim, and even though he was processing it with his therapist, Feyi could see the hollows forming under his eyes. He needed to resolve this, and Feyi knew she couldn't be there in his house while he did it. They would have to give each other some time and space, so he could mend what was broken with his children without Feyi, so Feyi could go home and cuddle on the couch with Joy and perhaps that was the only way to know that this wasn't a dream after all.

Alim came by the studio in the late afternoon, while Feyi was working one of the tear-soaked linen strips into the painting. Keya's lace was laid out on a table, weighed down by a small pane of glass.

"Give me a second," Feyi said, and Alim leaned against the doorframe, watching her hands move. Once the linen was secure, she stepped back and looked at the painting, then glanced over at him. "Hey, handsome."

Alim's eyes were slurried and hungry. "I'm beginning to understand why you licked my fingers in the kitchen," he said. "It is incredibly sexy watching you work."

Feyi laughed and wiped her hands with a cloth. "What did you have for me?" she asked. "I've been wondering all day."

Alim pulled a short length of copper wire out of his pocket. It had a touch of patina to it and was bent into a loose spiral. He held it like it was made of a breath and a thought, so gently. "This was Marisol's," he said, and Feyi straightened as he turned it over in his fingers. "She used to wear it in her locs. I wanted to offer it to you for the painting, but I didn't know if that was appropriate, if this was between you and Pooja."

Feyi rested her hip on the edge of the table. "It's my piece," she said. "I can put whatever I want in it." She gestured at the copper. "And I would love a relic from your heart in the painting, Alim. It's so generous of you to offer."

He glanced at the painting, then at the blood-soaked squares of chiffon Feyi had drying on a rack. "However it comes?" he asked.

Feyi frowned, but nodded. "Of course. However it comes."

Alim looked down at the copper wire thoughtfully, then jabbed it into the soft of his thumb, drawing a swollen bead of bright red blood. Feyi inhaled sharply, but said nothing, watching as he coated the wire with his blood then held it out to her, his expression shuttered. Feyi accepted the piece of copper gingerly and placed it gently on the glass covering Keya's lace, then took Alim's thumb and brought it to her mouth, pressing her lips against the brief wound, a drop of iron coating the tip of her tongue. Alim hissed in a breath and wrapped an arm around Feyi, pulling her in close to him.

"I've missed your mouth," he murmured, sliding his thumb past her lips and hooking it against her bottom teeth, applying slight pressure. It was enough to slacken Feyi's joints with a sudden and loud desire, amplified by the trace of his blood against the inside of her cheek. She knew Alim had been taking it slow because she said she wasn't ready, but in that moment, there was low-key nothing Feyi wanted to do more than sit on the edge of the table, hike the dress she was wearing up to her waist, and pull his wide dark mouth between her thighs. The visual was so clear and insistent that she stepped away from him, and Alim dropped his hand, leaving her mouth achingly alone.

"I'm sorry," he said, and Feyi wanted to protest, but she didn't trust herself to speak without saying too much. She grabbed his hand instead and squeezed it tight. Alim was so painfully beautiful to look at, not just his face, or his body, but the whole of him, the way he was relentlessly tender, the way he let pain pass through him like a current, the way he didn't run from it or try to divert it into something else. The way he offered blood-smeared copper as a gift, a consecrated object, alive grief.

"Let's watch the sunrise tomorrow," she said. "From the peak."

Alim raised an eyebrow. "Are you sure?"

Feyi cut her eyes at him. "What, you don't think I can handle a little trek?"

"A little—" Alim chuckled and shook his head. "Sure, sweetness." He looked at the painting again, the way it loomed against the wall. "It's incredible, by the way."

Feyi glanced back at it. "Yeah, I think I'm almost done. It feels close to finished."

"Ah." Alim's voice gave away nothing, but there was still a mass of unsaid things roiling in the air between them. "I can't wait to see it when it's complete. Pooja will adore it, I'm sure."

"I hope so," Feyi said. "It's not . . . pretty."

"It doesn't have to be. I don't think that's what she was interested in."

"Yeah. You're right."

They stood in the studio, just the two of them and the volume of the painting, until Feyi let go of Alim's hand so she could start cleaning up. He waited for her by the door, and when she was done, Feyi took his hand again and they walked back up to the house together.

. . .

The darkness was beginning to pale into a hint of morning when Feyi and Alim started the hike up to the mountain peak the next day. They walked in silence, concentrating on beating the sun, and made it up to the clearing just in time. Alim flung a blanket over the grass and collapsed on it. "I can't remember the last time I made the climb that fast."

Feyi sat next to him and passed over a bottle of water. "You'll survive, old man."

Alim cut his eyes at her. "I'd fight you for that if I had the energy."

He trickled the water into his mouth without raising his head, then returned the bottle to her, closing his eyes as he caught his breath. Feyi was sweating and taking deep breaths of her own, filling her lungs all the way to the bottom and then releasing the air through her mouth. Her calves and chest burned, but it felt good to be up there, higher than so many things, watching a bird wheel against the opening sky, the way the clouds were slowly starting to pick up colors. Her dress was sticking to her back, and her feet felt stifled in her sneakers. She leaned down to undo the laces, kicking them off and peeling her socks away.

"Mm, good idea." Alim sat up next to her and did the same, and Feyi rested her chin on her knees, watching his fingers work at the knots.

"I always wished I had hands like yours," she said.

"Like mine?" He took off his shoes and socks, flexing his feet against the blanket.

"Yeah, you know, piano hands. Long fingers. Oval nails. All those tendons and texture." Feyi held hers out to compare. "I've got such boring hands."

Alim took her hand and bit the tip of her finger. "That," he said, kissing her wrist, "is the most"—the inside of her elbow—"ridiculous thing"—her shoulder—"I've ever heard."

Feyi giggled. "You're sweet," she said. The fantasies of his mouth on her from the day before hadn't eased up. They'd shoved their way into her dreams, waxing lucid, and Feyi had come in her sleep, waking up wet in Alim's arms. He'd slept through it, and she'd felt like she was keeping a wonderfully indecent secret.

"Your hands are full of texture," Alim was saying as he traced the scar on her palm.

"Oh, that." Feyi shrugged. "I don't count it."

"It's yours whether you count it or not." He said it casually, his fingers flitting over the skin of her forearm, his eyes studying the angle of her elbow. When he glanced up at her, Feyi's breath caught at the smokiness of his eyes. "You're the most beautiful thing on this mountain, did you know?"

Alim was looking at her like she was precious and delicate and worth more than he could put together in a lifetime. His legs were long and cloaked in jersey, his arms dark wings, his mouth was a raw fruit. Every brush of his fingers sent a rattle of electricity through Feyi's skin. The sky was an immense stretch above them, and in the midst of all the dew and cool air, Feyi realized why she'd suggested that they come up here in the first place. Her pulse was hammering through her, quick and steady as she leaned in to kiss Alim, slipping her hand to the back of his neck, her mouth sure against his. He hesitated for a sliver of a second before kissing her back, and Feyi felt her body pool at his touch, the feeling curling in her belly and dropping lower as the slick heat of his tongue pushed into her mouth.

She made a soft sound and reached for every ounce of aliveness that she had, then Feyi pulled herself up, swinging one leg over Alim to straddle him, her dress riding up her thighs and her knees digging into the soft blanket.

Alim broke his mouth away from hers so he could see her face. "Feyi?"

There was no way she was going to have a conversation about this. Feyi started undoing the buttons that ran down the front of her dress, and a small evil thrill ran through her when she saw the panicked desire that flooded Alim's eyes as he tried to figure out what she was up to.

"What are you doing?" he said, his voice already tangled up, his hands moving to her hips. "We're outside."

Feyi laughed. "No one's coming up here." The buttons were falling open at her waist now, and her nipple rings pressed against the sheer black bra she was wearing under the dress. Alim's fingers dug into her hips and against her waistbeads as he drew in a sharp breath.

"Sweetness," he said, "you have to tell me what's going on."

Feyi leaned forward to kiss his neck, her braids washing over both of them. "What do you think?" she whispered into his ear. She could feel him growing hard under the thin cotton of her panties, his desire stretching out the jersey of his

281

joggers. Feyi hid a smile as she bit his earlobe, then gasped as Alim wound a hand in her braids and pulled her head back sharply, curving her throat open.

"Feyi," he growled, "don't play with me."

She wondered if he could feel how wet she was, if it was soaking through the jersey, pooling in the fabric, seeping to his skin underneath. Her face was pinned to the blooming sky, and a bird swooped across the blue. Feyi undid the last few buttons at the hem of her dress.

"I'm not playing," she said, her voice ragged. "I'm sure."

Alim released her hair. "You're sure?" He sounded like he was at the very edge of something, about to break or topple over.

Feyi bent her head forward, her braids cascading around his face, and cupped his jaw in her hands. She could barely think; being so close to him felt like a thousand welcome insanities against her skin. A breeze brushed over her collarbone and she felt so perilously alive.

"I'm sure, Alim." She leaned her forehead against his, their breaths knotting together. "Please," she whispered, and the word was barely out of her mouth before Alim's tongue replaced it, his hands multiplying hungrily on her body, his teeth clashing against hers with how hard he was kissing her. Feyi shrugged off the dress and Alim tugged at the strap of her bra.

"Tell me if you want me to stop," he said, kissing her neck, her collarbone.

It was a ridiculous idea. "Don't stop," she ordered, and he bent his head to take her nipple into his mouth, the gold rasping behind his teeth. Feyi gasped and clutched at his head, her fingers digging into his curls. Alim grabbed her ass and pulled her snug against him, so she could feel how hard he was, and Feyi couldn't help grinding helplessly against him, soaked and aching. The sky was brightening around them and there were birds now, a stream of song somewhere behind the blood rushing in her ears.

Alim slid up to her throat, all mouth and teeth and tongue. She pulled at his shirt so he leaned back to take it off, ripping it over his head and tossing it aside. He stopped to look at her, almost naked in the dawn, almost riding him, and Feyi blushed at the pounding hunger and adoration in his eyes.

"We're supposed to be watching the sunrise," she said, running her fingernails lightly down his chest, grazing his nipples, trying to sound more controlled than she felt.

Alim's eyes fluttered shut as he dug his fingers into her hips, grinding her against him, just as helpless and hungry. "Fuck the sun," he said. "Tell me how far you want to go."

Feyi reached down and slipped her hand beneath the waistband of his joggers, meeting him all hard and velvet and dew-tipped. He'd been telling the truth, she noted with a smile, Joy would appreciate the confirmation.

Alim hissed in a breath and looked at her, searching her eyes as she pulled him out. "Feyi. Are you sure?"

She nodded, not breaking eye contact as she lifted herself a little and tugged her panties over to the side. "You've had a vasectomy and I got tested before flying out here."

Alim's breath was coming harsh and fast, his pupils dilated. Feyi paused, hovering just over him. "Are you?" she asked.

The hunger in Alim's face blurred into a sharp edge and his voice was strained. "Yes, sweetness. I'm good and tested

283

over here." His fingers were still digging into her hips, but he let Feyi control it as she sank onto him, sliding down in excruciating and wonderful fractions. She stopped halfway, her breath short and broken, because she wanted it to last longer, this moment, this first time.

"Oh, fuck." Alim was breathing hard, his mouth against her shoulder. "You're so tight."

Feyi buried her face in his neck, against his salty skin. "Tell me if you want me to stop," she teased, and Alim let out a scattered laugh.

"Don't stop, I'm begging you." He kissed her shoulder, then groaned out loud as Feyi slid all the way to the base, her body falling flush against his. "Ah, fuck, sweetness." Alim wrapped her braids around his hand and pulled her head back to see her face.

"Look at me," he said. "Look at me, darling."

Feyi could hardly think. She felt like she was about to come just from being stretched around him, from the heat of his flesh filling her. Alim kissed her mouth, then raised her off him before pulling her back down and thrusting up, slamming them together. Feyi came immediately, crying out as she shook around him, and Alim pulled her even closer. "Yes, baby," he crooned, then he flipped her over onto her back, pulled out, and entered her again, hard and fast. "Come for me."

Feyi lost her breath and gasped out an incoherent moan as her orgasm folded over itself, waves and waves crashing through her, her braids spilling out against the blanket, the sky washing a light gold with seashell colors above her.

"I love hearing you make that sound," Alim whispered

against her ear, his lips brushing her skin as he pulled back. "Make it again."

He slid back in, and Feyi bit into his shoulder to dampen the sounds she was making, even as she wrapped her legs around his waist. Alim pinned her wrists above her head with one hand, looking down at her as she writhed. "My God, you're so beautiful like this."

Feyi tried to turn her head to the side, but Alim smacked her thigh lightly.

"No, look at me. Always look at me. I want to see you."

"Oh fuck, I hate you." Feyi laughed, turning her head back and blushing. Alim slid a hand down between them, stroking her clit and watching her mouth fall open, the small whimpers fall out, the way her back arched.

"Don't stop," she begged, and he obliged, sliding in and out of her, his thumb whorling circles, her hips hungry and grinding until she was raking welts on his body with her nails, her eyes wide as he looked into them, falling, and even then, he didn't stop.

"Yes," Feyi moaned, a hand tight in his hair, "just like that, please, Alim," and he was kissing her neck and shoulder, rocking against her till she put her lips to his ear and whispered, "Fuck, I'm coming again."

"I'm with you," he replied, their bodies frantic, and Feyi tightened her legs around him.

"Stay with me," she gasped, and Alim clutched handfuls of the blanket beneath her, his other arm around the small of her back, crying out against her collarbone as he buried himself as deep in her as he could go, spasms rocking his flesh. Feyi's body rippled around him and then they were spent, but he didn't pull out, and she didn't pull away. They lay in the clearing as the dawn made its way across the sky, holding each other tightly, like they'd just fallen through into another world and weren't ready to let go yet.

Chapter Twenty-Two

The finished painting was a glorious thing. Feyi always liked her work, but this was different, this had a precise weight to it. Pooja had insisted that Feyi not worry about packing or transport, she'd come up the mountain and have her people handle it.

"It gives me an excuse to share a meal with Alim," she'd said. "The man is impossible to pin down." Pooja had flicked her eyes up to Feyi as she said that, and she knew she was dying to ask about the rumors, but Feyi just smiled pleasantly back at her and said nothing, so Pooja shrugged and grinned and let it go. She was coming to pick it up the next afternoon, and Feyi was overwhelmed with the endorphin rush she got every time she finished a piece.

Her phone started ringing, and Feyi did a double take when she saw Milan's name on the screen. She picked up the call and said a tentative hello.

"Yo. It's Milan."

It still didn't make any sense. "You know you on an international call, right?"

"Girl, I know where you are." His voice sounded exactly the same, down to the note of exasperation, and Feyi hid a smile.

"Just making sure. What's up?"

"Aight, so I just spoke to Nasir, and he caught me up on all the shit that's been going down over there."

Feyi sighed. "Bruh, if you're about to go in on me, don't even start. I've had enough of that shit from him, I don't need it from you, too."

"Nah, nah. That's not why I'm calling. I just wanted to say, do what you gotta do, Feyi."

"What?"

"I mean it. Do what you gotta do to be happy. This world is literally on fucking fire right now. I didn't know about your husband dying in that accident and all that, but it makes sense. You had something that was hurting real bad inside you. I could feel it."

Feyi cradled the phone in her shoulder and walked to the studio window, staring out at the trees. "This is . . . not what I expected you to say."

"Yeah, well. Nasir's my boy and all, but he's had a good life. He doesn't know about the shit that cuts you up deep inside, you know? He doesn't know what that's like."

Feyi was quiet, not knowing what to say, what to ask. Defending Nasir or bringing up his mother's death didn't feel quite right, especially if he hadn't talked to Milan about it, so she said nothing.

Milan continued. "I felt you watching, you know. All those nights when you thought I thought you were asleep. I felt you watching me, but you never asked me about it."

She cleared her throat, nervous. "Nah, I didn't. Was that an asshole move?"

"Nah. It was perfect. I didn't wanna talk about my shit, and you didn't wanna talk about yours, but I dunno. I think we recognized something in each other anyway, you know?"

Feyi slid her back down the wall and wrapped an arm

around her knees. "You were hurting, too."

"Yeah. Lost one of my kids from group a while back. That shit stays with you, takes up a whole lotta space."

"Yeah. I know the feeling." There was a pause where it was just both of them on each end of the line, then Feyi filled the silence. "So you basically called to give me your blessing, is that it?"

Milan laughed. "I just wanted to make sure you were looking out for you. Nasir will be fine. He's got his boys, and yeah this shit is messy, but it's not like his dad stole his girl or some shit, you feel me?"

Feyi scoffed. "Yeah, well, I'm sure that's not the way he's telling the story."

"Eh. He's hurting. We know how that shit goes. It'll pass with time. Just don't throw away your life to make him feel better, you know? Me and the guys will look out for him. You look out for you."

Feyi felt tears well up. "You're being kind as hell."

"We friends, ain't we?"

"Shit, I thought you were just saying that."

"Well, I meant it."

She sniffled. "The guys are talking mad shit about me, aren't they?"

Milan whistled. "Whoo, chile, you do not wanna hear the half of it. They are some foul-mouthed motherfuckers."

"Damn."

"It don't matter. You don't really give a fuck what they think about you, do you?"

"Nah, I guess not." Feyi wiped at her eyes. "How's it going with you and your ex?"

"Yo, she got us in couples therapy. Shit is wild."

A laugh bubbled out. "You? Talking about your feelings?"

Milan laughed as well. "Ay, we all gotta grow, gotta keep up. It's the only way to build a better life, feel me? At least that's what she tells me. I just . . . I don't wanna lose her again over some dumb shit. Life is too fucking short."

"That's a word."

"Yeah. We gon' be all right. I gotta head to group with the kids, but text me if you need to talk, aight?"

"I will, and thank you, Milan."

"It ain't no thing. You deserve to be happy, Feyi. Catch you later."

Feyi hung up and shook her head. Of all the weird things to happen. She closed up the studio and started walking through the gardens, into the citrus orchard. Alim had a collection of finger lime trees that had started fruiting, and Feyi hoped that she'd be able to try one of them before she had to head back to New York. She still hadn't talked to Alim about that yet, but surely he could feel it, too, the way the time here was ending, the way life had to move on, continue. She didn't know if he would come with her, or if she'd go back first and he'd join later, or if they were even going to try long distance, but Feyi knew she had to step out of the bubble. Go back to her apartment, go back to Joy. Go visit her parents. See if the rest of the world had held up.

She was about to return to the house when she saw Alim walking over a small hill, toward the orchard. Feyi waved to him and Alim waved back, his face breaking into a gentle smile. She ran up to him and kissed his cheek. "Where are you coming from? I thought you were in town."

"Nasir wanted to talk. We walked around the grounds a bit."

"That's good, right? How did it go?"

Alim looked thoughtful. "Not too terribly. He did ask if this thing with you was my way of exacting revenge for how they reacted to Devon."

"Ouch."

"Yeah, he's still struggling to make sense of it. But at least now he's trying." Alim glanced over at her. "I think it might help if he spoke to you, actually."

"Really? You think he'd be down for that?"

"By tomorrow, who knows? But today he seemed like he could listen a little. Not a lot, but more than before."

Feyi looked over the hill. "Where did you leave him?"

"By the gazebo. He's always loved that spot. He has to walk back here to get his car, though, you could catch him then."

"Nah, it's okay. I'll go find him." Feyi stroked her thumb over Alim's jawline. "I'll see you back at the house."

"Of course." He kissed her mouth lightly and she felt him watching as she walked away, until the slope of the hill took her out of sight.

The gazebo was visible in the distance if you looked hard enough through the trees at the right angle, and Feyi took her time walking over, thinking of what she'd say to Nasir, wondering what he'd say to her. They hadn't spoken since that charged afternoon in Denlis's office, and Feyi had been surprised at how much she missed just having him around, as a friend, the ease they'd had. When she came up to the gazebo, Nasir was perched on a railing looking out over the mountain, one leg dangling down. He didn't seem all that surprised to see her.

"Hey," he said.

"Hey, yourself." She posted up at the entrance to the gazebo, at the top of the steps, leaving a healthy distance between the two of them. Nasir noted her caution and leaned his head against one of the posts.

"I'm not gonna wild out again, don't worry."

"You mean like at the museum or that first time at the house?"

Nasir looked almost ashamed of himself. "I shouldn't have treated you like that," he said, his voice grudging. "I've been meaning to apologize."

Feyi almost said it was okay, but then she remembered how scared she'd been, his spit flying in her face, her things tossed on the floor like they were nothing, like she was nothing, the rage at the museum, and she felt her neck tighten with anger again. "So apologize," she said, her voice stiff.

His jaw clenched, but then he took a deep breath. "I'm really sorry I pulled all that shit. It was out of line, and it'll never happen again."

Feyi couldn't quite find words or forgiveness, but she gave him a slight nod, and that felt good enough.

Nasir grunted, then folded his arms. "So. You two are actually a thing now."

Feyi tilted her head to one side, watching him carefully. "Something like that," she acquiesced.

"But you're serious. Like, you're both serious about this." Nasir looked like he was making a credible attempt to keep either disgust or contempt out of his voice and face as he spoke to her, and Feyi felt her hackles rise. She straightened her shoulders, refusing to look ashamed.

"Yes, Nasir. We're serious. Alim wouldn't be putting either of you through this if it wasn't serious."

Nasir raised a hand, grimacing. "Don't . . . don't speak for him. Please. It's really—" He took a second to compose himself then looked directly at her. "It's really hard to hear that without getting angry."

Feyi nodded. "Okay. I can speak for just myself, but—"

"That's between me and my father."

She raised her palms. "I hear you."

Nasir looked at her, his expression flickering between anger, hurt, hunger, and maybe still some hatred. Feyi wouldn't put that past him. "You look good," he said.

"Thanks."

"He fucking you right, huh?"

Feyi blinked, then turned to walk down the steps. "Okay, then. We're done here."

Nasir called after her. "No, Feyi, wait." She paused and turned, watching him bite down on his lower lip. "I'm not going to be able to be graceful about this," he said. "I'm not that big of a person, and I'm sorry. I just . . . I need to know some things. Okay?"

Alim was right, he *was* trying. Feyi came back up and leaned against the entrance, her mouth tight. "Go on, then."

Nasir nodded his head and moved his tongue over his teeth. "Why him?" He looked up at her and a flood of bitterness drowned out his face. "What the fuck did he have that I don't? We had chemistry, you and I. We were good together. You never . . . you wouldn't let me touch you, not like that. And I tried to make you feel safe with me, I tried to do all the right things, and none of it was enough, but you're here with him for barely any time, and boom, it's on? And you two are serious, and he's fucking up everything for this, for this thing y'all have?"

"He's not fucking it up, Nasir."

"Nah . . . you have no idea, Feyi. It used to be the three of us, for my whole life, and we've never, *never* come apart at the seams like this. And I don't understand why the fuck this would happen, why you'd do this to me, why *he'd* do this to me. And I'm sorry for being crass, but I legit cannot stop thinking, maybe that's what's happening—he's just fucking her right, that's why she left me for him, but that doesn't make sense, see, because I never got a chance to even get that far with you. I keep trying to imagine how this could have even started, and I can't come up with anything."

"Well, apparently you think I'm a groupie and a gold digger who seduced him, so that sounds like a great start."

Nasir met her eyes. "I was angry. I knew you were a fan, but I don't think you set out to do all of that."

"Shit, maybe pass the memo to your sister. Both of y'all were so obsessed with us fucking when we hadn't even—" Feyi broke off and waved a hand. "Never mind. It doesn't even matter."

"Nah, when y'all hadn't even what?" Nasir leaned forward.

Feyi cut her eyes at him. "Why don't you take that up with your father when you talk to him?"

"When y'all hadn't even fucked?" His face was sharp, an odd kind of hungry. "So, when was it then? When did you"—Nasir flicked his fingers at the air—"consummate this relationship with my father?"

Feyi looked at him, and she thought of the clearing and the sunrise and Alim's face bordered by a new sky, his smile, his body as he moved against and inside her. She blinked and leveled a cool stare at Nasir. "It doesn't belong to you."

He frowned. "What?"

"This shit you want to know, it doesn't belong to you. It's not your business."

Nasir raised his eyebrows. "It's not my business when you started fucking my dad?"

"No." Feyi bit out the word, anger spread beneath it. "It's not your business what I do with my body, or what Alim does with his. You have no 'right' to me, we weren't together, we weren't even exclusive. You're not entitled to fuck me just because you were a decent human being and went along when I wasn't ready to be intimate with you, or be mad because I ended up fucking someone else. You don't get points for waiting for me. I didn't use you, I didn't lead you on. I went as far as I felt comfortable, and I stopped there."

Nasir stared incredulously at her. "I'm not mad because you fucked someone else, Feyi, I'm mad because *it was my dad*! Because you did it in my home, as my guest! Because neither of you seems to understand how deeply fucked-up that is."

"I know it is!" She'd been trying to keep her composure, but it cracked under the weight of the things he was saying, things that she said to herself over and over. "You think I don't know how fucked-up it is, Nasir? He's your fucking *father*. I've spent hours thinking about what kind of person does that, what kind of person I had to be to do that, what

295

kind of person I am to still be doing it. And yeah, I've even hated myself a little, for doing this to you, for all this *bullshit* that's happened because of it."

"Then *why*, Feyi? Why fucking do it?!"

She looked at him and shook her head. "You don't wanna hear it, Nasir. I know you don't."

He leaned forward again, his eyes black and intent. "Try me."

Feyi bit her lip and smoothed her hands over her thighs. "Fine," she said. "Fine." She let out a deep breath and folded her hands together.

"Every day, I would hate myself a little, right? Like, I'd think all those things you said, every cruel and horrible thing, all the shit Lorraine said, and I wonder if they're true. Sometimes I believe some of them are. And I beat myself up for it, for being that person. But then . . ." She looked out at the hill, thinking about the orchard on the other side, and her voice snagged. "But then I see Alim. And he's smiling at me, and I don't understand why I'd throw the world over a cliff for him, but it's so clear, and every minute I'm with him, all those things drop off me like dead skin, and I don't feel like the ho who got with her friend's father or some groupie or the piece of shit who came to your house and repaid your hospitality like this." Feyi shrugged, her eyes shining with sudden tears. "I feel like the world wanted to remind me that it loves me, and so it gave me him. It gave me a chance, that possibility he's always talking about, and I seized it with both hands because I know, and Alim knows, how fucking rare it is for that door to open, even by a crack, and what it's like when it closes."

Nasir stared at her. "You're talking about Jonah. And my mom."

Feyi pressed her fingers to her eyes and willed them dry. "Yeah, them. But also me, and Alim, and how we—we collided. No one planned it. No one thought, *Yeah, what a great idea, Nasir and Lorraine will totally go for this; this is going to be fun and great and a fucking wonderful time all around.* But we'd crashed into each other and the door was open and we chose to take the chance." She looked at him and gave a half smile. "You were amazing, Nasir. Before all this shit went down. You were sweet and kind, and I'm sorry I couldn't feel about you the way I feel about Alim. It would've been a fuckton simpler if I could've chosen that, believe me."

Nasir stood up abruptly and turned his back to her, looking out into the trees. "Fuck." He put both hands on the railing and leaned on the wood. "You were right. I didn't want to hear that."

Feyi looked down at her hands. "Sorry."

She wasn't, not really. In fact, seeing this other side of Nasir had done nothing but justify her hesitation in jumping into anything more serious with him, but Feyi didn't think he'd want to hear that, either.

"Nah, don't be." Nasir took a deep breath and tapped his sneaker against the floor. "Don't be. I asked." The rubber nose of the sneaker bounced rapid-fire against the dark wood. "It's so fucking weird hearing you say his name, especially the way you say it."

"The way I say it?"

"It's just . . . the way it sits in your mouth." He stopped bouncing his foot and stood up straight again. "I keep imagining you saying it when you're . . . you know. With him. And it just . . . it does me in. It really fucking does, Feyi. Sometimes I can't sleep, thinking about you with him. Wondering if you look at him the way you used to look at me, back when you still wanted me. Wondering how your mouth falls open when he touches you, how your eyes close, how your body—that fucking body of yours—moves for him. And then I have to stop, because it drives me fucking crazy thinking about this shit, about my dad with you. Comparing shit. Whether he kisses you better. Your head on his chest like when you used to sleep on mine. If you chose him because he's more successful, more interesting." Nasir hissed in a sharp breath. "I just—I have to stop."

Feyi looked at his back, the gray T-shirt stretched across it. "I didn't choose," she said. "You're you. You're not a lesser version of him, Nasir. You're you. I'm just—I'm not the person you need."

He turned around and cracked a half smile. "Clearly."

"I mean." Feyi threw up her hands. "Go with a bitch who doesn't hook up with your dad, first of all."

Nasir rubbed his eyes and laughed. "Too fucking soon, man."

"I'm just saying." It was good to hear him laugh.

"Yeah." He dropped his hand and looked at her, several things swirling in and out of his face. "I should get back to town," he said.

Feyi nodded. "Thanks for coming over to talk."

"Yeah. Sure." He started heading out, then stopped. "You know," he said, "you called me your friend."

"Yeah," she said. "Maybe we can get to that again, one day."

"Here's the thing, though, Feyi. Put aside how I felt about you, even just as friends? What you did was really fucked-up."

"Yeah." Feyi looked down. She could at least concede that point. "I was high-key a shitty friend to you. I'm sorry I didn't wait to talk to you, and I'm sorry you didn't find out from me. But most of all, I'm really sorry I hurt you."

Nasir bent his head and put his hands in his pockets, his mouth tense. "Thanks. I'm sorry I hurt you back. It wasn't cool." They looked at each other, and to her surprise, Feyi found herself wishing she could hug him.

"You should probably tell him, by the way," Nasir said, trying and failing to keep the bitterness out of his voice.

"What?"

He pulled his car keys out of his pocket and tossed them lightly in his hand. "You should tell my dad you've fallen in love with him."

Feyi stared at him, and Nasir shrugged.

"He probably feels the same way, if it's any consolation." He walked past her and jogged down the gazebo steps. "Bye, Feyi."

Feyi watched his back retreat until it disappeared around a bend in the garden, leaving only his scent in the air behind him, and the shock he'd dropped in her hands.

Chapter Twenty-Three

Feyi walked over the hill in a daze. She wanted very badly to insist that Nasir didn't know what he was talking about, but what he said rang a small but extremely clear bell of truth inside her and Feyi couldn't unring it. If realizing this was supposed to feel exhilarating, then something was wrong, because it didn't. Feyi actually felt like crying—out of fear, and guilt, and just the sheer mass of feelings burgeoning inside her like an unruly collection of bewildering cells. The urge to return to Brooklyn was louder and stronger than ever, and now that Pooja's painting was done, Feyi knew it was time to go. She was walking through the citrus orchard, small fragrant blooms dotting the branches, and called Joy, even though it was going to run up her data charges like mad.

Joy was on their couch when she answered, and Feyi could see the glimpses of the apartment through the video call, the indigo throw on the arm of the couch, the wing of a monstera leaf at the edge of the frame. It was as if a window to another world was in the palm of her hand; she could smell the palo santo they used to cleanse the apartment, hear the music from the bodega wafting up through the window, taste the doubles from the spot around the corner. Feyi was literally standing in paradise, but all of a sudden, she was done with it, done with the endless sky and the rolling dark green of the trees on the mountain, done with the birds and the air and the yawning space, done with the gorgeous house waiting for her at the end of this walk. She wanted the brownstones again, the jogging route that led to the ice cream shop, her own bed in her own room.

"Babe." Joy's voice was worried, her eyes sharp with concern. "Babe, what's wrong?"

Feyi wiped her face roughly. She hadn't noticed when she'd started crying. "I just want to come home," she said, and her voice broke on the last word, swelling up into a sob.

"Aw, sweetheart." Joy didn't ask any questions. "Come home, then."

She made it sound so simple and maybe it was.

"What if that ends things with Alim? Like, what if we can't survive long distance?"

"I think you're worried that it's not real," Joy offered. "But, babe, if it's real, the distance won't change it. You can't stay there forever just 'cause you don't wanna break the spell. If y'all have something, you gotta give it a chance outside the bubble."

Feyi sniffled and tilted her head back, trying to catch her breath. "Fuck!"

Her voice echoed over the mountain and Joy cracked up laughing.

"Bitch, get your ass home. I miss you like mad, you know?"

"Shit, I miss you, too. How are things with Justina? She still ghosting you?"

A flush of rose fed into Joy's gold cheeks and she ducked her head. "I'ma tell you about it when you get home."

"Oh snap! Come on, you can't leave me hanging like that. Did she leave her husband?"

Joy smirked. "The sooner you're home, the sooner you get the tea. Send me your itinerary when you have it!"

"Fuck you very much." Feyi laughed.

"I love you, too, baby. I'll see you soon?"

"Yeah, I'ma go talk to Alim now, but I'll get a ticket as soon as Pooja picks up the painting. In the next few days for sure."

"Sweet. I can't wait to see you."

"Big same." Feyi blew Joy a kiss, then hung up. She hadn't said anything about her talk with Nasir or what he'd said to her; Feyi needed to admit it to herself first, and then if she was going to say it out loud to anyone, Alim should be the first one to hear it. Feyi didn't even trust herself to go into the house and face him yet, so she found a patch of grass instead and lay down on it, letting her muscles and spine relax into the mountain.

"Thank you," she whispered into the breeze. "For holding me this long. For giving me Alim."

Feyi called back to the first time she saw him, standing in front of the airport, dressed in white, power rolling off him in waves. How was it possible that the same man now shared his bed with her? There was so much she had learned of him since the mountain and none of it felt like enough. They hadn't been able to keep their hands off each other since that morning, coming together again and again in the sprawl of his bed, against the tiles of the shower wall, and in their midnight garden with moonlight streaking their naked skin. Feyi had called it fucking and Alim had pinned her down, kissing her lightly all over till she was soaked and begging.

"You say that like you're not my whole heart," he'd said, finally dipping his mouth between her thighs as she trembled with need. "But as you wish. I'll fuck you after you've come a few times." He was—as she was discovering—a man who kept his promises, who could be as rough as she wanted or as soft as she feared, but Feyi hadn't let herself drown all the way yet. The aftershocks of their first time on the mountain had flooded her heart, and she was waiting for it to dry out, hoping it could be as simple as fucking, but knowing damn well that it wasn't.

To be honest, that's how she knew that Nasir was right, because up under the dawn, when Alim had moved inside her, swamping her with his eyes, when Feyi had cracked apart in his arms, looking up at his face, his blinding face with the sunspots on his cheekbones and the silver in his hair, she had felt something huge rear up in her heart, like a planet shifting her lungs aside, flattening them against her ribs. Alim had held her for a long time and checked in with her after they uncoupled their bodies, asking if she was okay, how she felt, soft worry in his hands and voice. Feyi had told him she was perfect because that was how her body felt—sated and languid, fed with pleasure. She hadn't told him that her lungs were flat, that something alive was breathing in her chest. It had been so long since she'd felt like this, Feyi didn't recognize what it was until Nasir said it like an ambush, and fuck, he was right.

She loved Alim. Somewhere in all of this, she'd fallen in love with him, with how gentle he was, with a thousand things about it ranging from the wrinkles in his eyes when he smiled to the way he looked when he was fast asleep. She'd fallen in love with him, and it was too much, too overwhelming, how dare she love someone else after Jonah? Feyi pressed the heels of her hands into her eyes and sunspots

303

danced in her dark vision. He would have wanted that for her, sure, but he wasn't *here* and that was the whole fucking point. He wasn't here and Feyi had promised to love him until death ripped them apart, and then death had ripped them apart and she hadn't stopped loving him; she still loved him, her first best friend, her first love. When the accident had happened, Feyi could have sworn she would never love anyone ever again. It wasn't even a possibility. It was like a fork in the road had closed, shut off by an avalanche of grief, choked with rocks and a broken heart. It wasn't supposed to open, and honestly, it still hadn't, but somehow, an entirely new path had formed, green and creeping.

Despite Nasir's flippant reassurance, Feyi decided not to worry if Alim felt the same way or not. It didn't matter. Her therapist would say to only control what she could and Alim's heart belonged loudly to him. Feyi had lost too much to feed herself daydreams, and she was tired of feeding herself fear. The only thing left was whatever was true, and in this case, it was two things.

She was in love with Alim Blake.

She was going home to Brooklyn.

That was the solid ground she could stand on, no matter what. Anything else was unpredictable, a current careening past, seizing and discarding whoever and whatever it wanted. Feyi sat up and braced herself to return to the house. It didn't matter how this went—it *couldn't* matter how this went. She had a life in New York. She had Joy, and her work, and it had been enough before this, so it would be enough afterward. Feyi shook out her braids and left the citrus grove, her heart pulsing in her mouth.

. . .

Buika was playing in the house when Feyi pushed open the door and stepped inside. This time the music loudly filled every room, pouring through a centralized sound system Feyi hadn't even realized existed, piano chords striking against the walls and glass. Buika's voice rasped against the paintings, against Feyi's skin, climbing up to scratch against the ceilings of the rooms Feyi was walking through as she searched for Alim. The kitchen was empty, as were the living and dining rooms, the lower courtyard, the corridors. She finally found him in the library, wearing one of his usual outfits, a shirt open to the chest and rolled up at the sleeves, loose trousers. Feyi watched him silently, her heart alive in her chest. Alim was humming along to the music, intermittently singing a line or two in flawless Spanish. His voice sounded like smooth waves of deep amber honey pouring and folding over on itself. Feyi had never heard him sing before, and it pierced through her, lancet sweet. Leafy vines crept up around the window frame and Alim reached up to a shelf, running his fingers over the spines of the books before angling and lifting one out. He was flipping through its pages when Feyi took a step forward, her air cutting into his.

Alim lifted his head, and Feyi watched the small shifts that lit up his face, the stretching curve of his mouth, the wrinkling around his eyes, the gladness that filled his body as he turned to her, dropping the book on a table.

"How did it go with Nasir?" he asked, and Feyi had to catch herself—she'd already moved past that, it seemed so trivial now.

"It's fine," she said automatically. "We're cool. He apologized."

"Are you okay?" Alim caught shifts in her mood easily. Feyi smiled to reassure him, but even she could feel the sadness catching behind her teeth.

"I have to tell you something," she said, twisting her fingers together.

Alim sat on the edge of the table, one leg dangling easily in the air.

"Well, two things, really."

"I am listening for both of them," Alim replied, looking amused at her formality.

Feyi glanced at his collarbone, jutting out from the open mouth of his shirt. The night before, they had gone for a swim, and Feyi had kissed his collarbone until Alim pressed her against the side of the pool and fucked her slowly, until she was coming apart around him, her cries falling on the water. She couldn't imagine him outside this mountain, off this island. Maybe he didn't exist anywhere else. Maybe he turned into someone else—the celebrity chef, the version of him the rest of the world saw. Joy was right—Feyi was never going to trust if this was real unless she left this bubble, took this into regular air to see if it'd asphyxiate then.

"I have to go home," she said. "Back to Brooklyn."

Alim just nodded. "When?" he asked.

"In the next couple of days? I just—I need to be back in my life, you know?"

"Of course." He seemed unruffled, his hands resting gracefully as he listened to her. "You said there were two things?"

Feyi usually hated when his feelings were shuttered—he was impossible to read, infuriatingly neutral—but in this instance, neutral was helpful.

"I think—" she started, then broke off. It was harder forming it in voice, but there was also no need to inject uncertainty where there was none. Fuck fear. She loved him, and she was going home, come hell or high water. It didn't matter if he loved her back, that wouldn't change anything. She'd still love him anyway. The thought flooded her heart again, but Feyi leaned into it, into the ache and aliveness of it all.

She smiled at Alim, and this time there was no sadness there, just the bursting love and its thundering pulse and the way it expanded her, made her ring with life, heartbreaking cloth-rending life. Surrendering to it felt effortless, like floating on great salt, like calm and peace and everything was going to be all right in the end, even if he didn't love her back, because her heart could do this. After everything it had been through, her heart could still do this.

"I love you," Feyi said, and it felt easy in her mouth.

Alim straightened up, and Feyi held out a hand to stop him from talking.

"You don't have to say it back. You don't have to say anything. I just wanted to tell you because it was true and it felt right, that you should know."

She walked up to him as Buika sang over a plucked bass, her voice stripped and cascading upward. Feyi slid her hands along Alim's jaw, marveling as she always did that she could, that his eyes darkened at her touch, that he leaned into her palm as if they'd spent a lifetime touching each other already.

307

The late-afternoon sun came through the library window and illuminated the muddy sclera of his eyes, the gray ringing his pupils. It broke against the steep slope of his nose and cast a shadow on his opposite cheek. Feyi traced his lips with her thumbs.

"You are so beautiful," she told him, and Alim held her wrists, encircling the fine bones with his fingers.

"Feyi," he said, cramming half a world into her name.

She leaned her forehead against his. "You don't have to say it back." It was enough to feel his skin, know that he was alive under her hands. If there was a miracle, it was complete like this. Feyi didn't need anything more.

The song that was playing wound to an end and another began, rippling keys before Buika's voice brushed through, snagging on breaths like she was standing there, the sounds of her throat and mouth close to them. Alim stood up when the languid horns started playing.

"Dance with me," he said, and Feyi let him pull her close to him, his arm snaking into the small of her back, his thumb pressing into her palm as he spun her around, into the center of the room. Feyi laid her head against his chest and Alim kissed her braids. Together, they moved as if they'd had years to form the habit, flowing in slow steps. Feyi closed her eyes, breathing in his lemongrass scent, the gentle musk of his skin underneath, the rumbling of his chest as he hummed along to the song.

"I have two questions for you," he said eventually, still dancing.

Feyi smiled to herself. "Go for it," she said.

"Would you ever want to get married again?"

Feyi jerked her head back to stare at him. "Why would you ask me that?"

Alim smiled at her, and it was like the sun was fighting to push through his skin, he was so bright with feeling. "Because I'm in love with you, Feyi. And I was just curious, if you could see yourself doing it all again."

"Hold up. Are you proposing to me?" Feyi asked it with a raised eyebrow, so he'd know she was being light with it, even though her heart was galloping against her long-suffering lungs.

Alim kissed her temple gently. "Not yet," he said. "It depends."

Feyi wasn't ready to process what he'd just told her. How could he be in love with her? Then again, how could she be in love with him? It was easier to fall back on logistics.

"I don't know if I'd get married again," she said. "I guess it depends. What was your second question?"

"Would you mind if I came back to Brooklyn with you?"

This time, Feyi stopped in her tracks, even as the music continued around them. "What?"

"Just for a short visit. I know I have to come home and do some work with Nasir and Lorraine, but I want you—I want us to know that this is real. That it survives the mountain, that it can cross the sea and still be there, in our hearts."

Feyi stared up at him.

Alim lifted her hand to his mouth and kissed it. "I'm in love with you," he said again. "I love you, Feyi. I love how you skin fear and move through it. I love how you lean into grief and somehow use it to be even more alive. You've shifted my whole world, brought me light and company and a joy I forgot I could feel. I'm not letting a little distance get in the way of this."

Feyi had thought the bursting in her chest couldn't take up more space, but it stretched through her limbs, rushing warmth into her hands and feet. "And you'd want to get married?"

"In time," he said. "Only if you want to. I'm happy just to be with you, however you'll have me."

"Nasir and Lorraine would never go for it, Alim."

Alim pulled her back into their slow step, spinning her around and collecting her into his arms. "Ah, well," he said, his voice light. "Maybe one day. What does it matter, when we love each other?" He nuzzled her neck and jagged bolts of electricity sped through Feyi's skin. "Imagine that, Feyi. We're alive, and I love you."

Feyi felt tears sharp behind her eyes. He was right.

"I love you," she said, and it sounded truer the second time because it was mirrored, they were together on it.

Alim inhaled a rough breath. "What a fucking blessing," he said, wonder filling his words. "Thank you for coming into my home."

Feyi laughed softly. "I can't wait for you to see mine." He was coming home with her. They were going home together. "Fuck, I have no idea how we're going to do this."

"That's fine, my love." Alim's breath was warm against her skin. "We have time."

Acknowledgements

You made a Fool of Death with your Beauty is my seventh book in my fifth genre, and, at this point, just four years into my career as an author, I can safely say that I wouldn't be here without you all. I am so grateful for the readers who've been there since my Tumblr days and even earlier, the readers who discovered my books along the way, and the readers meeting me for the first time with this romance.

Thank you for holding these worlds with me, for hand selling these books, for slipping them to the young readers who need these stories, for spreading the word, getting extra copies for your friends, teaching the books in your classes, requesting them from your local libraries, writing reviews, and much, much more. Thank you for being here with me. A story is not quite a story until someone listens to it, completing the circle, and I am very glad to be telling stories with you all. I hope we get to keep doing this for many more years, books, and genres to come.